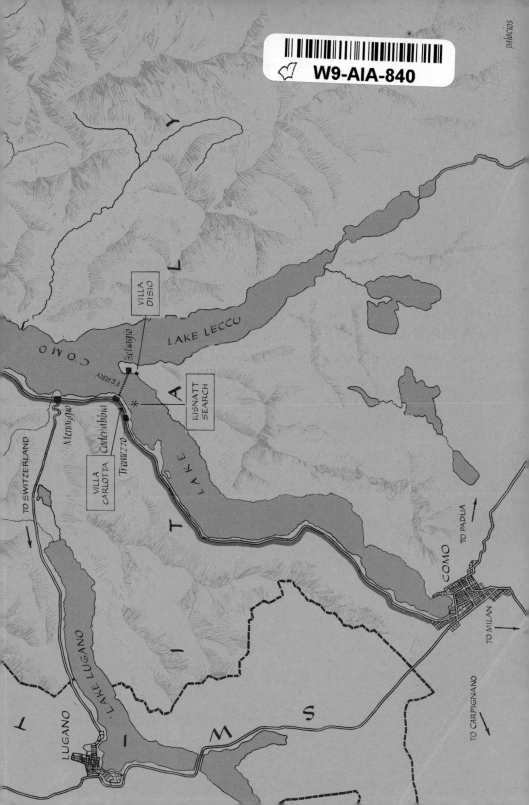

palacios

TO SWITZERLAND

LUGANO

LAKE LUGANO

Menaggio

Cadenabbia
Tremezzo

VILLA
CARLOTTA

COMO

FERRY

Bellagio

VILLA
DISIO

LAKE LECCO

KISNATT
SEARCH

LAKE

COMO

TO PADUA

TO MILAN

TO CARPIGNANO

Books by A. E. Hotchner

Treasure
Papa Hemingway
The Dangerous American
The White House (a play)

TREASURE

TREASURE

A. E. HOTCHNER

 RANDOM HOUSE/NEW YORK

FIRST PRINTING

9 8 7 6 5 4 3 2

Copyright © 1970 by A. E. Hotchner

All rights reserved under International
and Pan-American Copyright Conventions.
Published in the United States
by Random House, Inc., New York and
simultaneously in Canada
by Random House of Canada Limited, Toronto.

Library of Congress Catalog Card Number: 77–102337

Acknowledgment is gratefully extended to Tom Lehrer for
permission to include lines from "Alma."
Copyright © 1965 by Tom Lehrer.

Manufactured in the United States of America
by Kingsport Press, Inc., Kingsport, Tennessee

Book design by Mary M. Ahern

*For Holly and Tracy
with love*

A man there was, though some did count him mad,
The more he cast away, the more he had.

The Pilgrim's Progress

TREASURE

preliminary

During three fateful and bizarre days in the spring of 1945, Benito Mussolini made a frantic and almost successful attempt to escape the hangman's noose. He failed, but his wild flight created a mystery involving the vast treasure that he carried—a mystery that has endured to this day.

On April 25, 1945, the Allied forces were only fifty miles from Milan, and Mussolini, whose headquarters was in the Milan prefecture, hurriedly convened all the members of his cabinet and announced his desperate plan to try to reach Switzerland, where he hoped he would be given political asylum. To that end Mussolini instructed the Secretary of the Treasury to go to the vaults and bring the entire contents of the Italian Treasury into the conference room. The wealth distributed included:

Gold ingots Kgs. 51,649   *French francs 22,551,300*
Gold pounds sterling 2,750   *Portugese escudos 11,000*
British pounds 2,653   *Gold marengos 21,179*
Spanish pesetas 10,000   *Swiss francs 803,903*
U.S. dollars 149,345   *Italian lire 1,000,000,000*

In addition, all the great jewels that had belonged to

past royalty were brought in as were the entire Italian operational funds of the German navy, quartermaster and Luftwaffe. The value of the total treasure is estimated to have been between $80,000,000 and $120,000,000.

Besides these official assets, each member of the cabinet had with him all his personal monetary wealth and jewels. Mussolini impetuously and haphazardly distributed to each cabinet member part of the official currency and jewels heaped up on that conference table; then he ordered all of them to descend to the courtyard, where thirty staff cars had been assembled to take them from Milan. Mussolini himself carried—in addition to his portion of money and jewels from the treasury—two large leather briefcases which contained another kind of wealth: all his personal papers, his diaries, and his extensive correspondence with Hitler and Churchill.

Mussolini's plan was to drive north to Como, then follow the road as it ran north along Lake Como to the Swiss border. In a more ordinary time the journey would have been an easy day's drive, but in the spring of 1945 it was partisan territory and Mussolini knew that he would have to be cautious. In about an hour he arrived in Como, where he led his convoy directly to the prefecture. He tried to find out about partisan conditions along the road to the north, but there were no reports he could really rely on.

Following the narrow twisting road that runs along the lake, the convoy threaded through the mist-heavy fog; the going was slow and it was seven or eight in the morning when they arrived in Menaggio. Mussolini immediately went to the Villa Castelli—the owner, Emilio Castelli, was the Black Shirt leader of the district—for the Duce was anxious for word about General Pavolini and five thousand loyal Black Shirt troops whom he expected.

Pavolini had arrived, but instead of the thousands of men Mussolini had dreamed of, the sum total of Pavolini's army was twelve—the great Mussolini reduced to an army of twelve stragglers.

But later that night, a counteracting bulletin arrived: word from Como that a German motorized column, over three hundred men, was coming north on its way to Austria. Mussolini made immediate plans for his convoy to attach itself to this German column. The partisan reconnaissance, however, was also aware of the German unit, and passed along the information to the Fifty-second Garibaldi Brigade, which controlled the road north of Menaggio.

The commander of the Nazi column, a Major Kritz, tired of the war, wanted only to get himself and his weary men out of hostile territory and back onto the Aryan soil of the Third Reich. The sight of Mussolini, who spelled trouble, was not welcome to Kritz, nor was the prospect of taking on a convoy of the most wanted men in Italy. But Mussolini ranted and raged and Kritz reluctantly agreed. Early the next morning, they set out—due north, along the lake, headed toward Chiavenna, which was beyond the partisan domain and was the place where Mussolini planned to separate from the convoy and make his run for Switzerland. During the night, Mussolini's mistress, Claretta Petacci, and her brother Marcello, had arrived; in Claretta's possession was a red leather cask that held all the sensational jewels lavished on her by Mussolini over the years. Preceded by motorcycles with machine-gun mounts, Major Kritz led the way in his big armored car, then came the thirty-eight Nazi lorries, followed by Mussolini's entourage.

By 7 A.M. they had reached the little town of Musso, a few hours from the Swiss border. But as the road turned into Musso there was a solid barricade across it manned by a handful of partisans of the Fifty-second. Unaware that Mussolini and his cabinet ministers were part of this convoy, they were interested only in the Fascist cars.

Kritz could have easily shot his way through, but, fed up with the war, he had absolutely no disposition to fight. Thus he made a deal with the partisans: he would surrender all his Italians if the partisans would grant him safe passage to Austria.

The full convoy was ordered to proceed a few kilometers further north where a larger partisan force under the control of the commanders of the Fifty-second would be waiting for them.

The partisans still did not know that Mussolini, who had kept himself well hidden during the negotiations, was part of the exchange. When Mussolini discovered what Kritz had agreed to, he slipped out of his car—leaving his military cap and gray-green uniform overcoat on the rear seat—and into one of the big German lorries. There was a spare Nazi uniform in this truck—that of just an ordinary enlisted man —and Mussolini put on the overcoat and helmet and a pair of spectacles which he had with him. Disguised now as a German private, he sandwiched himself between other Nazi soldiers far back in the lorry.

Kritz led his column, as agreed, to the next barricade between the adjoining towns of Zonico and Dongo. The barricade itself was in Dongo, but the convoy was so long it stretched around the curve, out of sight, with its tail in Zonico. The Italians were all arrested, and Mussolini might have slipped through in his disguise if the partisan who inspected the German lorry in which Mussolini was hiding had not noticed that this one lowly Nazi private was wearing highly polished, expensive officer's boots.

So Mussolini was unmasked and taken first to the Dongo City Hall, then, with Claretta, to a nearby villa in Azzano, where they were stood up against a wall and shot. Later their bodies were taken to Milan and hung by the feet in front of a gas station.

The ministers were lined up in the Dongo piazza, and

with the local population jammed in as spectators, they were executed by a partisan firing squad. At this point all trace of the fabulous treasure of gold, jewels, money and documents disappeared. Despite occasional leads—all of which have turned out to be false—from that time to this, June, 1969, when this narrative begins, no one has ever laid eyes on any of it.

1

POINT OF ORIGIN

You see the ways the fisherman doth take
To catch the fish; what engines doth he make!
Behold how he engageth all his wits;
Also his snares, lines, angles, hooks, and nets:
Yet fish there be that neither hook, nor line,
Nor snare, nor net, nor engine can make thine:
They must be groped for, and be tickled too,
Or they will not be catched, whate'er you do.

                              The Pilgrim's Progress

chapter one

The *maggiordomo* at Dan Reeder's wore a white tight-collared jacket with a delicate twist of gold braid along the shoulders and sleeve cuffs, and he looked at me not so much with disdain or arrogance as with pain. He looked first at my rounded, crumbled trousers with their prominent knee bulges, and then at my shopping bag, cracked and soiled from being hauled in and out of third-class compartments between Santo Stefano and Rome. With a touch of mercy he passed quickly over my lop-sided jacket and out-sized shirt collar, but his eyes rooted on my haircut which was close all around with no sideburns. In fact, when he finally spoke he addressed the bristles at one naked temple, his eyes clearly showing, as I said, pain.

I had asked whether Mr. Reeder was at home; in response the *maggiordomo* inquired about the nature of my call, and looked openly cynical when I described myself as an old friend. But no matter, Mr. Reeder was not at home; he was at the criminal courts on Via di Villa Giulia and would not be back before six. Would I like to leave my card? Sardonic amusement in the eyes.

Via di Villa Giulia, I discovered, was at the other end of

the Tevere and I had to traverse the length of the city to get there. The fumed bus traveled slowly along the Lungotevere, and although there was a continual pageant of passing Roman splendors, I was too impatient to find Dan to enjoy them. It was early June but Rome was already hot and as I searched along the Via di Villa Giulia for the courts, I could feel sweat running along my body under my heavy wool suit.

I had presumed that Dan was at the courts on some coverage and that the television cameras would lead me to him, but there was no sign of television equipment. As I passed along the clusters of men standing outside the courts, lawyers, clients, witnesses, all tensely discussing impending trials, I was not at all sure I would be able to recognize Dan if I saw him. We had been good friends during the Paris time when he was with *Yank* and I was with *Air Force* magazine, but the last time we had seen each other was in Milan in 1945, and there was no telling what twenty-four years had done to him.

Dan was twenty-one years old when I had last seen him, a wiry, black-eyed, black-haired, black-tempered man with a strong laugh and a natural gift for intimidating Italians. In 1948 he had gone to Paris as a stringer for a couple of American newspapers, and eventually became a commentator for one of the television networks. In the 1950s he was transferred to Rome, where he was made chief of his network's Mediterranean Bureau. During his long Rome residency he had developed powerful contacts in high and low places; he was especially well placed in the Vatican, where he could virtually guarantee any visitor who "counted" an audience with the pope on forty-eight hours' notice.

I had accumulated this information over the years from various items that had appeared about Dan in the Italian press. He had married an American shortly after his arrival in Rome. She had achieved a certain amount of success as an artist and sculptor, first in massive wood blocks and currently in stainless steel, several of her spiraling structures having been commissioned for the far-away lobbies of New York office buildings and for shopping plazas in Kansas City and Des Moines. But her *succès fou* was in having become autocrat absolute of Rome's *stranieri,* the expatriate community. According to an article I had read about her in *Corriere della Serra,* any American contemplating going to Rome to live shouldn't squander money on a passport before he had a strong letter of introduction to Natalie Reeder. For there had apparently been instances where couples had settled in, and after months of vainly maneuvering for an invitation to one of Natalie's parties had finally pulled up stakes and sadly moved on.

"For Christ sake—Paul?" Dan had spotted me first but, no matter, I would have recognized him immediately, he had changed so little. The widow's peak on his forehead had eroded somewhat but that was more than compensated for by a cascade of thick hair at the back of his neck that spilled over his collar. Big, strong teeth grinned at me now as he was pounding me on the back with one arm over my shoulder. He stood back and looked at me. "You son of a bitch, you look like you've been preserved in a deep freeze."

"I have."

"Not a frigging wrinkle. You're older than I am, aren't you?"

"A year younger."

"You look thirty. Come on, let's get out from under this judicial shit." He took my arm and guided me toward a bar on the opposite side of the street. "Nothing worse than guinea justice. Christ, a few weeks ago I drove to the movies with Natalie and a couple we know; as I parked in a space across from the theater, two cops, standing there, ordered me to move on. There was a whole line of cars parked there but me, *straniero,* I'm given the finger. I got in a little argument about it, but finally I started up the god damn car and as I pulled out I happened to say, '*Va fa un colo*,' and the *carabinieri* heard me."

"You told them to stick the parking place up their ass?"

"Not so they'd hear, but they had ears like foxes. Come on, I need a drink." It was essentially a coffee bar but they had whiskey. "Of all people, *I* should know what gods the Italian cops are, especially the *carabinieri* with their Napoleon hats and their faggy swords. They're still protected by the Mussolini cop laws—you realize that? So just now the prosecutor read my indictment. There's to be a trial." He lifted his glass. "Here's luck." We drank.

"My first drink of scotch in twenty-four years," I said. Its fingers immediately spread out all over my insides. Dan looked at me as though realizing for the first time who I really was. I took another sip. "We would get wine occasionally, mostly reject Frascati, so heavily preserved with sulphur that afterward you could scrape it off your tongue with a knife. But the taste of scotch—it's like the first drink I ever had."

"You better take it easy."

"I've been taking it easy for a hell of a long time."

"I don't just mean the booze. I mean the whole scene. Have you seen the girls on the Veneto? Paul, you're sprung at a felicitous uncovered moment in history—top and bottom. Only the pubic hair is still protected by the last shreds of modesty. I'll take you on Reeder's Special Tour for the Raunchy and Degenerate but only if I can muzzle you and keep you on a leash. When I think of you without tail since . . . when was it, 1946? Can that be? Is it humanly conceivable? I slipped a disc and had to be hospitalized immobile for two weeks, *two weeks,* mind you, and it was driving me out of my mind until one of the night nurses, attracted by the tent over my groin, came to my rescue. But years—*years!*"

Dan was so deadly serious I had to laugh. "Well, it was not quite as bad as it sounds," I told him. "When I was first sent to Santo Stefano there was a new warden who allowed wives to visit every Sunday and gave the men the freedom of the island."

"But you weren't married."

"No proof was required. You remember the girl I was going with back then—Gisella? She would bring a picnic and we had our place in a little copse of scrub pines on a rock shelf that hung over the water. Every man had his Sunday stakeout. Gisella was so beautiful and cheerful and the best damn wife who came to the island. She got up at six o'clock in the morning, her one day to sleep, in order to get to Naples in time to catch the boat."

"How far is Santo Stefano from the coast?"

"Thirty-four miles, and she did it every Sunday, there and back, for ten years. I tried to persuade her not to—well, I guess I didn't try very hard, to be honest. As you can imagine, my heart wasn't really in it. All week long I'd think about her coming along those slippery rocks toward the gate, the picnic hamper over her arm, her long legs with their hard, smooth thighs moving across the rocks, her breasts and her long black hair moving in rhythm to her walk. All week long I'd think about her right up to the Sunday climax. God, what a girl she was!"

"Okay, ten years—then what?"

"Well, in 1956 one of the men attempted an escape with the help of his wife. They slugged a guard and got away in a little fishing boat, using his shirt for a sail. They made it all the way to Ischia but the police were waiting for them when they landed. After that, the guards were increased from forty to a hundred and eleven, wife privileges were withdrawn, and a tough warden took over."

"What about Gisella?"

"We wrote each other but, as to be expected, without our

Sundays in the pines to hold her to me, she wrote one day that she was going to marry an olive oil dealer in Brescia. That's the last I heard of her."

"So that leaves thirteen years—what the hell have you done for thirteen years?"

"I'll tell you, Dan, with no women around, in the dead world of the prison, on that God-forsaken rock in the middle of the sea . . . I went as dead as the twelve-foot cell I lived in. Besides, I had a hell of a lot to think about. They were taking my years. My good years. I couldn't get them back. But they are going to pay for them."

Dan looked uncomfortable. "I got you a ten-day stay on your deportation order, but, Paul, as for the rest of it . . . all the stuff in your letters . . ."

"I know it sounds far-out but just give me a chance to go into it with you, will you, Dan?"

"But for Christ sake, you're talking about twenty-four million dollars!"

"That's right. A million a year. Would you have traded your last twenty-four years for twenty-four million? Suppose someone had made the offer back in 1945? Would you?"

"No, I guess not."

"Okay, so the price is not exorbitant."

"I don't say you don't *deserve* it, don't misunderstand . . ."

"Then give me a chance to spell it all out for you. That's why I wanted the ten days."

"But even if you convinced me, you'd need more time . . ."

"I'd need four months."

"How in God's name could I get you four months?"

"The same way you got me the ten days. What if you had the possibility of ten percent, fifteen percent, of twenty-four million?"

"Good Christ, you talk like you know the rock it's buried under! From what I can tell, this whole thing is a spitball. Give up this nutty obsession, Paul, and go on back and find a woman and see if you can make some kind of life for yourself."

"Doing what? Great advice from a fat-cat in a solid job with twenty years' experience in back of him, not to mention pension funds and severance pay and hospitalization and stock options and all the other beautiful feathers they put in your cap. I've read all about big corporation largesse in the year-old *Epocas* and *Oggis* we used to get. Here he is, Paul Selwyn, forty-four years old, fluent in Italian prison jargon, dis-barred from the practice of law before he practiced it, convicted murderer, dishonorably discharged from the United States Air Force and stripped of his rank, absolutely no experience in any field of employment, here he is, going to the highest bidder. Do you know what the hell you're talking about?" I realized I was coming on much too strong, but the scotch had set me loose and I felt desperate. Dan was the only contact I had, not just in Rome, but my only contact with the entire outside world. And the world was still "outside" even though I had now been released into it. I had no relatives—my father had died while I was in high school and my mother during my ninth year in prison—and except for Dan, and a fellow I had been pals with in college and who was now head of a large shoe concern in St. Louis, I had not one identifiable person I could even communicate with, let alone rely on. As for the St. Louis shoe pal, he had sent me a check for two hundred dollars and had tactfully but clearly let me know that that was to be the extent of his involvement with my rehabilitation.

So poor Dan, who certainly hadn't hired on to be my keeper and who was anxious to dispatch me back to the U.S., was nevertheless the desperate target of all my long and arduously assembled plans. My dilemma was that if I didn't pressure him, he would perhaps avoid my difficult demands, and if I over-pressured him, he might permanently dump me.

"Don't get your nuggets in an uproar," Dan said, corroborating my thoughts. "How long have you been out, less than twenty-four hours? Give yourself a few days to unravel, to absorb. You were damn good to me once, when I was a basket case, and I mean to reciprocate. But for Christ's sake don't blast me into the Tyrrhenian."

"I'm sorry, Dan. Twenty years of frustration builds up a mean head of steam."

"Do you have any money?"

"Two hundred St. Louis shoe dollars plus three thousand lire handed me by my grateful and affectionate warden."

"Well, that won't get you far. I'd like to put you up but my daughter, Lisa, is sheltering all four members of The Orgasms."

"The *what*?"

"Part of the new culture you've missed out on. I can get you a good cheap room at the Inghilterra—the manager owes me a favor. We're having some people tonight for dinner—come around nine. You'll meet Natalie and some pretty good chicks you could score with. But not in that clown costume."

"I'll have you know the prison's master tailor personally executed this garment."

"Yeah, well you might win the First Annual Lucky Luciano Tailoring Award with it, but tonight leave your sartorial splendor to me." He gave a long, exasperated look at my haircut. "Maybe you should wear a turban," he said, and then, as we got up to go, he spotted my shopping bag, which I was trying to keep out of sight. "That's a beautiful piece of matched luggage you have there," he said. "No one can accuse you, Paul Selwyn, of not starting from scratch."

* * *

The room in the Inghilterra was on the top floor, and it had glass doors that opened onto a common, narrow, geranium-festooned balcony that ran the entire length of the building. The sensation of walking from the small dark room, which was triple the size of my cell at Santo Stefano, onto the brilliantly sunny balcony, with open sky above and bustle of street traffic six stories below, was rather like my first drink of scotch that afternoon. I broke off one of the big red geraniums, and its distinctive pungent smell contributed to the surge of the moment. On all sides the old, irregularly shaped Roman roofs, with their gnarled pipe vents and ceramic-crowned chimneys, presented a horizon not unlike Paris'. As I looked down at the street I realized I had expected to find Vespas everywhere, but apparently that was a passed phase of the fifties; now little Fiats covered Rome like termites on a log.

I went back into my room and pulled back the coverlet on the bed, knelt and put my cheek against the cool, soft sheet. The day had been full of sensual experiences which I had isolated and reacted to as one would pick a particular flower in the garden, smell it and inspect it before placing it carefully in the cutting basket. But the soft, taut sheet with the peculiar clean fragrance a hot iron leaves, was the flower that tipped the basket; tears ran down my face, leaving a wet circle on the white sheet. I had not wept since I was a boy, and I didn't really know why I was weeping now. Perhaps for all the nights my body shuddered as it first came in contact with the unironed, burlap-like covers on the prison cot. There are many things in prison one never adjusts to and every single night my body rebelled at those abrasive, wrinkled covers. Maybe I wept for the nights I had had to sleep alone and all the mornings I awoke without a woman's head on my shoulder and my whole body in erection. Twenty-four years times 365 equals 8,760 nights on that cold strawed burlapped lousy cot, and that many times not to have heard a concert or taken a hot bath or swum or chosen dishes from a menu or browsed in a book store or slammed into a tennis ball or danced or hunted pheasant in November corn fields or sat in a theater or driven a car or smelled perfume. Not once to have gone to bed voluntarily or awakened voluntarily or to have gone to the toilet in privacy or even, would you believe it, to have shaken hands —not even that—in a prison no one ever shakes hands.

Up you get, Paul, old man, dry your eyes and stop feeling so fucking sorry for yourself. You're sprung, aren't you, so cut out the misery inventory. They owe you 8,760 days and you're going to collect.

Ever since I stepped onto the government launch that went the thirty-four miles from Santo Stefano to Naples, all through the long steamy wait in Naples and then the cattlecar ride to Rome, I had been savoring the thought of a bath in a tub filled with hot water. At Santo Stefano we were permitted one shower a week with brown laundry soap, cold water severely rationed so that if you soaped completely there wasn't water to wash it all off. I unpacked my shopping bag: a bottle of aspirins, hair brush and comb, toothbrush and toothpaste, razor, prison-made handkerchiefs and two pairs of prison-gray underwear and socks; and the lucky piece Giorgio, my one prison friend, had given me when he left a year ago—a metal disc off a package of Russian tobacco that had been given to Giorgio by a whore in Palermo who adored him. I left the cardboard box that contained all my papers in the bottom of the shopping bag.

I undressed, freeing myself of the sweated, heavy, leech-like garments, and I stood naked for a moment in front of the open doors, enjoying the feel of the warm breeze on my damp body; but then I realized I would have to put those terrible clothes back on in order to go down the hall to the bathroom.

*   *   *

When I returned to the room after what must have been a two-hour soak (I emptied and filled the tub twice just for the sensation of feeling the rushing water against my body), I found a package on my bed. It contained a dark blue suit of a light textured material, two shirts of fine cotton and two silk ties, socks, handkerchiefs, underwear, a leather belt, a pair of black shoes, and a wrist watch, not new, but very respectable looking. I rolled all of my prison clothes into a compact bundle and later, when I left my room to go to Dan's house, I pitched the bundle into the deserted linen room.

chapter two

The sum of Natalie Reeder was greater than her parts. She had good, wide-set eyes but her nose and chin were too angular, as if the tips of them should have been sandpapered. Her hair was a shade of dark red that somehow did not flatter her face and yet it seemed to suit her personality, which was vivacious, complimentary, warm and lusty. She was wearing a dress made from Israeli prayer shawls (I learned later that she had recently been to Israel to inspect the installation of a giant menorah which she had designed for the summit of a hill that faced a new museum) and around her neck she wore a heavy piece of tangled, tortured metal which was a product of her jewelry-sculpting period. Watching her move around the room, introducing her guests, I was impressed with how effective she was.

I felt terribly self-conscious in my borrowed clothes and prison looks but none of the guests took particular note of me and handshakes were perfunctory. Dan's shoes and suit fit surprisingly well, although my legs were longer than his and I had to compensate by pulling down the waist of the pants tight over my hips. The names were an incomprehensible jumble but in the course of the evening I was able to identify some of the guests. Among others there was an American novelist and his wife, who was a correspondent for an influential magazine, an English actress who subsisted on small parts in British and American films made at Cinecitta, an oceanographer from Key West, an Israeli functionary, an American actress whose principal income came from dubbing Italian films into English, two protocol clerics from the Vatican, a lady photographer with short hair, a French anthropologist, and an Italian designer who was a current rage with what were described to me as his "man-woman look alikes." As Dan had predicted, several of the chicks were pretty good, and the entire group glistened with a kind of frosted chic that I felt coldly out of. But it was easy to see why, if this gathering was typical, Natalie Reeder was Queen of the Social Realm.

On a terrace outside the main salon where we were (every room in the house, scalloped out and remodeled by the Reeders from what had been a slum tenement, had its own terrace), a white-jacketed servant attended a baby lamb, a Roman delicacy called *abbacchio,* which was crisping on a spit over a charcoal fire. Needless to say, it was not a dish I had ever encountered on the Santo Stefano dining table. I was served a drink by the *maggiordomo,* who showed no sign of having seen me before; as a result of my encounter with the afternoon's scotch I was careful to sip this drink very slowly.

The novelist's wife was telling about her experience that afternoon with the income tax collector. Income tax in Italy is a joke, she explained, but one must go through some kind of formality. In the case of foreign journalists, all of whom belong to an organization called *Stampa Estera,* a tax collector comes to the *Stampa Estera*'s offices and the journalists go before him, one after the other, to make a declaration of earnings. By prearrangement with the collector, they all declare the same earnings—700,000 lire for the year (around a thousand dollars)—as if all foreign journalists were on a fixed wage scale like assembly-line workers. The wife said that she had worn her oldest clothes, and when her turn came she not only declared that she, like everyone else, had earned a paltry 700,000, but that her husband, the novelist, had had no earnings for three years. "Ah," the tax collector had sighed, "why, Madam, did you not send your husband?"

"Speaking of husbands," the English actress who subsisted on small parts said, "I was walking down the Via Veneto yesterday when a man whom I had never seen before came up to me and greeted me effusively and carried on until he saw that I was looking quite blank. Whereupon he said, 'Well, ducky, just how many ex-husbands do you run into on the Via Veneto?' Would you believe? Married for ten years, had my only child with him, divorced six years ago, and I didn't even recognize him."

New sensations were rolling in on me: the looks of the women, the good cooking smells, cigarettes in an open box, the brilliant colors in the pictures on the walls, the touch of a woman's hand as I held a light for her cigarette, the strangeness of hearing conversation in English, the feel of carpet through my shoes, the eeriness of large windows.

"We have a problem here with Ingrid," Dan said to everyone, his arm around the shoulders of the lady photographer. "She went to the Thieves' Market last Sunday with her dog, also named Ingrid, and the dog was kidnapped."

"Dognapped," Natalie corrected.

"She was a black Labrador," Dan continued, "and just about the greatest dog ever lived. She fiercely guarded the Land Rover which was always full of photo equipment and no one ever went near it, but away from the car or the house she was very gentle and so they were able to nab her. Of course, we all know about the dognappers at the Thieves' Market and we never take our dogs, but poor Ingrid didn't know and now we have to try to help her to get Ingrid back."

"She did everything but load film for me," Ingrid said in a deep voice cracked with emotion.

"I'll tell you what we should do," Natalie said; as she talked she ran her hands over the tops of her thighs, smoothing her short skirt. "Next Sunday, we all go to the Porta Portese and we'll carry placards advertising a reward and hand out flyers and I'm sure they'll contact us before the morning's over."

They began to discuss what to put on the placards and how much reward to offer and I took the opportunity to move out onto a terrace. I was unaccustomed to the density of the cigarette smoke that hung in the air (in Santo Stefano cigarettes could only be smoked in the open exercise yard) and for a moment there I had started to feel asphyxiated. The clear warm air washed the smoke out of me. The night sky, heavy with stars and a late-rising moon, was another startling experience; cells had been locked at sundown and the *bocca di lupo* windows, high on the damp stone walls, were viewless.

"You look sad." It was the American actress they called Iris. She was tall and large bosomed; her long brown hair hung loose and her dress, very short, was made of a silver metallic fiber that reflected the light from the sky.

"There's too much up there. It overwhelms me."

"All that never bothers me because I never look up."

"Never?"

"That's why New York was such a waste. I look down and around but hardly ever up."

I looked up at the Milky Way and pitied her.

"What happened to your hair?" she asked.

"Ran into an insane barber."

"I got caught in a brush fire once and after they got through trimming away what was singed I looked like that."

She studied my hair closely, turning her beautiful face from one side to the other. "It's cute, though. After seeing all these hairy types all the time, I mean it's all right on kids but hairy jobs on guys your age, like Dan with his hairy look, not that you're so old, but it's cute to see a real *haircut*, for God's sake, even though you are awful bristly."

"I understand you dub films."

"Well, I'm primarily an actress, but I do dub films."

"That's acting, isn't it?"

"Not really. I mean, anybody who belongs to the union dubs."

"The union?"

"The English Language Dubbers' Association," she said in a tone that indicated I should have known about it. "All you need is a Mid-Atlantic voice."

"What the devil's that?"

"Well, they don't want voices that sound English or Bronx-y or southern or any of that—that's so an Italian movie can be shown in London or Los Angeles and you'll just have this Mid-Atlantic voice coming out of Marcello Mastroianni."

"And you do that for, say, Sophia Loren?"

"Right. What do you do?"

I knew we'd come around to that. "Oh, I just arrived."

"Going to stay around long?"

"That depends."

"But you're not just passing through?"

"No, I hope to be around."

"We could use you at the dubbers. There's a ghastly shortage of men."

"Am I Mid-Atlantic?"

"Oh, definitely."

We were called in to dinner, which was served from a silver serving cart. There was prosciutto and fresh figs to start with, then gnocchi with wild boar sauce, followed by

the *abbacchio* served with little Roman artichokes, so
delicate as to be completely edible, not just the heavy
ridges along the bottom of the leaves. There was a fine white
wine, *Est!Est!Est!*, with the first courses, followed by
generous pourings of a Capri chianti to go with the
abbacchio. My poor mouth and stomach didn't know what to
make of this sudden epicurean onslaught. It was as if the
rusted spigots on all of my senses had suddenly been pried
open, with an exultant outpouring of response to all these
forgotten delights.

Some of my senses were jolted, however, by the appearance at the dinner table of the Reeder daughter, Lisa,
and The Orgasms whom Dan had mentioned. Four Orgasms,
to be exact. I had, of course, seen pictures of the pot-pop-op-
rock people, but pictures are one thing and it's quite
another to see four mustached males in the flesh with matching goatees and shoulder-length hair-dos, jackets out of
Sherwood forest, adorned with beads, rings, bangles, brace-
lets, tattoos, ruffles and medals, silks cascading out of
pockets, silver and gold buckles on their patent leather
shoes. Although I tried to keep my attention on Iris, who
chattered at my right, I'm afraid The Orgasms and Lisa—
Dan's beautiful teenager with chalk-white makeup and eyes
made up like sunflowers—were too much competition for
her.

I suspect I became more drunk from the food than the
wine; I should have pulled myself out of there right after
dinner, but Dan had indicated that he had something to tell
me so I hung on. More people arrived after dinner. Well
dressed. Interesting faces. I kept to myself, sitting on a high-
backed chair near the balcony doors where the fresh air was
a help and where I had a good sweep of the room. A man
in a white silk turtleneck was sniffing after Iris but she kept
drifting back to me, bringing me gossip from her forays

into the thickening crowd, the way a platoon scout brings back reports from where the action is.

"Jesus, you won't make any connections sitting on your ass over here!" Dan had come up on my blind side, one of the perils of taking a position where your flanks aren't covered. "Do you know how much hungry pussy is prowling around this room dying to snatch somebody like you? And *you*, hell! if you got laid ten times a day for ten years you couldn't catch up. Listen, there's one—you can get your nuts off right away—see that blonde there, in the leopard-kind-of sheath? Upper-case English married to that tall British with the crazy mustache—veddy proper and all that but actually sour on each other. She's always goosed on grass and how she gives it to him is a party like this she sets up with some guy—let's say you—makes sure her husband knows it, and then she glides off with you into the john and locks the door and goes down on you. That's her big charge—always in the john, there's no way to get her to do anything else—she loves it and take it from me she's sensational—just what you need. Come on. I'll put you two together."

"I better give it a pass, Dan. This has been a heavy day for me . . ."

"Well, lighten your load, for Christ's sake! That's the great thing about a blow job, no put, all take. All right, maybe you can score with that Iris. I notice she's been smelling around you, but I warn you she's pretty low voltage." He suddenly grabbed my arm with such intensity I thought he was having a heart attack. "Look at those two! Would you just look at those two over there! I don't know who brought them but have you ever seen boobs and legs like that? Matched snatch. Why wasn't I born with twin pricks so I could give them a simultaneous bang?"

"Listen, Dan," I said, "I may fold off pretty soon"—his

sexual Baedecker was wearing me out—"all that great food
and wine and everything came on me so fast . . ."

"Yea, I guess it's a lot to handle if you're not used to it.
Well, a few things to tell you . . ." He led me through the
crowded living room and along a hallway into a small library. He threw himself down on the couch and unbuttoned
the top of his pants. "Oh," he exhaled, relieved, "I simply
refuse to give up a thirty-two waist but it's murder. Now—
I've been working my ass off for you. Why are you such a
goddam nut, Selwyn? All right, you are, and after what
you've been through you should get a crack at *anything*—
but you're sure pushing it. I talked to Elaine Gribble—she's
the Embassy woman who's here tonight. I think she can get
you the four months—but that's just the American part;
that's the easy one. It's the Italian *permesso* that's the bitch;
I figure it will require six ounces of wheedling, four ounces
of threats, and two pounds of money. Man, Roman intrigue!
That's what the whole town is, political intrigue. That's the
only industry here—nothing is manufactured in Rome except the machinery of politics. It's a city of civil servants.
Can you name one Roman product? Just political skull-
duggery—or should I say buggery?"

The door opened and an attractive, heavily jeweled
young woman poked her head in. "There a powder room in
here?" Slight accent.

"Come here, Vana," Dan said. She came there. "Lie
down." She laid down beside him. He put his hand on her
stomach and began to caress her. "I will soothe your bladder.
You won't need the *pissoir*." She giggled and snuggled
against him. One of her diamonded hands went to rest on
the inside of his trouser leg. Dan moved his hand aimlessly
over her stomach and thighs and breasts as he talked to me.

"You probably don't know what's happened to prices and
you may think your two hundred clams are going to carry
you awhile but they're not. And I don't want you to think

I'm a good touch because I live so fucking classy; the truth is my ass hole's up against the hilt and I couldn't raise an extra hundred lire even to get this luscious virgin to put out for me." He bit her neck and she giggled again. "So what I'm saying is if you don't get a sponsor you are out of business in a hurry."

I said I understood. "All right," he continued, "I went over all my names and one guy stands out over all the rest. In fact, the only possibility. Name is Constantin Gibio. Been here for years. First met him on an assignment, then he got the hots for Natalie, wound up buying some of her big sculpture. Well, for all the years I've known him, I don't know much about what Gibio really does. Import-export is all I know. He has power, contacts, money, and he knows how to keep his mouth shut. He is also smart. Let me say he is *first* of all smart. He won't double-cross nor can he be double-crossed by anybody who has any kind of a life expectancy. He is a gambler, but the odds must match the risk. How does he sound to you?"

"I would very much like to meet him."

"You will. Tomorrow at five o'clock. I'll pick you up at your hotel. Do your homework, Paul, because, frankly, if Gibio turns you down, you've had it." Vana's hand wandered under Dan's shirt. "Just what are you doing under there, baby?" Dan asked. She ran her nose back and forth along his neck. Our meeting had obviously lost its focus. I closed the door softly behind me and started back toward the living room but as the heat and noise and smoke came at me, last straws on the load of this long, new lop-sided day, it was suddenly too much and I just made it to the bathroom in time. Ephemeral delights—but not this ephemeral. From dining table to toilet bowl in under two hours. I sat on the edge of the tub and held a cold cloth to my face and wondered where I'd get the strength to maneuver myself back to the hotel.

Someone tried the door. I put my mouth under the tap
and let cold water flush out the sour taste. Again the door
handle rattled. I dried my face and combed my hair and
opened the door. The upper-case English blonde in the
leopard-spotted dress was waiting in the hallway with the
French anthropologist who had his arms around her from
the back. The sticky smell of marijuana hung over them.
I eased my way through the compacted living room without running into Iris, and luckily a little flat-nosed Fiat
taxi was just discharging its passengers as I came out on the
street.

chapter three

Bells ran the system at Santo Stefano. Six o'clock bells for rising, bells for cleanup, bells for breakfast, bells all through the day to a lights-out bell at 10 P.M. So the following morning I was up on my feet at the second bell; it took five rings before I realized where I was and that the bells were coming from a telephone on the table next to the bed. The phone, so long absent from my life, had an exotic feel as I put it to my ear.

"Hello, Paul—that you?"

"Yes."

"It's Iris. You snuck out on me. You know how long I looked for you?"

"I'm sorry. I . . . ."

"Look, it's okay—you didn't bring me but a girl likes her good-nights."

"If you think I could find you in that haystack of people . . ." There was a cacophony of amplified voices in the background. "Where are you?"

"Oh, you hear that? That's the dubbers at work. That's why I called you. Spoke to Signor Riselli. He'd like to audition you. He has a Vittorio Gassman that starts Friday."

"That's very nice of you, Iris. But me as Vittorio Gassman? Well—if you say so . . . Can I do it tomorrow?"

"All right. Why don't you meet me here at ten o'clock? I'll tell Riselli." She gave me the address. She also gave me her own telephone number and address.

I washed and shaved and dressed in Dan's finery, appreciating each piece of clothing even more than I had the night before. The terrace doors threw a golden block of sunshine on the mirror above the sink, and as I combed my hair I had the remembered sensation, in that amber light, of being on stage during my Thespian turns at Washington University.

I went downstairs to have breakfast, but the little coffee room off the lobby was deserted and not cheerful so I left my heavy brass room key at the desk and went out to find a better place. The narrow streets were busy and full of good smells emanating from the trattorias, coffee bars, food stores and flower stalls of the area; I felt wonderful and completely confident that a day that started so splendidly would surely culminate in success with Constantin Gibio.

Albergo d'Inghilterra, to use its full name, is just a few steps from the Via Condotti, the most fashionable shopping street in the city, and as I walked along the single-file sidewalk I was dazzled by the endless panorama of clothes, leather, silver, glass, jewelry, watches, furs, porcelain, statuary, antiques, rare books, tobacco, candy, silks, and other parading luxuries that decorated the windows. In the impoverished Italy I had last known, possession of a full box of pasta had been considered a mark of affluence; but these bedazzling riches had the curious effect of making me not want them. There was simply too much, and so much of what there was seemed to have a pointless costliness that vulgarized the object itself. A Ferrari flashed by; now *there* was costliness with a point to it, beauty with a function, with power, with an emotional wallop. For me, beautiful cars are feminine gender. The Lancias, Maserattis, Lotuses, Facel-Vegas and Aston-Martins whom I had fallen in love with on the pages of prison magazines were all females. Cadillacs were males.

I found a fine, old coffee house on the Via Condotti, its century-old smells of coffee and pastry imprisoned in its walls and tables, so that the very wood exuded the aroma of espresso from its pores. I ordered a *cappuccino* and found myself enthralled with the coffee man's ritual—banging the old wet coffee into a wooden drawer that caught the rejected grounds, then dipping in fresh, black coffee, and the man working the big brass handles on the machine, bringing forth tears of fresh, pungent coffee that dripped slowly into a cup. Then milk poured into a pail and bombarded with a jet of steam until it worked itself into a froth and this thick white froth poured atop the ebony coffee and crowned with a sprinkle of cinnamon. A crisp soft-centered *cornetta* to eat with it, everyone around me pleasant and well-mannered and handsomely dressed and in this euphoria I could see Gibio writing out a check for all I needed.

All that day, without a break, my papers (some of the news clips yellow-brittle with age) spread out on the bed and the floor and the most important ones on the wooden table that served as a desk, I rebriefed myself for the five o'clock meeting with Gibio. I tried to anticipate the kind of questions he might ask, and every so often I found myself on my feet in front of the mirror over the sink, giving Gibio a forceful answer to some straw query I had set up. If you spend enough time alone in a cell, talking to your mirror-self is as accepted a part of life as masturbation.

Dan arrived promptly at four-thirty with a look of gray hangover about his gills. He was in a surly, silent mood, a man trapped in a situation he would have liked out of. He sat hunched over the wheel, his handsome dark features shrouded in storm clouds, driving aggressively even by

Rome's reckless standards, grunting at his automotive com-
batants, not saying a word to me. I was thankful for that,
for I was so nervous about the impending interview that
conversation would have been virtually impossible. The assurance I had felt that morning was now draining off in the
face of reality, and a cold numbness had started to hit my
extremities.

Dan parked the car on Via Ludovisi, a block away from
the Gibio address. As we left the car we were accosted by
a gypsy woman in rags, holding a baby also swathed in
filthy rags, with open sores on its legs and face. I started
to put a few lire in the woman's outstretched palm but Dan
pushed my arm away. "Don't," he said. "She rents the baby.
The sores are deliberate." That's all he said to me from the
time we left the Inghilterra to the moment he rang the bell
on the top floor of 21 Via Ludovisi.

Constantin Gibio. The name had conjured up a dark-
visaged, stout man with smoky glasses, diamond ring-finger,
opal pinky, unfathomable, urbane, pronounced accent of
indeterminate origin—conjuration one hundred percent
wrong.

Dan and I were led into a circular, high-ceilinged (must
have been thirty feet) salon by a thin old retainer who wore
a black silk coat not unlike those worn by *valets des
chambres*. The room was sumptuously but sparingly furnished: silk brocade Regency sofas and chairs; giant armoirs
of unbelievably intricate inlaid woods flecked with ivory,
placed against the walls like majestic guardsmen; much free
space so that individual pieces—a mother-of-pearl chess
table, a tiered desk with veins of silver and gold running
through the ancient woods, an ebony Chinese harp—stood
as distinctive as jewels on their velvet beds in a Cartier window.

Constantin Gibio went with the furniture. He was a tall,
thin, ascetic man, with two heavy furrows running from his

nostrils to his mouth corners, gray hair white at the temples, combed flat back, an arched nose so thin one doubted he could draw breath through it, clothes so fitted they must have been sewn on his body.

"Dan, you look more *paparazzi* every time I see you." Indefectible English. Oxford or Cambridge, but acquired, not native. Dan and Gibio shook hands heartily, beaming at each other. The grayness lifted from Dan's face as he introduced me volubly and then started to discuss with Gibio some mutual friend who had recently, distinctly out of character, hacked off the left arm of his wife's lover with a meat cleaver. The ancient retainer wheeled in a liquor wagon from which we were served whiskey. Gibio was charming, laughed easily, and offered me no clue as to how I should deal with him—my one and only target of opportunity.

"Well, Mr. Selwyn, perhaps we should start our discussion. Dan said it would take some time. Why don't we take our drinks into my study where we can be more private."

My legs felt numb and I had to move them consciously, my own puppeteer. The walls of the study were covered with beige leather, as were the chairs and the sofa and the top of Gibio's arc-shaped desk. Gibio and Dan sat on the sofa, and I sat in one of the two soft leather arm chairs that faced them. The room was lighted by recessed fixtures in the ceiling, the lights set in such a way as to fall directly on the sofa and on my chair, thus making us players on a stage set, each basking in his own light. As I started to talk (I addressed myself directly to Gibio throughout) a profound change occurred in him. I could literally watch the bonhomie of the moments before begin to evaporate; his blue-gray eyes changed to slate; the twin furrows deepened and set. Before me was the man whom Dan had described.

Gibio knew about Mussolini's flight with the Italian treasury in his possession, which shortened the need for explanation. I informed Gibio that I had come into Milan with the vanguard of the Allied forces after Mussolini and all his ministers had been executed.

In late May of 1945, the Allied High Command decided to appoint a team to investigate the treasure. I was then a captain in the air force, with a background in air force intelligence, and before that law school. At the time of the investigation I was chief European correspondent for *Air Force* magazine. Our missions usually involved assignment to some air force outfit—for example the Eighth in England—where we'd stay for a tour of three or four months, writing articles about its exploits for the magazine.

I was in Paris just before it was liberated, and during this time I had met Dan, who had spent the war on the staff of the infantry journal *Yank*. Our paths were constantly crossing and we had some great times together.

As I explained this Dan broke in to describe how we met. "I think you could say that our friendship was forged in the heat of my stupidity and Paul's guts. It was the Marseilles area, tough district. I had a great, juicy, red-haired, freckled-faced *poupée* on ice there; and I'd been away for two months and I was on my way to heat her up again. I had loaded a jeep with boxes of rations—the big dining-hall rations with chocolate bars, beef stew and toilet paper, not the little dehydrated K stuff— and passing through that tough, bombed-out starving area in that open jeep with all those rations on display, I was the number-one moving target of the world. Rocks in the middle of the road, I have to stop, bunch of toughs jump me. I have a side-arm but they're on me before I can use it. They drag me out of the jeep and start beating the holy shit out of me. It wasn't just that they wanted the rations, although they wanted them all right, it was also this big American hate they had and I was getting it for the whole U.S. Army.

"It was incredible that these were French, not Germans,

and I can tell you they would have beaten me to death, the way they were going, if Paul hadn't happened along at that minute. He was coming from the opposite direction. Also in a jeep. His headlights picked up that gang giving it to me, and Paul came on with the greatest reflex I've ever seen. He didn't hesitate one second, but he somehow managed to squeeze his jeep between the rocks and the edge of the road, and he just kept coming, right into that pack of rats. He must have hit them going thirty miles an hour and *wham!* there were frogs flying through the air in every direction. I still don't know how he avoided running me over, but he did. He was out of his jeep with an automatic weapon, dragged me away with his free arm, stuffed me into the jeep, fired a couple of bursts to make the few frogs who were able to run, run faster, and had me in a base hospital twenty minutes later. It took me three months to mend. That's how we met."

They had beaten Dan's face so badly that I didn't know for six weeks what he looked like. But he was back on his feet in April, when the Allies went into Milan. I was in the vanguard, working on a wrap-up for a long, retrospective piece I was doing on the air war over Italy. It was then that the Allied Command discovered that the Italian treasury had been wiped out and appointed an investigative team. I was fascinated with the situation, and I thought it would be an interesting few weeks up in the lake country, so I managed to be part of the team. The British appointed a Major Ted Middlekey; the French member was Captain Louis Lefevre; the Dutch named an underground commander, Bis de Jong; and the Italian partisans chose a vice-deputy, Arnoldo Disio.

The five of us, plus Enrico, a former partisan captain we had hired as an assistant, spent about a week in Milan, following leads, taking depositions, and, in general, working out a *modus operandi*. The Britisher, Ted Middlekey, was in charge; he had Scotland Yard in his background and was clearly a professional in investigative work, while the rest of us were amateurs. Bis de Jong came from counter-intelligence, Lefevre from underwater demolition—try to figure out the Gallic reasoning in that appointment—and Disio had been a liaison leader between the French and Italian undergrounds.

By tracking down key people who handled the treasure at the Milan level, we began to get detailed background and leads we could pursue. The cashier for the Fascist chief of police, a man named Raffaele La Greca, gave us an important deposition: "In 1944 the Mussolini government used the Chief of Police secret fund to buy large quantities of foreign currency and gold. The currency was bought in Switzerland and the gold was collected from various jewelry shops in central Italy. The gold was purchased at its current price, then was partially transformed into ingots, the rest placed in small bags with tags indicating the quantity and the name and address of the jeweler from whom it had been purchased. All this was deposited with me for quite a long time; then, on a certain day, before the war ended, the Finance Secretary, Pellegrini, came to me and withdrew all of it, leaving me a regular receipt for it."

Depositions like these began to provide us with precise inventories of the various components of the treasure. One of the most important contacts we made was with the partisan Pedro, a leader of the Garibaldi Brigade, who had been in charge of the arrests in Dongo. He told me that the Nazis had managed to secrete a little of the treasure in their lorries, but when they realized they were going to be searched, they had jettisoned everything in the Mera River. Apparently a fisherman had found some of this treasure in the river bottom and turned it over to the partisans. When Pedro opened the bags, he found gold that weighed 35,880 kilograms. He was amazed to find that one of the bags contained the wedding rings and baptismal medals which Mussolini had asked the Italian people to contribute during the Abyssinian War.

In tracing the fate of these three bags of gold, we found that the partisans Pedro and Moretti, and a mysterious Swiss, Luigi Hoffmann, whose name kept cropping up again and again in our inquiries, had deposited the three bags at the Casa di Risparmio of Damaso. The police headquarters at Como heard about this and immediately sent an officer to pick up the bags. But when he arrived he was told that the three bags had just been picked up by a group representing themselves as partisans; Luigi Hoffmann was probably a member of this group.

Our tracking got as far as identifying the driver of the partisan lorry that was supposed to transport the bag to the general command of the Communist headquarters in Milan, but there the trail ended. The driver, Moretti, had disappeared into thin air. He had never appeared in Milan and there were no leads on him.

The leads on these bags of gold were just a few of the many leads we began to develop and which we pursued when we moved to Como and set up field headquarters there. During the first three weeks at Como, we began to make some recoveries. We conducted a search of the Villa Mantero, which was right in Como itself, that's where Rachele Mussolini and the Mussolini children had lived just before the abortive attempt to escape to Switzerland. We found a clumsily hidden leather case in which were nineteen Italian and foreign citations conferred on the Duce during his lifetime. There was the Order of the Annunciation, which was decorated with a chain of solid gold covered with fine diamonds; the Persian Order was even more impressive—an expanse of diamonds set in an exquisite gold shield. Experts said that the diamonds were unique and of enormous value. There were two German orders, also in gold and diamonds, and several of the others were set with rare emeralds and rubies.

We had established ourselves in a villa, right on the lake, which had been the Fascist headquarters during the war. It was furnished sumptuously with the choicest objects that had been plundered by the Fasciti from neighboring villas on the lake. One wall of the living room was covered with fluted silver organ pipes but the organ was out of commission and the pipes were badly dented as a result of drunken officers hurling empty bottles at them. It was underneath the platform on which the organ stood that we found an ideal hiding place for the valuables we had collected. The trap door that led to this space was covered by carpet, and in the space itself there was a maze of organ machinery, under which we were able to fit these treasures. We also kept our unit funds there—approximately $90,000—because at that time the banks could not be trusted.

What we found out, pretty much at the outset of our investigation in Como, was that the vanished treasure really divided itself into two parts: one found its way into the partisan coffers of the Communist party, and the other stayed in the lake region. The part that was funneled by the partisans into the Communist treasury eventually wound up in Rome, where it financed postwar Communist political activity and purchased a massive headquarters building which Romans promptly called the Palazzo Dongo. From what we determined, however, most of these Communist-directed funds were in currencies. Very little of the heavy treasure—gold, jewels, all that—very little of this heavy stuff was involved, probably because its source was too easily identifiable.

As to that portion of the treasure that stayed in the lake region, there again there was a division: the part that was looted from the convoy when it was halted along the road outside of Dongo, and the part, mostly heavy treasure, that disappeared into hands other than those of roadside looters. We also discovered that a detailed inventory had been made in Dongo of every treasure item as it was unloaded from the vehicles in the convoy. Here again the name Captain Neri cropped up: he was the partisan inspector of the military command for the Lombard region, and he had arrived in Dongo to supervise the unloading of the vehicles. His mistress was a partisan named Gianna who had fought by his side during three years of underground warfare and who had been tortured and somewhat disfigured when she had been briefly captured by the Fascists. Officially, she was the liaison officer for the Fifty-second Brigade.

Neri issued orders that everything unloaded from the vehicles was to be taken into the city hall, where Gianna had set up an inventory check-point and a storage area. As it was brought in Gianna herself entered each item onto the inventory sheet, which was then typed up, with either four or five copies—the exact number was never established. The inventory was then witnessed and signed by five persons: Gianna, Neri, the two partisans Moretti and Pedro, and the daughter of Dongo's mayor, who was a close friend of Gianna's and who had helped her prepare the inventory. We knew that if we could get our hands on a copy of this inventory we'd have precise information as to just what we were looking for.

But we discovered that Neri and Gianna did a lot more than just preside over the loot inventory. It was they who whisked Mussolini out of Dongo in the dead of that April 28th night, when assassination intrigue was beginning to boil. They hid him at a nondescript farm, and were also intimately involved in a series of complicated shuffles involving the most valuable booty on the inventory. Midnight transfers that involved silently arriving lorries, and daytime transfers to banks carried out openly. From reports of those in Dongo at the time, it seems that both Neri and

Gianna were scrupulously honest in their overriding resolve to return the treasure to the Italian people and the government. They wanted none of it for themselves, and they would not tolerate anybody else's lust.

Under the circumstances, that kind of honesty paid a deadly price. About a week after the Dongo capture, Neri disappeared near Como under mysterious circumstances. Gianna received anonymous warnings not to go to Como to look for him, but when she disregarded them and she arrived in Como, she too disappeared. When her brother, Cesare Tuissi, went to look for her, he was ambushed on the Como road but luckily escaped a machine-gun burst. A short time later the mayor's daughter, who had worked on the inventory, also vanished. Moretti had disappeared on his way from Como to Milan, and as for Pedro, reports persisted for several years on his whereabouts, and it's possible he's still alive. No one, however, has ever been able to locate him. Gianna's body was eventually washed up on the shore of Lake Como between Menaggio and Acquaseria. Thus, all those involved with the inventory and the inventory itself had disappeared.

Middlekey decided that he, Bis de Jong, Lefevre and the partisan assistant, Enrico, would go on up to Dongo and start trying to unravel things there, especially the mystery of the disappeared inventories, while Arnoldo Disio and I stayed on in Como. Arnoldo knew the area and the people well, as he came from Bellagio, a few miles to the north, on the tip of the promontory that separates Lake Como from Lake Lecco. We went about our business slowly, at first. Letting the locals get used to us, Arnoldo seeking out old friends, probing a little, but not prying. First-rate man, Arnoldo. Sensitive. Intelligent. I admired and respected him very much. On several occasions we drove up to his small, attractive house in Bellagio, where he had a lovely wife and a little daughter, whom he adored as only Italian fathers can adore daughters. His old mother and a brother also lived there. The brother, who had been a novitiate priest, was a sour, bitter man who had also fought with the partisans, and had been badly wounded. He was dead set against Arnoldo's working for the Allied Commission because he felt the treasure rightly belonged to the partisans and the new government.

We became good friends, Arnoldo and I, and really quite effective in our work. Information began to pile up. Jigsaw information, much of it contradictory, but continued reference to Luigi Hoffmann, the Swiss who had lived in a lush villa just outside the city. The police told us they had fine-combed the place—Hoffmann himself had disappeared —but had found nothing but personal possessions. Nevertheless, Arnoldo and I methodically conducted our own search day after day: the gardens, the verandas, the three floors of the house, and on the afternoon of the third day, the cellar. It was a clean, uncluttered cellar that quite obviously had nothing to yield but a wine rack that covered most of one wall. In those times a single bottle of good wine was a rarity, but there before us was an entire rack of choice bottles. While inspecting them one of the bottles slipped, fell to the floor and broke. As we bent down to pick up the pieces, we saw marks, symmetrical lines where rollers had moved forward. Set back underneath the racks we found the metal rollers that had made the marks. So it was just a matter of figuring out what released the racks which were so beautifully engineered they effortlessly moved forward and swung to the side. Set behind them was a walk-in wall safe, forbidding, complicated mechanism. We needed help for that, two experts sent from Milan, and we stayed right there in the cellar until they got there.

There was a lot of stuff in there that belonged to Hoffmann, and a lot that didn't—at least, not rightfully. The three bags of wedding rings and other gold which the fisherman had scraped off the bottom of the Mera River. A velvet-covered box that contained twenty-two of the crown jewels. Several wooden ammunition boxes in which was a total of thirty-three million lire in neatly stacked one-thousand-lire bills. We knew about the bags of gold and the crown jewels, of course, but the boxes of new lire puzzled us until, in his quiet, confidential way, Arnoldo got the story from Hoffmann's gardener, an ancient but vigorously straight-backed gentleman whose affection for Mussolini was unabated by recent events. It seemed that a partisan came to visit Hoffmann, who confidentially (but not quietly enough to avert the gardener's ear) told him that when the German motorized column was passing through Como, two of the officers came to see Hoffmann, whom they had known slightly when he lived in Bremen. They carried suitcases in which they had thirty-three million lire in new thousand-lire notes, and they proposed to give Hoffmann a third—eleven million—if he would promise to deliver one-third shares to their two Italian girl friends, one of whom lived in Bologna, the other in Montecatini. Hoffmann readily consented, with no intention of relinquishing the money.

By removing some of the organ machinery—it didn't function anyway—we were able to snug all of this new treasure in the organ pit. We left enough of the machinery to provide complete cover. We informed Middlekey, by pre-arranged code, of our find, and we sent word to Milan to send an armored vehicle to remove the treasure as soon as possible. As far as we knew no one on the local scene knew anything about our discovery.

That evening, around twilight, a boy came to the door of our villa with a note. I had to surrender it at the trial but I remember it only too well: "What you found at Hoffmann's villa is chicken feed. I am in possession of information that can lead you to the bulk of what you seek. Meet me tonight,

Leonardo's Trattoria, 11:30. Sit at table by yourselves. Be sure you come alone. Bring 15 kilograms of gold as first payment."

Arnoldo and I were shocked that our security had been so easily penetrated. Obviously someone had a pretty good line on our activities in Como. My inclination was to disregard this note—I didn't like the smell of it—but it didn't put Arnoldo's nose out of joint. He felt that this was an opportunity that had to be explored—after all, we had no Como leads beyond the Hoffmann villa—and that we had nothing to lose in keeping the rendezvous. I argued that we did have something to lose—what if this was simply a ruse to get us out of the villa so that it could be searched; what we had assembled in our secret organ drop had considerable total value. Arnoldo argued that the risk of losing our assembled treasure was outweighed by the possibility of getting to the really big booty.

We finally solved our differences by doing both things: I would stay in the villa while Arnoldo went to Leonardo's. There was no reason why both of us had to be there, and if an immediate decision of some kind had to be made, the most that Arnoldo could commit would be the fifteen kilograms of gold. We knew Leonardo's very well, having eaten there several times; it was a busy, well-lighted restaurant on the Lungo Lario just beyond the lakefront, certainly a respectable and relatively safe place. Arnoldo wore his inseparable Beretta-bearing underarm holster and, at my urging, put a second gun under the gold, which he carried in an attaché case. He left at eleven o'clock in the enclosed jeep which had been our transport from Milan, and I locked up behind him.

In my recounting for Gibio, I had dreaded this next moment in the narrative, which was, in effect, a sudden gap into which everything that had gone before could tumble and collapse.

What happened in our villa that night is of necessity vague—from the time I started to type up the daily report I have no recollection of anything that happened after Arnoldo left. My next awareness was that it was morning and the maid, who had arrived at her usual time, was waking me for breakfast. I had a headache that ran in a band across my eyes, and a dry-mouthed drowsiness that was hard to chase off. I had an uneasy awareness that something disturbing had happened, the way one wakes aware of an almost-remembered dream, and I kept reaching inside my head, stretching memory fingers that almost touched the disturbances, but not quite.

Then, with a jolt, I did remember Arnoldo and his mission at Leonardo's. But his room had not been slept in, and there was no sign that he had returned to the villa. The maid said that the door had been locked as usual when she arrived. I telephoned Ted Middlekey in Zonico, and our headquarters in Milan, but neither had heard from Arnoldo. I asked the maid if I could borrow her bicycle to go into the town, but when I went outside to get it, there, to my surprise, was our jeep in the garage. It was perfectly all right, the key in the ignition. I searched the jeep carefully, found nothing. I walked around to the rear of the villa, in fact I circled it, but there was no sign, either along the sides where giant hedges formed fences, or in the rear with its lawn and flower gardens, that anyone had been there.

I got in the jeep and drove to Leonardo's. It was closed, but the man in the shoe store next door told me where I'd find Leonardo. Yes, of course, he knew Arnoldo very well. No, he had not been in the restaurant the night before. Yes, he was positive; he, Leonardo, was always very attentive to his clients and no eater as well known to him as Arnoldo could have escaped his attention, especially at that late hour.

I put in a call to Arnoldo's house in Bellagio. His brother,

Pietro, hostile the minute he head my voice, answered the phone. No, Arnoldo was not there, but immediately Pietro demanded to know what was wrong, began firing questions at me. I got off the phone quickly and put in a second call to Ted Middlekey to tell him to come down to Como as soon as he could, but discovered that he was already on his way.

Driving back to the villa, I intended to search Arnoldo's room carefully and to check on the treasure trove. As I turned into the driveway of the villa I came upon the two police cars without warning. The cars were empty but a policeman stood in the driveway in front of the villa's doorway and when he saw me he immediately came over. He asked me who I was and then said that Chief Orsatti was very anxious to talk to me. I followed him into the living room, and a few seconds later the chief entered the room from the garden-side doors. He was very polite and deferential, as Italian police invariably are toward the military, and he explained that he regretted having to interrogate me, but that the tragic circumstances required it. The tragic circumstances were that the neighbor's dog, an amiable brown-and-white Pyrenee who had been spending more time with us than with his master, had discovered a newly dug section in our garden, and in digging up the recently turned soil had unearthed the shallowly buried body of Arnoldo Disio. The maid had come out into the garden to chase the dog away and it was she who called the police. The chief explained that a local doctor who functioned as official medical examiner was at that moment making his examination.

I told the chief the truth about Arnoldo's mission of the night before but then I began to realize, looking ahead, how awkward my own position was, remembering nothing from the time I started typing, so I asked if we could delay his questioning until the head of my unit arrived and I could get his permission to participate in this inquiry. Perhaps this was a matter solely within the jurisdiction of the military . . . The chief said he was perfectly willing to postpone his inquiry, but asked if I was aware that Arnoldo, as a partisan, had no official military standing, even though he was cooperating in a military project.

As soon as the chief returned to the garden, I opened the hiding place under the organ. There were no signs that the carpeting that covered it or the camouflaging machinery in the pit had been disturbed, but the treasure was gone. All of it. The thirty-three million lire in thousand-lire notes, our $90,000 operational funds, the twenty-two crown jewels, the leather case with Mussolini's priceless medals, and the three bags of scrap gold and wedding rings. Not a trace of them. That was the first and only time in my life that I experienced a cold sweat. I suppose at that moment, without yet knowing details of how it would happen, I had a terrible premonition of what was in store for me.

It didn't take long for me to find out. In searching the house, one of the chief's men had come across my service revolver hanging on a hook where I kept it in the armoir in my room. One bullet was missing from its chamber. It had been recently fired. Arnoldo had been killed by a single shot fired into the base of his skull. The examining doctor had established the path of the bullet which had traveled through Arnoldo's skull and partially emerged over his right eye. It was of a caliber that fitted my gun.

Shortly after Middlekey and Bis de Jong arrived from Dongo (Lefevre had been hospitalized with jaundice) and before they had been able fully to assess all that had happened, another discovery was made that drove the spike into me even further: a trail of blots of dried blood ran from the hallway outside my door along the upstairs corridor, down the back stairs, and out the garden door right up to the area where Arnoldo had been buried. Middlekey and de Jong never for a second doubted that I had been made the victim of an elaborate frame-up; that the theft of the resident treasure was just incidental to the bigger purpose of getting rid of our investigative team. As long as we were around we threatened the main treasure, and well-organized, clever and ruthless people were determined to get us out of the way. What better way than to impugn all of us by the criminal misdeeds of one of us?

The chief, however, was not interested in our speculations. Arnoldo Disio had been an old boyhood friend of his. Middlekey and I argued with him over whether he had proper jurisdiction in a matter that involved the military, but the chief was firm in his belief that the murdered body of Arnoldo, who in the chief's eyes was a Como civilian and not of the military, had been found buried in Como soil and therefore jurisdiction over the body and the murderer was his. The chief explained that he would make the arrest but he would be available at any time for conferences with any Allied military who wished to discuss this matter of jurisdiction with him; in the meantime he would consult with his own higher authorities for a ruling.

The immediate effect of the arrest was precisely what, we were sure, our unseen enemies had had in mind—Allied Headquarters in Milan suspended our activities pending an investigation of the charges lodged against me. Middlekey and de Jong were ordered back to Milan for interrogation.

One of the pitfalls of Italian justice is the absence of habeas corpus—a defendant can sit in jail for months, years in fact, without knowing the charges against him or having his day in court. What the army's Judge Advocate lawyers were trying to do was to force the Como prosecutor to indict me formally and set a date for the trial.

I think that if there had been no further negative developments, considering the ardor with which the Judge Advocate's staff was working for me, that I might have come out of the trial not too badly. But there *was* a single further development.

At the time of my arrest, my personal possessions at the villa had been confiscated and impounded. When it was finally determined that the Como authorities, not the military, had jurisdiction over my case, these possessions were released to the Como prosecutor's office. Among my things was a log book, which Middlekey had suggested each of us keep of our activities, findings, interrogations. The regular daily entries pretty much supported the account of my activities that I had given to the police, but in the back of my log book, on the inside of the cover, there was a notation: "Nationale Lugano MLZ-674." It was printed in ink, but not by me.

It didn't take much detective work to decipher it: a numbered account with the Bank Nationale in Lugano. In those days, just after the war, there was just enough laxness, and just enough collusion between Swiss and Italian officials, to permit access to a numbered account on the grounds that the account was involved in a criminal proceeding. What the Como prosecutor discovered was that account number MLZ-674 with the Bank Nationale, about which I knew nothing, was registered in the name of Paul Selwyn, and the assets deposited in the account were thirty-three million lire, converted into Swiss francs.

None of the other treasure that had disappeared was there, but the thirty-three million was all that was needed. Although the Judge Advocate did not formally withdraw its lawyers, they did in fact disappear soon after the numbered account's identity was disclosed. Dan had come up from Milan and hired a local lawyer to fend for me but there was not much he or anyone else could do. The investigation of the treasure was abandoned. Middlekey and de Jong came to see me before leaving to let me know there was no doubt in their minds but that I had been

elaborately framed. Without proof, their belief was mean-
ingless. I wasn't brought to trial until 1948, three years
sweating it out in the stinking medieval sewer that they
use for a jail in Como, and by then the few people who
had been trying to help me had given up.

"So there you have it, Mr. Gibio," I said. "The fact is
twenty-four years in Italian prisons—all my young manhood
—and the only way I know to get repaid in some measure
for it is to have what's left of my life financed by the very
thing that did me in to begin with. That's where you come
in, Mr. Gibio, and you, Dan. I need a certain amount of
money, and I need contacts and information. And to get
them, I'm willing to give you a good chunk of whatever I
find."

"But, Mr. Selwyn," Gibio said, "granted your motivation
and your determination, do you have any plan of action
other than to go back to the Como-Dongo area and hope
for the best?"

"Yes, I do. I have spent the last fifteen years working on
nothing else. What I want to do, to start with, is to locate
Ted Middlekey and Bis de Jong and convince them to join
me—naturally for a participating part of whatever we get
our hands on. *If* I can find them and *if* I can persuade them
to throw in with me, then the next thing needed is a cover
for our operations. The one that I've worked out, in complete detail, is that of an archaeological team."

"Doing what?"

"Have you ever been to Sirmione on Lake Garda—the
town that's on a promontory that juts into the lake?"

"Yes—to see the Roman spa that's been excavated there."

"Well, now, if the Romans had such a spa and resort on
Garda, it seems credible, doesn't it, that they might also have
had a spa on Lake Como? Of course, to get the necessary
permissions for our expedition I would have to present a

compelling case to the Italian authorities . . . and, thanks to the prison library I have read and studied a great deal about Roman and Etruscan archaeology. The library was able to obtain on loan virtually every important book I wanted. I'm perfectly confident that the Fine Arts Council will accept both my role as a professor of archaeology and the scholarly leads I've developed to justify digs in the Dongo area. With the ten years of research I've put in, I doubt anyone on the Council knows more about Roman activity in this area than I do."

"Then your overall plan would be to set up headquarters there under the guise of an American archaeological expedition . . ."

"An international expedition . . ."

". . . that is seeking the remains of an ancient Roman spa, but in reality you would be following leads toward locating the treasure—leads that either you know about or plan to create."

"That's part of it. Equally important, I should think, would be the psychological pressures that might build up when word gets around about the real purpose of our mission. I imagine there will be people who will get very nervous about us. And perhaps other people who, under proper cover, might want to talk to us out of the sides of their mouths."

"A little while ago you referred to Dan and me in relation to your plans in rather general terms; can you be more specific?"

"Yes, quite specific. I need a four-month extension of my *permesso* to stay in Italy. I need a proper presentment to the Fine Arts Council, and permission from them to set up the archaeological stand as soon as possible. The expedition has to be outfitted with a special van and equipment, and we have to be financed for the four months. I must find my prison friend Giorgio in Naples and hire him for the expedition. Through Giorgio I will be able to get all the forged documents I need. Also, he has very special skills, most of them frowned on by the law, which the expedition needs. And I must also locate Ted Middlekey and Bis de Jong—I presume they're in London and Amsterdam—and go see them about joining on. I also must find the Disios, who may still be in Bellagio or not. If all goes right, we will need a villa in Zonico for our headquarters, and we will need supplies."

Dan was on his feet now. "For Christ's sake, Paul, what do you think's going to happen when you start nosing around again—especially with this outfit you want to assemble. Talk about risk! Why, hell, I don't have to get you four months— a couple of weeks are all you need because by then you'll be laid out in the Como mortuary."

"But you're talking about *my* risk, Dan . . ."

"And your friends Middlekey and de Jong and Giorgio and anybody else you lure into this."

"But all those risks are calculated. Don't you think those men know exactly what's involved? And as for me—I appreciate your concern about my safety—but what's the difference if I'm one kind of corpse or another? I've been a corpse in a prison cell for twenty-four years. I've already told you I intend to make up for that lost time. If I put my ass in jeopardy that's my business. It has nothing to do with the kind of risks I am asking you and Mr. Gibio to take."

Gibio got to his feet, and so did I. "Mr. Selwyn," he said, as if Dan's outburst hadn't occurred, "I understand your proposition very well. You have been honest and explicit and I am intrigued by the possibilities you have offered. I would like to give it some thought, for it is a rather large undertaking; within a day or two I shall give you an answer." He started to walk us toward the door. "Just one thing, Dan," he said. "In view of these rather intense feelings you have, if I should decide to participate would you go along with us? Obviously your involvement would be an asset and I would like to know if it can be counted on?"

Dan looked at me, hesitated. "Well—I'll think on it," he said. "If there's no stopping Paul, I guess I'd like a potful of jewels as much as the next guy."

chapter four

Iris initiated me into the society of English dubbers—masters of the baffling process by which language substitution is achieved. I decided to pursue the dubbing opportunity because, as Dan had warned, my small funds were disappearing at an alarming rate and there was no telling if or when Constantin Gibio might come through. I first had to join the union—the English Language Dubbers' Association—which deducted its five-thousand-lire fee from my first day's pay. Next I had to learn the exhaustingly patient technique whereby a line of English is mouthed in rhythm to lips on the screen that are speaking Italian.

I was immediately put to work on a picture called *Blood Is Red,* dubbing the dialogue for the Italian actor Vittorio Gassman. It was a costume film about feudal war in medieval Lombardy, and Gassman (and I) played the part of a villainous prince. The first line which, in my Mid-Atlantic voice, I was to deliver in the first sequence was: "Say no more! You speak heatedly but your words make my blood run cold." The sequence was repeated so often (primarily because I couldn't get the hang of moving my lips at the same time Gassman moved his) that my neck froze from looking up at the screen so long and my voice got throat-bound and reedy.

Iris was very adroit at this and tried to help me all she could; but in addition to not having what the dubbers called true sync, I also didn't have any true acting ability, so that most of my lines sounded like announcements over an airport public address system. At lunch, that first day, Iris massaged my neck and coached my delivery so that in the afternoon session we were able to do three sequences (six was par). Iris was like my big sister on my first day at school, and quite removed from the Iris of Dan's party. She was friendly, but when she massaged my neck it seemed to me her chiropractical fingers were being deliberately nonsensual.

"There, that ought to ease it," she said, suddenly moving away and into the chair across from me, as if she had felt the rush of my blood under her fingers. I rotated my neck to show how she had bettered it. She was not wearing a bra under her thin summer dress, so that the nipples of her high, tight breasts left two exciting punctuations on her dress. But what was it Dan had said at the party? Warn you she's pretty low voltage; very accurate; but I had the feeling that it was not so much a normal low output as a throttled one. Iris seemed to sit ambivalent in her saddle, digging her spurs into her flanks while pulling hard on the restraining bit in her pretty mouth.

"I'm sorry to have to leave you on your own but I have a two-day on an oater in Calabria," she said.

"What language is that?"

She laughed. "Paul, you're so out of everything. Why don't you tell me where you're from? Where you've been? You're so mysterious, so . . . what should I say . . . old-fashioned. Maybe you're an Amish—where's your beard?"

"What's a two-day on an oater?"

"It means I have a stunning part in an Italian western

that will require two days of shooting in the peace-loving province of Calabria."

"When do you go?"

"This evening."

I showed my disappointment. I had keenly anticipated this coming night with her; finally, finally, finally, a woman, my whole body on a sharpened edge of expectancy.

"You won't have any trouble with the part," she assured me, misreading my disappointment. "Just don't push too hard. Try to make your voice sound more casual."

"When will you be back?"

"Probably Friday."

"I'd like to have dinner with you."

"Fine, but I can't be sure. Once they see what a great cow-girl I am, they may pad my part."

"Well, if they can part with you and you do get back . . ."

"I'll phone you at the dubbery."

Four days passed and despite stiffness of neck and hoarseness of throat and nervousness of stomach I was grateful that the 8 A.M. to 8 P.M. hours with Vittorio Gassman kept me preoccupied. There was no word from Constantin Gibio, Dan had gone to Florence to cover an incipient student riot at the university there, and Iris, who must have wowed them in Calabria, did not come back on Friday.

I moved from the Inghilterra to a small *pensione* off the Piazza del Populo, no balcony but one-third as expensive, and I found a couple of alley-street trattorias that served hearty workingmen's dishes at workingmen's prices. Dan's warning about the insufficiency of my capital funds had been quickly corroborated, and the daily wage from dubber's heaven was a godsend. I was adjusting to this "outside" life more sure-footedly than I had expected but that is not to say that I didn't have my surprises and problems. Every day the streets, the shop windows, the newspapers, the talk, the movies, the beauties of antiquities, sky, flora, fountains, the kiosks, the restaurant smells, the fringed-topped horse carriages in line on the Via Liguria, the immaculate white-suited opéra-bouffe cops—such things were a source of continuing excitement. I actually enjoyed crush-hour on the bus that carried me from *pensione* to dubber-ville, enjoyed being part of that free-moving mass of people. The best evening I had was the one I spent sitting in the Excelsior lobby watching the ebb and flow of arriving and departing humanity.

Those were my diversions and they took me away briefly from the mounting pressure of my treasure project. I spent much of my free time at the dubbery reading books old and new, and reviewing my prison notes in preparation for my interview with the Fine Arts people when the time came (I hoped!) to get the all-important archaeological permit. My moods varied from despair, because I had not heard from Gibio, to resolute confidence that I could pull it off even if I had to go it alone.

Physically, my primary problem was adjusting my twenty-four-year-old diurnal cycle away from the prison routine— up at 5:30 A.M., lights out at 10 P.M.—to the languid Roman life which provided siestas and emphasized night life that began at just about the time prison lights were going out. In fact, when my poor confused stomach began to demand attention at its accustomed feeding hour it was virtually impossible to find a restaurant that served before nine or ten. Also, I found it very difficult to keep my eyes open past the ten o'clock darkness that enveloped my cell every night when, at the sound of the final bell, I turned off the bulb.

I had one other physical problem—sweats—not an easy one to describe or certainly to explain. These were not simply night sweats—I used to have those in prison occasionally and I attributed them to bad dreams. But now these first days in Rome, I experienced day sweats, at the strangest times, the most peculiar feeling to be talking to someone or sitting in a coolly shaded café or even in an air-cooled movie, my mind not on anything distressing or feeling any conscious anxiety but suddenly the sweats, all-over sweats, even my scalp wet and my fingers probing inside my shirt, soaked, and my hand run up from my ankle under my trouser leg came away covered with heavy moisture. Sweat so heavy on my forehead it ran down my temples and when, under unwarm circumstances I had to fish out my handkerchief and mop away, I would get uncomprehending looks from people that made me embarrassed.

Then with the same abruptness with which they had appeared, the sweats would disappear, as if I had some kind of pore-operated irrigation system that could exhale and inhale its output. I realized they must be anxiety sweats, but this explanation did nothing to alleviate the distress I felt when, at times, I would get as soaking wet as if I had just stepped from a shower.

Then the other distress was about a woman. That was the strangest feeling of all. I was certain, after that party at Dan's, that Iris was going to be my touchstone, and all through the afternoon of that day I thought I was going to go to bed with her, I thought about her mouth and how her breasts would feel and the unbearable sensation on entering her. I thought about her small flat ass and narrow hips and my anticipatory senses could actually feel her skin on mine. All through that day my skin and groin were sensitized by this anticipation, and then when it did not come off the desire continued to nag at me. But with Iris away there was nothing I could do about it. Even as a young man I was not much good at foraging; now the prison years had left me feeling that there was some kind of indelible stamp on me, a tell-tale tattoo for all the world to see that I was a convict. The whores that patrolled the Isedra fountain chirped at me, but whores had always repelled me, and especially now.

Natalie Reeder phoned me twice. The first time to invite me to what sounded like a pretty formal dinner party, where I knew I'd feel out of place. But I accepted her second invitation, which was to accompany a group to the Porta Portese in quest of Ingrid, the dognapped Labrador for whom Ingrid, the photographer, was grieving.

The Porta Portese is perhaps the last genuine Thieves' Market left in Europe. The police do not inquire into the genesis of any of the wild range of items that are offered for sale there—anything from a hunk of Renaissance plaster bearing the portrait of a Medici nobleman unceremoniously and hurriedly hacked out of a wall of some Palladio villa in Florence, to an old warped phonograph record of Rudy Vallee singing "O Solo Mio"—and there is no regulation on who may sell, what he sells, or how. For the most part it is a jungle of junk but if one has a good eye, patience, and that rare gift of being able to plunge one's hand into a compost heap and pluck out a rose, then, from what I observed, one can come away with exciting bargains. But I was certainly not there to buy, and the others were all intent on Operation Dognap. Natalie split us up into six groups and we dispersed to various sections of the market where we distributed handbills on which were a picture and description of Ingrid. Our group had been hard at it for over an hour when we were informed that contact had been made by a group at the opposite end of the market and the four-legged Ingrid had been retrieved for a paltry six thousand lire.

Afterward we regrouped at the Reeders', both Ingrids drank champagne, and for the first time I felt that I was not a complete outsider. Natalie showed me a United States

embassy letter on Dan's desk to the effect that my applica-
tion for a four-month stay would be approved *if* the Italian
authorities concurred. She also gave me a large cardboard
box, prepared by Dan before his departure, that contained
what he had described as excess wearing apparel.

Later Natalie took me out to see her studio, which was in
a small, high-peaked structure at the end of a little court-
garden to the rear of the main house. There were a few
canvasses here and there, remnants from her painting
period, but the emphasis of the place was on big, powerful
pieces of machinery and the polished stainless steel sculpture
which they helped execute. I could feel no relation between
the feminine Natalie who stood there in her Pucci and her
Gucci and talked about the huge, boxlike pieces in her
graceful voice, and the very masculine artist who had
created them. I felt that I would actually have to see her at
work to believe that she really manipulated those Goliaths.

She must have sensed this skepticism in me. "One thing
about a lady sculptor, she may not have big sales but she's
sure to have big forearms. Just take hold. No, really take
hold, there below the elbow, is that not a thing of beauty?
Dan says I'm the only woman in the world with Venus
mounds on her forearms. It really comes from chiseling
hickory—that was before my love affair with stainless steel
—I used to put in ten hours a day. Don't you adore this
one? It's called 'Narcissus Reversed.' You want to feel something sexy—just run your hand under here . . ." She
took my hand and guided it along the smooth, sensuous
undersurfaces of the cold steel. Nothing overt, mind you, but
the way she had put my hand on her forearm and now guid-
ing my hand with hers as her left breast, quite casually, perhaps innocently, soft-touched my arm, I felt uncomfortable
and wanted to avoid anything that could cloud my relation
with Dan. Perhaps I was misreading the signs, very likely

I was, so long out of it, but I moved us out of there, not very adroitly, I fear, and back to the main house to join the others.

The day before Iris returned, my career as a dubber came to an end. On completion of the last loop of *Blood Is Red,* the production manager gave me the name and address of a drama coach who, after a few lessons, he felt sure, could give my untutored Mid-Atlantic monotone the vitality it needed.

So I was at liberty to meet Iris for lunch. She was bronzed and her hair a half-tone bleached from the Calabrian sun. She met me at a restaurant she suggested, Pasetto's, just off the Piazza Navona where she lived. On seeing her—white piqué dress with a high waist that accentuated her breasts and a high hem that accentuated her good legs—smiling at me with her full lips imperiously disdainful of lipstick, all the feelings that I had banked when she left rekindled. She suggested a Pasetto specialty: a rich fondue which when brought to table was delicately blanketed with paper-thin chips shaved off a huge white truffle that was handled by the waiter with great care. When Iris urged the waiter to add more truffles, he said, his face very serious, "All right, signorina, but be careful—the white truffle is very aphro-disiac."

"Warn the gentleman, not me," Iris said, and the waiter laughed and gave her the look of approval she deserved.

Fresh asparagus, wild raspberries in cream, espresso, a light Orvieto, the very essence of a languid lunch leading to siesta, but not destined to be, for during lunch Iris had discovered that I had not done any formal sightseeing—I even had to admit I had never been inside St. Peter's— and, treating it as a state of emergency, she became deter- mined to save my cultural soul. At another time it would have been pleasurable, touring the great ecclesiastical show places, St. John in Lateran, Santa Maria Maggiore, St. Peter's, the Pantheon, Santa Maria Sopra Minerva, Iris prattling on in her crisp actressy voice, actually knowing a surprising lot about the history, architecture, works of art, burials, artifacts and all the other minutia churchophiles dote on. I myself had never cared for churches, but now on entering these I was moved by their splendor. By late afternoon Iris' voluableness had gradually subsided, and as we walked silently through the carpet of pigeons in the spacious piazza leading away from the basilica of Santa Maria Maggiore, I felt that I had been truly touched by the grandeur that was Rome.

"One more," Iris said.

"No. I'm over-churched."

"Well, this is different. This is for the good of your soul."

"If you really care about my soul, we will sit down somewhere with our feet up and our shoes off and a drink in our hand."

"I promise you—right after San Salvadore."

"I'm over-apsed, I tell you."

She took my arm and snugged it against her as she measured her steps with mine. "How about *my* soul? A little indulgence for poor little Iris' poor little soul?" We were back to her red Fiat 850 coupe. "I'll tell you about it on the way," she said.

What she took me to was the Scala Santa, which is inside the church of San Salvadore. It is a long flight of marble steps, reputed to be those which Jesus climbed in the house of Pilate in Jerusalem, and brought to Rome by boat by the Empress Helena, the mother of Constantine the Great. There is open access to the stairs but they may only be ascended on one's knees. The prize for this act of devotion (and it is quite an act for there were at least seventy stairs),

is that the church grants each knee-sore ascendant an indulgence from penance for one thousand years. It seemed
like such a bargain for so little relative effort that, although
I was not connected to any religion, I decided to get in line
with Iris and make the ascent. Two priests at the bottom
of the stairs controlled traffic, placing the worshipers four
abreast for the ascent. They constantly exhorted those in line
to move forward and moved each quartet onto the steps with
such efficiency that there was not one vacant step between
the ascenders. There were thick planks of walnut over each
step in order to protect the marble which bore deeply eroded
cups from the centuries of knees that had passed over their
surfaces. Even the planks were knee-pitted and Iris said they
had to be replaced every few years. I felt sorry for the nuns
and monks with their long, copious robes entangling their
knees at every step. It was an awesome sight, the silent
throng undulating upward; there were those, mostly the
aged or infirm, for whom the ascent was too punishing and
they had to be led back down to the bottom, the promise of
one thousand penance-free years lost to them.

As Iris and I knelt side by side to start our ascent, I
noticed a sign on the wall to our left: "Beware of Pick-
pockets." I moved my wallet to the inside coat pocket of my
suit.

It was quite awkward and painful, especially with bony
knees like mine, to kneel my way up. It was also terribly
boring. The slowest ascenders inhibited the pace of the
others and it became necessary to maneuver around the
immobile. Many of these pilgrims had come great distances
for this penance dispensation, and they were determined to
force themselves to the summit, no matter how painful or
how long it took. The hot air in the stairwell was redolent
with the odors of luncheon breaths, sweat, perfumes, lina-
ment, sour wine and stale tobacco. I presumed that since

most of the ascenders kept their heads down they were praying (or watching their knees get bruised); my form of praying was to think about Gibio and his discouraging silence.

"Listen, Iris," I whispered. She turned her head and looked at me through the curtain of her hair. "Do you feel like you're on your way to heaven?" She smiled and nodded and we kneed up a stair in unison. "Do you know who I hope to meet when we get there?"

"No, who? Don't whisper so loud."

"One rich man—who wants to get richer."

"Why?"

"How are your connections? Know any of the moneyed class?"

"No . . . not really. I know some titles . . ."

"Think hard. Don't have to be Italians. Prefer they weren't. How about you? Are you an heiress?"

"I haven't spoken to my father in eight years."

"I just thought you might know an adventurous gentleman with capital—who would like to make more."

"Are you a con man? They say they're the ones who least look it."

"And I don't look the part?"

"Not the least. You want to know how you strike me?"

"Yes."

"Like a man who's been rescued from drowning and can't make up his mind whether to go back in again."

"Tell me, Iris, is the thousand-year indulgence transferable? What's it worth on the open market? How about a ten-thousand-year indulgence? Ten times up and I'd have it, although I'd probably wind up looking like Toulouse-Lautrec."

At the top of the stairs, nuns handed us certificates guaranteeing our thousand-year penitential absolution; we walked along the upper corridor on stiff, numb legs, and I bought Iris a pink plastic Scala Santa at the souvenir stand as a memento of our ascent.

"This rich party you mentioned—is it for a business you want to start? I mean, were you being serious?"

"Yes—double yes. It's for . . . yes, you could say a business, and yes I was being serious."

"Well, I do know someone. I don't much like going to him . . ."

"I have another possibility. I was just covering myself. And I wouldn't like you to ask favors."

"I don't mind asking a favor if I don't have to give one. In this case I wouldn't have to. So let me know and we'll see."

We went for drinks to Iris' apartment, where, as a surprise, she had planned an all-American dinner, pandering to a longing which she ascribed to all Americans who had been too long absent from the land of the hot dog, the hamburger, the bag of hot buttered popcorn and the toasted marshmallow. Little did she realize how long absent *this* American had been or how much a treat it was to taste these long-forgotten culinary obscenities.

Her apartment was on the top floor of a five-story building, facing directly down upon the Bernini statue that centers the Piazza Navona. The place was simply and tastefully furnished with a mixture of antiques and modern. While we waited for the espresso pot to bubble its essence into its upper chamber, we sat on the little balcony and finished the Verdicchio. Down below us a white-aproned boy, holding a silver tray high above his head, darted between the traffic in the piazza, bringing us ice cream *bombas*.

From the moment we walked in, Iris had talked constantly, at first general talk, then increasingly intimate, about her loneliness, her inability to relate to people, and the business

of being an attractive woman alone in an attractive apartment in a city where attractive men are all married and
extramarital hanky-panky an accepted part of life. "There'll
never be divorce laws here," she said. "The men have it too
good. They keep wife and kids to one side and have all the
affairs they want with the excuse that they are trapped by
the church in a loveless relation. Even the Americans are in
on the act. Your friend, Dan Reeder, he was hot up here the
day after I first met him at a cocktail party at his house.
Virtually undressed on the way in. Couldn't understand why
I didn't hop in the sheets with him. Decided I was frigid.
Or a lesbian. Spent an hour analyzing my queerness. Makes
cracks about it every time I see him. What did he tell you
about me? Don't tell me. Probably that you were wasting
your time since I only get in heat over amorous billy goats
with green beards."

"How do you know I'm not married?"

"No, you have an underfed bachelor look. Married men
get a kind of fat look around the eyes. I don't know, maybe
you *are* married but for some reason you caused a rise in me.
It's been a long time. The movie crowd are such bed hoppers
and that's not my style either." Her breath began to quicken
a little. "You're so . . . I don't know . . . an island . . .
I wish you would talk to me and tell me something . . .
maybe you will . . . I'd love to hear . . . I really
would . . ."

But we didn't talk. The *bombas* melted and the espresso
bubbled away and kissing her and feeling her was an unbearable excitement. I have no recollection of clothes coming off, just the rising swirl of blood that filled my head and
my eyes, and my hurting breath caught in my chest and all
the years of fantasy and frustration carried to the cool white
brocaded coverlet, her body surprisingly hot against mine,
moving and begging, and then at the point of taking, finally
taking, at that moment: those terrible sweats, pouring from

spigots that opened inside me, running down my face, biting my eyes, drenching my hair; I tried and tried and strained and heard myself groan aloud from the terribleness but the sweats poured from me and I could not, could *not* make love. I don't honestly know if the sweats started before or after my impotence. My whole body charged with desire, plugged into a yearning for Iris, whose body was even more beautiful than I had imagined, everything feeling absolutely alive outside this incongruous deadness. Then panic, the rise of panic, never experienced in my life before. She tried to help, little whimpers coming from her as she tried to make it happen, but the persistent nothing, nothing, nothing finally defeating her and she pushed with her hands and slid away, her body soaked from mine, my sweat the only wetness, and she began to sob. Panic drained to defeat, my head buried deep in the coverlet, wishing suffocation.

Through the sobs, words barely distinguishable: "You don't find me attractive. Why, why don't you . . . don't you see it's important? I have this thing—even as a girl—it comes from my son-of-a-bitch father, I guess, loathing me, made him feel old or cramped his leching or I don't know what but he called me Ugly Fruit—that was his endearing nickname for me, charming isn't it? Have you ever seen an ugly fruit? Mrs. Klemp, take Ugly Fruit upstairs or outside or to the movies or . . . or . . . or . . . take her, take her, Mrs. Klemp . . . never *wanted,* you understand, that's the whole thing, I can't believe any man really wants me . . . it doesn't matter how I look now, pretty, not pretty, it's just . . . God damn it! The men who have wanted to make love to me . . . really wanted . . . and the few times I have tried with them but never felt anything. I felt they were using me and not *really* wanting anything or giving anything or god damn it *feeling* anything, just their own little pops, and they call that making love. All I ever felt was used. Oh, it wasn't all that often—maybe five of them,

and only one of them more than once. He was warm and
cared a litle and I saw a lot of him but he didn't really want
to go to bed with me—oh, he said he did and he was always
so hot for me but then when I did it would be over for him
before it really happened. But I didn't know what bad was.
I was so aroused for you. I really thought that I'd have it
with you, finally get turned on. Am I really that repulsive?
I thought men could walk into a whore house and do it with
any old slut who spread her legs. Why go this far if you don't
want me . . . what the hell kind of queer is that? Oh, go on,
oh please, please, please, oh please don't . . . no, no, I
realize . . . get out . . . now . . . just get up and get
out of here . . . now . . ." Her voice was rising to anger.
I raised my throbbing head, tremendous effort, and looked at
her, trying desperately to find words to speak; I wanted to
say, Look, I've been in prison for twenty-four years and
they wrecked me, nothing to do with you, it's me, I didn't
know, how would I know, that that's gone too—you're wonderful and exciting and a hell of a woman but they've killed
everything I had as a man . . . But none of it would come
out and interfere with her sobs, the deadness in me everywhere complete, a different panic now like an animal cornered and wounded and wanting only to get to its tunnel
and hole up in the safe dark to die.

I reached out to touch her, to comfort her, console her,
but my hand would only go so far and I could not even give
her that; she was spread-eagled on her belly, her arms
thrust upward, a clutch of bedspread in each hand, her face
obscured by the fall of her hair. I have no memory of
dressing, as I had none of undressing, but I felt the snap of
the lock at my back as I let myself out, felt it as you'd feel a
knife run between your ribs.

Out in the piazza it was quiet. A few sidewalk diners at
the Tre Scalini. The sweats had not stopped. I felt like they
never would.

chapter five

Dan's trial, about which there had been much joking and to which all his friends had gone rather festively, turned out to be dead serious. The courtroom was strangely proportioned, quite wide but so shallow that when you entered you were only a few yards away from the judge's dais; this wide-angled nearness greatly magnified the judicial presence. In large black embossed letters on the white wall behind the judge's high-backed leather chair was the legend, LA LEGGE E UGUALE PER TUTTI, beneath which was a large, black crucifix. The judge, who sat elevated, wore a heavy black robe of an expensive material with silver tassels; the bailiff, who sat a step lower and to the right of the judge, wore a thin black robe of cheap material with red tassels; the prosecutor, on the judge's left, also a step lower, although not robed or tasseled, wore a perpetual, fierce scowl and an imposing beard, the bristles of which moved even when he was not speaking. The whole thing was like sitting in the first row before a wide movie screen on which the action is slightly out of focus.

The testimony of the two young cops, nattily dressed in civilian clothes, was very positive and serious; Dan's attorney scored nothing on cross-examination, and the prosecutor demanded a minimum of six months as a punishment for this influential foreigner who had debased these venerated public servants. By the time Dan stood before the witness rail he was white and visibly nervous, his legs seemed unsteady, and he had the stricken look in his eyes that I had seen only once before—in Marseilles.

His deep, robust voice was constricted to the point of being hardly audible. In a way it worked in his favor, for it was hard to believe that a man so wan and soft-spoken could have been capable of shouting such a vile epithet at two guardians of the law. Dan's explanation was that whatever was said in the car that night had been spoken to a friend in the rear seat, and was in no way directed toward the policemen.

"You told your friend, in connection with something, to stick it up the ass?" the prosecutor asked, an edge to his voice.

"No, sir, he was an American and we were speaking English. The English words probably sounded like *va fa un colo*."

"What English words sound like that?"

"I wouldn't be able to recall exact words . . ."

"What was your friend's name?"

"Louis Addams."

"Will your friend be here to testify?"

"No, sir, he is hospitalized with a bad back."

Dan's lawyer got to his feet. "I respectfully suggest, Your Honor, that we postpone this trial until the witness Addams can testify."

"Why did you not take his deposition, Counsellor?"

"I thought he would be recovered."

"Then you should have requested the necessary time before this trial started. It is now too late."

I had met Dan's friend, Lou Addams, who was a sculptor

and who was indeed currently afflicted with a troubled sacroiliac; his absence at the moment was ominous not just for Dan but for me, because if Dan were found guilty and sentenced to jail, all my hopes and chances would be sentenced right with him. A free Dan Reeder was vital to my existence in Italy.

No one had paid any attention to me; at least, I *hoped* they hadn't. I had come late, after the small courtroom was already crowded with Dan's friends, so I decided to take a gamble, a desperate gamble, that I had been unnoticed. I suppose my lawyer background is what gave me the courage. Before I fully realized what I was doing—just some kind of reflex action responding to Dan's (and especially *my*) predicament—I had slipped out into the corridor, contorted myself into a posture that I imagined would reflect a painful sacroiliac, and, feeling whisked back to the Washington University Thespics (my forte was character parts à la Paul Muni), entered the courtoom slowly and painfully.

Dan's jaw dropped and he went a shade paler.

"I am Louis Addams, Your Honor," I said in very deliberate Italian. "I have come here against my doctor's orders but I would rather be crippled for life than let an innocent man spend one night in jail undeservedly. I must sit down. Will someone help me?"

The bailiff got up and carefully helped me into his chair. The judge gave me a glass of water from his carafe and I drank it gratefully, holding the glass with both hands. In between my bouts with the pain waves that racked my body, I forcefully corroborated Dan's testimony that he had been talking to me as we drove away from the policemen and I remembered his asking me, in connection with my bad back (at that time not as bad as it is now, your Honor), if parking down the street was "very far for you, Lou," which, come to think of it, could have sounded to Italian policemen who spoke no English like *"va fa un colo."*

The prosecutor started to question me but the spasms in my back suddenly intensified and the judge, fearing that I might come to some messy end at his feet, excused me. Several of Dan's friends, now wised up, came forward and literally carried me from the courtroom.

Five minutes later, after a stern admonition from the judge, Dan was acquitted and we all converged on his house to celebrate. While the champagne was being poured, and I was being mock-ministered to while reclining on a bed of pillows which Natalie had arranged in the middle of the living room floor, Dan brought me the message, received by his *maggiordomo* an hour before: Signor Gibio would like to see me at his place at five o'clock.

chapter six

"I'm sorry to have taken so long," Gibio said, "but when I go into a thing I must know, but really *know*, whom I deal with. You understand, no matter how attractive a proposition, it is only as good as the man I must trust. And I learned long ago that one cannot, without serious corroboration, rely upon a judgment based solely on the man as he appears. The man before you is always a distillation of his past, the essence of him steamed from the materials of what he has done and been, but it is a distinct advantage to know as much as possible about those basic materials. So therefore the delay in getting back to you.

"Needless to say, your presentation fascinated me—and I reacted favorably to you as a person. Now that I have a rather complete dossier on your background"—he picked up a thick, flapped folder, the kind lawyers use, and weighed it in his hands—"I am satisfied that you are a man I can deal with."

My hopes rose. "I'm very glad to hear you say that."

"But I must tell you that despite these favorable auguries, there is one doubt that keeps chewing on me. It is very basic, and actually I don't know how you can answer it except with rhetoric. I don't say it is fatal, but it is critical. It is this: you have been wrongfully deprived of twenty-four years of your life and you want to be compensated for that loss in terms of money, recovery of the very treasure that did you in—to that extent our interests are mutual; I, too, want that treasure recovered to compensate me for the sizable amount of money I would be required to risk. But now there is an additional element: in the course of your inquiry into the treasure's disappearance, it is reasonable to assume that you are going to develop some leads on people who were involved with its disappearance, and inevitably that inquiry can encompass a quest for the person or persons who framed you. It then becomes a vendetta that distracts you from the original mission that involves me. To put it bluntly, I don't care who did you in, but you, of course, do, and why isn't this a near-fatal weakness in the proposition you make to me? I cannot believe that any man who has suffered at the hands of another as you have suffered, does not have revenge in his heart, and revenge is one of the emotions I want nothing to do with. It blinds and can provoke an insanity of self-destruction that is comparable to the hyena eating his own entrails when he is wounded. That is the only matter for us to discuss, Mr. Selwyn. All else is settled in my mind."

My immediate reaction was shock—shocked that so obsessed had I been all these years with desire to recover the treasure, I had never really thought of tracking down my persecutors (I always thought of the enemy as plural). Of course, before the trial my entire effort had been in trying to exonerate myself primarily by trying to figure out who might have fashioned the noose which had been slipped around my neck; but once the hanging was over, I can honestly say the prison corpse never again thought about his persecutors. But I felt that that explanation, although the truth, did not necessarily preclude the eventuality that Gibio was talking about; it's one thing to have had a prison point of view, but what if I had an opportunity to find the sons of bitches who had fouled me and wrecked my life? Who says that I would not berserkedly follow that pursuit to the detriment of all else?

"You're right, Mr. Gibio—rhetorical protest is my instinctive reaction. But you have already ruled that out as a convincer—and rightly so." I got up for a moment and circled my chair. "That dossier you have there—how far back does it go?"

"Quite far."

"I mean, boyhood and all that?"

"Well, it is mostly focused on your adult life—let's see . . . from college on."

"Do you know about the depression—the great depression that occurred in the States from 1930 until the outbreak of the Second World War?"

"Yes, of course."

"Well, that's my argument—that's why you can trust me to stay dedicated to our cause. Those depression years were all the years of my life—plus the military."

"I don't quite see how the depression can have any bearing on the question I posed."

"The bearing, Mr. Gibio, is that I have never known anything but poverty and struggle—nothing else. My father was an ineffectual man who lost his jewelry business right after the stock market collapsed in twenty-nine and was reduced to being a traveling salesman for a wrist watch company. Watches, during the depression, were hardly a necessity. My mother had jobs off and on—selling cheap lingerie door-to-door, part-time secretary, cashier—but when I was nine she developed a lung condition and had to go off as a charity case to the Fee-Fee Sanitarium on the outskirts of St. Louis. That's what I was told, 'lung condition,' which, I suspect, was tuberculosis. We were then living, all four of us—I had a younger brother—in one room in the Deluxe

Hotel, a run-down, semi-whore hotel with a taxi dance hall in the basement. My brother, who was killed in the Korean War, was sent off to an aunt in Keokuk, and I lived alone in that hotel except when my father came home from the road for a day or two each month. He had what was called a 'drawing account' to pay for his expenses against his earnings. Of course, he never had enough earnings to justify the expenses, but he went from job to job, each time lasting just long enough to use up the drawing account.

"I don't intend to make this a long autobiography of my early miseries. But you say you must know this man, Paul Selwyn. Not just what he says he will do, but what he *will* do. I think how he existed at age nine will tell you better than anything else what he'll do now. So—that hotel room, living alone, meals at the Greek's Dew Drop Inn at the corner, my father bartering a sample watch (not his to barter) for the meals, sitting on a spin-top stool at the white counter, getting a plate of whatever Jimmy wanted to get rid of. After school sometimes, the hotel owner's son, Kenneth, would come to my room with his bee-bee gun and we would take turns shooting the cat-size rats that prowled in and around the open garbage cans at the end of the black cinder parking lot. I was a hell of a shot.

"When I went every Sunday on the Creve Coeur streetcar to see my mother she warned me about the social workers who might come and find me living alone and put me in an institution; she warned me not to risk using any more of the federal food stamps for relief groceries."

I wanted to tell Gibio much more, but he was a stranger and these boyhood hurts were too intimate. "Does this make any sense to you, Mr. Gibio, my telling you this about my mother and father and living alone in that hotel when I was only nine?"

"Yes, it's the other dossier. I suppose it does have a certain strength—to have come from that background, to bring from it the desire to have . . ."

"Believe me, Mr. Gibio, it overrides everything else. That's exactly what it is—the desire to *have;* I have no desire to be someone—what I suppose you would call power desire; big-shot desire. I have no desire to belong— what would that be?—social desire, let's say, friends and all that. Only to have. That's all I feel. It possesses me, this desire to possess. And that's your insurance. Scholarships got me through college and an N.Y.A. job paid fifteen dollars a month of which I paid twelve to my mother. And when I finally got my law degree, ten days after I passed the bar exams I was drafted; the rest you know about."

"All right, Mr. Selwyn," Gibio said, standing and offering his hand, "we have a deal." I rose and we solemnly took each other's hand. "The business of getting you an Italian visa is for Dan, but I shall deal with most else. I have a good entree with the Fine Arts Commission and will arrange your interview for your archaeological license. As I understand it, you will take care of your own identity papers—I mean, whatever papers have to be 'created,' shall we say? I will purchase the van and other items you need; I will need a complete list and as complete a budget as you can assemble at this time. As for my return, it will depend somewhat on what is recovered. My primary interest is in documents: the diaries, correspondence, citations, whatever may be recovered in that area. If only money is recovered, I would expect one-fourth of the total. I like to be very explicit about finances. I am corrupted by money and it helps to be very direct about it."

"You've got that wrong, haven't you? It is those of us who need it who are corrupt."

"No—once a man fully understands what other men will do for money, then that man is truly corrupt. Not they—not the ones who debase themselves for it—but I—the debaser.

"One last thing—under no circumstances am I to be personally involved; neither by actual presence, nor by mention of my involvement. No one but you and Dan are to know that I am in on this. I don't wish any reports from you. The only contact between us is to be when I contact you. I will establish your operating funds in a numbered account in Zurich, and you will draw against that. There will be no written agreement between us, but despite my absence, you may be sure that I will have eyes. Of course, we are playing roulette, but I have a good feeling about your number coming up; if it does not, you will find I am a good loser."

Before going to sleep that night, I began to think about all the boyhood things that talking to Gibio had stirred up. Like the sweater. I had never had any new clothes, not one thing ever bought new for me, everything I owned passed along from someone; this nubbly sweater was in the window of a men's store I passed every day walking home from school, and all my subconscious desires—I would never permit myself *consciously* to want anything because that was beyond reality and the wanting hurt too much—so all this frustration and poverty-fear, fixed itself on this sweater which cost $9.99. The reason I permitted myself to hope about the sweater was that the St. Louis schools had a savings system, The Students' Savings Bank, and once a week you took your savings book to school and gave your teacher anything from a penny on up, and she marked it in your book and you were paid a little interest, but the big thing was that nobody could get at that money but you; the school promised you that. When I got up to $6.50—money I earned from odd jobs and errands—I began to see myself in that blue sweater with its red piping around the neck and sleeves. I dreamed of myself in that sweater. I even went in one day and tried it on—I had never been in a clothing store before and I was very nervous—and it looked even better than I had imagined. But when The Students' Savings Bank failed, all they finally paid us was one cent on the dollar and I wound up with seven cents in my hand and the teacher taking my book and stamping it "Canceled."

To sustain myself during those awful boy years, I used to have this fantasy—so strong, so embellished, so *real,* it became reality and the dismal reality of my life became fantasy. Living alone in that hotel room, always afraid after school of finding a padlock on the door for rent arrears, and with the raucous sounds of the Good Times taxi dance hall seeping up from the basement and mingling with the drunken sounds through the transom from the room across the hall where a big blonde whore brought her clients all through the night, I used to fantasize that my mother and father were in reality extremely wealthy but that they felt that they should make me live tough in the beginning of my life so I wouldn't grow up a soft little rich kid; that they were away so much because they kept returning to their "other" life, but that any day, when they felt my steel had set, they would finally end this masquerade and tell me the truth; I could see the truth in clear detail, the truth about my real life: I knew the house we really lived in, a mansion on Millionaires' Row facing Forest Park; I could see how life really was and I knew the names of the help from gardener to chauffeur, and the names of my teachers at the exclusive Country Day School to which I would be transferred. I knew everything about that "real" life, every article of clothing, my summer camp, my toys, and I even had a large oak chest with a leather lid that was filled with nothing but sweaters.

So even after my mother was released from the sanitarium and went to work for the Bell Telephone Company and we moved constantly, one squalid flat and one school after another, and even after my father had become a semi-invalid and finally died on my first day of high school, even then— the fantasy persisted. Nothing could shake it.

We had to keep moving to get in on the concessions.

Landlords were having a rough time like everyone else. Couldn't rent their places. So they offered what were called "concessions"—you signed a lease for a couple of years, paid the first month's rent, then got the next two or three months' free (one place we rented on Lawn Avenue gave us a five-month concession, as I recall); well, what the Selwyn family did, apartment after apartment after apartment, was to pay the first month, use up the free concession months, and then move. Of course there was no fear of being sued under the lease because we had no assets.

And that's how it was for a long time, and when it got better it only got better to the extent that we finally managed to live in one place, a dismal three rooms over a delicatessen where they killed chickens in the back, outside our bedrooms, the rabbi making them kosher, slitting their throats with his knife, and then the two shirtless Negroes plucking their feathers, the white feathers sticking to their sweated black skins in the St. Louis heat until they looked like prehistoric birds.

chapter seven

At night it bothered me about Iris, not about Iris really, but how I'd been with her. I felt as though my penis had been taken over by some outside force over which I had no control. In prison there is no way to turn yourself off—down, yes (the kitchen was very liberal with potassium nitrate), but not off. The choice was to join the homosexuals, if you were built that way, or to take care of yourself. As school kids we had been warned by Mr. Glendale, the physical education instructor who also taught hygiene, that if we masturbated we would ruin our manhood and we all laughed among ourselves and put this down as bullshit; but it looked like Mr. Glendale was right about one of us. Some nights I'd have a recurring nightmare about the experience with Iris; my penis would be missing and frantically I'd be searching for it, or there would be some object like a book—a *book*, for God's sake—hanging between my legs. In these dreams Iris' reaction was always amusement, smiling at me coolly, sometimes giggling with some of the dubbing people, and I invariably awoke heavily sweated.

Some of the inmates who masturbated indulged themselves as regularly as if they had a woman, but for me it was a release I sought only when the sexual tension of my body became unbearable. Curiously, in my masturbatory daydreams I never laid a woman I had actually fucked. I suppose I was so humilated by being forced to masturbate that I wanted to make it as unreal as possible by reaching back to girls who were only figments of frustrated memory.

I did see Iris one more time. Dan gave a party to celebrate his victory over the evil forces of law and order and I found, to my embarrassment, that because of my impetuous impersonation at the trial I had become a hero in the eyes of Dan's friends. Iris arrived, yellow dress and shoes and quite beautiful, bearing a small package for me. It was my thousand-year certificate framed in gold with glass over it. She was pleasant and chatty and I felt a surge of some kind of hope (for myself) as we talked; her perfume made the talk seem intimate. But a thin young man with long sideburns and a Zhivago jacket came to get her, and when he arrived she turned from me and kissed him on the mouth and you could tell it was all there between them. They left shortly after he arrived and this time she didn't bother to look for me to say good-bye.

Gibio lost no time getting underway; items were purchased almost as fast as I turned in my requests, not to Gibio himself—there was no further direct contact with him —but to a Federico Amatelli, who ran an office called International, Ltd., certainly a perfect sobriquet for an anonymous nonentity.

My appearance before the Fine Arts Commission was brief, and it was obvious that the members had been favorably conditioned to my request. After I gave a short summary of why the shores of Zonico gave promise of being another Sirmione, the commission chairman asked a perfunctory question or two and that was it. I was to fill out certain forms and submit certain documents. The conditions were that the Fine Arts Commission would have first refusal on all items excavated; in general, the Italian government and my excavation team, the Associated Colleges Expedition (ACE), would split fifty-fifty either proceeds or objects, depending. Of course we were talking about Roman treasure, not Mussolini treasure.

The only personal advantage I took of the Gibio financing was to move back to the Inghilterra, on the grounds that a phone in my room (this time with a bath), had become a necessity.

Dan had as much trouble as he had anticipated getting a four-month visa for me, even with the large amount of lire provided by Gibio for the purpose. But Dan, whose years of experience had made him an absolute master of Roman politics, kept at it doggedly, turning one official around another, turning them round and round until finally the convolutions tightened and he was able to pull the cork from the bureaucratic bottleneck.

But the need for the creation of other inaccessible documents was growing acute and I prayed that Giorgio would still be at the address in Naples he had given me when he had left Santo Stefano. Dan said he knew a pretty good counterfeiter who posed as a ceramics-maker on the Via Margutta, but Giorgio was a great artist as well as a hundred percent trustworthy, a percentile rarely encountered among Romans. Besides that, he was warm and amusing and he was my friend, someone I didn't have to pretend with, an ally, fellow alumni of Alma Mater Santo Stefano. And Giorgio's skill as a counterfeiter applied to his personality as well as his drawing board. He had the imagination, the talent, the buoyant brass, to carry off almost any masquerade, and his mind was as quick at making the unlawful seem lawful as his hands were in executing the thimblerig and three-card monte.

* * *

The feel of things moving was exhilarating; I even received a phone call one morning from the Dubbers' Association with an assignment to dub the dialogue of a French actor named Belmondo (unknown to me, for no film of his had ever been shown at Santo Stefano) who had spoken Italian in an Italian film. I pointed out that I had not improved my monotone, but the Dubbers said, never mind, they were desperate; I felt bad having to refuse them.

The days were packed busy, but the nights were lonely. There is something mournful about eating alone in an Italian restaurant, especially a trattoria. Italian food needs the flavor of conversation, between eaters, waiters, eaters at other tables, and owners; conversation and laughter and a splash of music evoke the sensual qualities of a lusty pasta. To eat alone in a lively trattoria in Trastevere, bubbling with sounds and the effervescence of its *camerieri,* no matter how *al dente* the pasta, is overwhelmingly lonely, and at times, sitting there, envying the lively tables around me, it made me wonder if I would ever get out of solitary.

2

POINT OF DEPARTURE

Some are shy of the ditch, yet can
Lie tumbling in the mire;
Some though they shun the frying pan,
Do leap into the fire.

The Pilgrim's Progress

chapter eight

Ted Middlekey was a very talkative Englishman, an enthusiastic raconteur who laughed easily, drank quietly and discussed his physiological problems excessively.

He had changed astonishingly little since the war. Dan had located him through the network's television bureau in London, and Ted seemed genuinely cordial and hospitable when I first telephoned him to say I was coming to London. He had warned me, however, when I explained the general nature of my visit, that he doubted it would be of interest to him—or to Bis de Jong.

I was met at the airport by Ted's gray-liveried chauffeur, who drove a silver Daimler that had a crystal vase with two roses in it attached to the right side of the dashboard. I sat beside the chauffeur and was immediately, and silently, driven to Ted's offices on Regent Street. PR, Ltd., it was called, the PR standing for Public Relations, and from its size and expensive, but rather garish, decor, it was obvious that Ted had struck a treasure lode of his own in London.

Except for an imperceptible roundness about the middle and moderate puffs under the eyes, he seemed unchanged; his dark hair was unreceded, ungrayed, and there was not a discernible line on his face.

"Paul! Paul, how damn nice to see you! No visible signs of wear and tear although, daresay, there are a few chops underneath. Cigarette? Sit down, sit down. Where to begin?"

"Tell me about your company. Great offices! How'd you go from Scotland Yard to this?"

"Fact is, never went back to the Yard. A policeman's lot and all that, and besides, toward the end of the war I had met a gaggle of American hucksters, in uniform of course, all of them in Public Relations—army PR, but they had been PR men in civvies, too, and I was absolutely astounded when they told me what U.S. public relations blokes did and how much they earned at it."

"I don't know much about them even now."

"Damn, Paul! It's hard for me to realize it's been twenty years. Whatever is it like—suddenly Rip van Winkled into a new world?"

"Well, it's not so much the extent to which the world has changed, as it is the extent to which I haven't. I'm astonished at how quickly I've come to accept so much of what was overwhelming on first impact—but that doesn't mean that I'm able to cope with it."

"Well, one thing we can do right off is to rid you of those clothes you're wearing. Gifts from a hostile warden, no doubt. I mean, you don't have to be Cardin, but Jean Valjean is something else again." I started to defend Dan's wardrobe but Ted sailed on, without stopping. "Fact was that back in 1946 American-style public relations had not yet penetrated the dense fen of British traditionalism. I decided to run the kite up and see if it would fly. Six years of military duty had conditioned me to taking large risks—in exchange for large returns. A flyer in PR was therefore much more in the spirit of things than back to the Scotland Yard dole."

"But you knew nothing about PR, did you?"

"I knew nothing about underwater demolition or counterspy infiltration when I joined the army but I did rather well at them. So, chum of mine brought me my first account— Restoration of Damaged Monuments—and I was off and running." He pressed a button on a button-board on his plexiglass desk, and the white-on-black bas-relief map of Europe that covered the wall behind the desk lit up with a myriad of blue stars. "There you are—the far-flung offices of PR, Ltd. As the sun set on the British Empire it rose on Middlekey's Dominion. I have more outposts now than England had colonies at the height of her glory."

"You certainly made up for the six years *you* lost . . ."

"Yes, indeed—but, you know, I do envy you one thing —don't misunderstand—positively ghastly being holed up like that all those years—but what an opportunity to write, and you a writer. That's my frustration—not to have time for writing. The joy of it! One's thoughts leaping through one's fingers and onto the paper, seeing it all concrete and real, and there it is for other men to read, the feedback going, as it were, from one's fingers through their eyes—brain to brain, direct transfusion. Glorifies the ego. Actually, I did do one book—you know about that? Three weeks in Marbella—kissed the tots good-bye and took a cottage at the club there and locked the doors and didn't surface for three weeks. Lost the British Woolens account but God knows it was worth it. Most exhilarating experience of my life. *In the Heat of Passion,* it was called, very detailed account of a series of sex murders I tracked down; sold rather well, and the reviews were most kind."

"I'd like to read your book if you have a copy."

"By the dozens. That's the only writing I've had time for, though, and it's frustrating. I do hone the creative edge a bit with book reviews I do for the *Daily Mail,* and I'm a regular on a TV panel discussion show called 'Bull's-eye'— its detractors call it 'Bullshit'—it does tend to run on and on —but how about it, did you write the great prison novel?"

"I wrote absolutely nothing. 'When my heart is heavy, I cannot put my words in the air.' Well, Christ, my heart was zinc and my ass was lead and sorghum ran for blood. It was twenty years to life, don't forget, and no assurance it wouldn't run the whole course. No, not a line. Besides, my whole thrust was in another direction—and I read and wrote plenty about that."

We were finally around to the subject of my visit, but as if on push-button cue, there was a discreet two-tap on the door and Ted's secretary came in to remind him that we were due at White's in ten minutes.

Ted's chauffeur was waiting at the curb with the Daimler's door open, but Ted said, "Thank you, Hines, but a brisk walk might be just the thing." The way he said it, it was Ronald Coleman right out of my movie youth, a line I have used ever since when transport was scarce and slogging it was in order; but I was a bit disappointed not to drive up to White's, which is London's (and, as far as I know, the world's) most exclusive men's club, in a silver Daimler. I had been to London during the war, but an officer's billet at Grosvenor House, with the whores as thick as pickets in front of the hotel, and meals at the officers' mess, was as far from the world of Ted Middlekey as Santo Stefano was from Mayfair.

As it turned out, we had only a Bloody Mary at White's, in the small bar just beside the billiard room; the dining room was being painted, and members were to take lunch at Boodles, White's almost as illustrious brother club down the street. I felt ill at ease in both places, especially in view of Ted's summary rejection of my Dan-given clothes; but there is something about the way the regulars look at an outsider that, apart from how well one is accoutered, is demoralizing. It is not that they stare you down—not at all; it is the barest glance, casual, the eyes hovering for a moment, then sliding on, like a humming bird that has paused, cased the flower as worthless, and moved on, seeking nectar.

Sitting there in Boodles' elegant upstairs dining room, straining to remember forks and manners, distinguished ancestry staring down from their gold frames, surrounded by present ancestry sibilantly discussing the affairs of the day, which they had the power to affect, and perhaps control, sitting there with a second Bloody Mary magnifying reception, my ears by-passing Ted's account of the last time he and de Jong spent a weekend in Paris, and listening instead to the affluent conversation around me—well, my resolve to make my treasure project work became more intense than ever.

"Look, Ted, it's nice of you to want to take me around to your tailors and all that, but I really don't care that much about . . ."

"It's not that. I know that it's relatively unimportant, considering what you've got on your mind right now. But you'll be surprised how much good it will do you, turn you into a top bugger, no doubt, and besides, it's good for *my* soul, if you know what I mean. The office doesn't expect me, this is my afternoon to indulge myself about you, so just relax and be indulged."

The afternoon was a cascade of indulgence. Benson, Perry & Whitley, 9 Cork Street, Mr. Whitley himself, white waistcoat, white mustache, adroitly measuring, suggesting the fabrics, four buttons on the sleeves, no cuffs, a slight pinch at the waist, snug on the hips, no belt. Across the street, 27 Cork, C. J. Cleverly, Bespoke Shoemaker, tall, gaunt, ancient, showing the pages in the big book, upon which once stood the Prince of Wales, Clemenceau, Leslie Howard, Lloyd George, the Duke of Argyll, and now stands the Hon. Paul Selwyn, Esq., flat feet close together as old Cleverly creaks and cracks to stoop, the sound of a venetian blind running down, then his tracing pencil in and around the toes of the Hon. Paul Selwyn.

Around the corner, Mr. Fish, and then Blades, but aside from one necktie at Blades, bright colors criss-crossed and zagged, a technicolor explosion, I convinced Ted I was not ready for the costumes on display. Certainly not ready for Mr. Fish.

But Turnbull & Asser on Jermyn Street, shirts of Sea Island cotton as fine as silk, lustrous ties, and what the twinkle-toed salesman euphemistically referred to as "silken body garments," ready for that all right, by then wallowing in Ted's indulgences, in and out of the shops on New Bond Street, Mr. Middlekey received grandly, his Dunhill thin Havanas, his Signoricci aftershave scent, duplicates of his cuff links and so on, by now thoroughly seduced, self-indulgence, I suspect, turning into greed. *A memory stirred: nine years old, Uncle Brody, the successful haberdasher from Keokuk, visiting St. Louis on a buying trip over the fourth. Not enough to eat, ragged clothes, busted Keds, but Uncle Brody only concerned about firecrackers. "What the hell kind of a fourth is that for my nephew?" The giant roadside stand, "An Acre of Fireworks," and Uncle Brody up and down the aisles, piling the firecrackers into a wicker arm basket they gave us at the door, sparklers, rockets, pinwheels, torpedoes, Chinese crackers, nigger babies, Roman candles, snakes, everything, and I began to put things in the basket, too, the beautiful pile mounting, so exciting I began to giggle and I couldn't stop and Uncle Brody kept loading things in the basket and I was giggling so hard I could scarcely keep up with him as he hurried up and down the aisles, plucking those beautiful firecrackers from their heaps and tossing them in the basket, and at the end they filled two big brown paper bags and cost $9.65.*

The afternoon with Ted stirred that long-forgotten spree with Uncle Brody; I experienced that same feeling of mounting intoxication as the shops and their things piled up like firecrackers, but I found that an urge to thump people on the back (successfully contained) had replaced the giggle.

Finally sated and exhausted, into the grandness of the Royal Automobile Club, descent to the steam rooms below, assigned small curtained rooms, each with bed and dresser, then towel-wrapped into the marble-walled steam chambers, not steam, really, but dry heat, a succession of them, one hotter than the next, canvas sling chairs, attendants to bring ice water or drinks, a few bellied members in the corners, reading newspapers, the papers wilted from the heat and sweat drips.

"I really think the Royal Automobile Club has saved more Englishmen from extinction than William the Conqueror, Wellington, Dunkirk, the stiff-upper-Blitz and the Drunk-o-Meter combined. 'Open the flood gates of your pores, let last night's gin roll down your shores, all that raucous mirth and muddle, reduced to one small Beefeater puddle.' "

We were sitting in canvas sling chairs in a medium-hot alcove devoid of members. In steam-room garb Ted's roundness was more pronounced, a tribute to his tailor's (I should say *our* tailor's) skills. "I think it's shitty, Paul, that Bis and I didn't keep touch with you all these years, but the truth is, I suppose, although we didn't know you very well, we did have—and still have—a good deal of guilt over what happened."

"You mean about my conviction?" I was startled. "How could you possibly feel guilty about that?"

"Because, look, there were five of us involved—four, really, because Lefevre's jaundice took him out of it. So, four men, one murdered, one framed into paying for that murder with twenty-odd years of his life, and the remaining two not scathed. Why us? Just the luck of the roulette. But don't you see we are made to feel helplessly guilty? In all these years Bis and I have been seeing each other—he comes here quite frequently on business, and I have a big office in Stockholm—we never once mentioned your name. Not until I received your phone call asking us to join up with you on this treasure hunt. I've discussed it with Bis. We would really do anything to help you square accounts for the raw deal you got, but don't you see that this obsession of yours is tantamount to suicide? Look how many people are already dead because they started to poke around this treasure business."

"You told me that beginning with the war you gambled high stakes against risks, didn't you? Well, do you realize what the stakes are here? Your take could be in the millions."

"Yes, but the silt of twenty years covers a lot of traces. And what about our businesses? This isn't just a week on the shore of Como. Now look, Paul, I've talked this out with Bis and we want to help you—first, by keeping you from going ahead with this wild scheme of yours, and second, by detouring you into something that promises a little longevity, and a little of all the good things you've missed out on. We will stake you to any reasonable enterprise that . . ."

"God damn it! Everybody trying to save my ass!" I was out of my chair and I yanked the towel off the back of the chair and flung it across the room in my naked anger. "What in Christ's name could you stake me to? If you and Bis haven't got the balls to go in there and take what's coming to us, then okay, but don't give me that sanctimonious shit about saving me from my own destruction. I don't want to be lectured. I don't want to be staked. I've been on the cross once, and that's staked enough. You're both fat cats and you don't need the money. You've made it and it's rolling in and there's no reason for you to run the risk of being blasted. I can understand that. You've got plenty, and you don't have to go for more, even for really big stuff."

"Yes, I suppose that's it," Ted agreed. "But since we are

in a position to, we'd like to start you off with some capital."

"No, I've got financing for this project, and this project is all there is for me. At Santo Stefano, as you entered the prison courtyard, there was an arch you passed under, and above the arch was a big plaque with this inscription: 'As long as the holy law holds so many scoundrels in chains, the state and private property are secure.' Well, this scoundrel is no longer in chains, and the state and private property are going to catch hell, with or without you. But whether you join me or not, what you can do is to tell me what you remember, what leads you had, what you might do if you *had* joined me. Bis, too. That would help."

"And you'll do this, even if you have to go it alone?"

"Sure. Why not? What have I got to lose? My life? What life? And if I do lose, there's just me. It affects no one else, it's my life, or my death. But you didn't answer—will you tell me what you can? And something else. There's some information from Scotland Yard I'd like to get. Last year they sent information to the Italian police that located some of the treasure on a farm near where Rachele Mussolini now lives. I want to get the details on that, where the information came from, exactly what motivated the search."

"Well, I'll certainly tell you what I remember of the leads we had, and I'm sure Bis will, but as for the Yard, the man in charge of that division is C. O. R. McDermott, who is an old friend of mine but sorry to say, the Yard has an iron-clad rule against disclosure of file contents except to Yard officers and working members of accredited police departments."

"But wouldn't McDermott tell you, as an old friend?"

"McDermott wouldn't tell, and I wouldn't ask. Now what say we cool out, in more ways than one? How about a dive in the pool, then the Olympic one, get a brisk rub, sack out for an hour, and then on to the Middlekey manse where you will meet my wife, who despite three children and a husband who adores to eat, has a figure that will raise your temperature faster than this room."

I retrieved my towel and re-draped. "I'm sorry I blasted you, Ted. I really do appreciate all you're doing for me. Despite your cock-eyed guilt, you owe me nothing. Today's shopping binge was a great catharsis. I'm really grateful."

Ted started out of the room. "You'll be all right, Paul. Maybe conquer Dongo—who can tell? Now, off for our swim like baby barracudas."

"No, afraid not."

"Afraid not what?"

"About the swim . . ."

"Don't feel like it?"

"No—simply can't. Never learned. No swimming holes in South St. Louis."

"But, my word, I don't know *anyone* who can't swim. Not a stroke?"

"I had intended to learn but I never could fit it into my busy schedule at Santo Stefano."

The Middlekey house was splendid. Narrow four-stories on Juniper Street just two blocks from St. James's Park, two graceful white porcelain greyhounds flanking the entrance; antique furnishings picked with care, an open purse, and a shrewd eye as to homogeneous nonconformity. Susanna Middlekey was thirty, and as Ted had rather pridefully announced, her body generated a voluptuous heat. Ted made numerous homageable references to her "cleavage," and her expensive wardrobe was obviously designed (I suspect by Ted) to promote this blessing. She spoke thick English, with *a*'s of remarkable flattage, and when she spoke to you she spoke in a low voice with her lovely head quite close and her cleavage disconcertingly making little electric contacts with your arm.

We had dinner at The White Elephant, a posh eating

club around the corner on Curzon Street, and went on to Annabelle's, the opulent discotheque cellar that somehow managed to look like it once was part of the *Île de France*. I felt overwhelmed by the frenetic dancing and high-decibel music, and although Susanna tried valiantly, it would have taken more than wild cleavage to have dragged me onto that dance floor.

If it had not been for my successful impersonation at Dan's trial, I would never have had the courage to tackle Scotland Yard. But with the negative prospect of not having Middlekey with me in Zonico and Dongo, it was doubly imperative to get all the information I could, however I could manage it. Besides, if my project went forward, impersonation was to be a major factor, and the more practice, I figured, the better.

I bought a leather card holder, slipped into it a facsimile of a police credential (bearing the name of Detective Lieutenant Fabbio Auri, with my snapshot pasted over his face) I had snipped from an Italian crime magazine, and presented myself in my Italian-made suit, speaking only Italian, at the Scotland Yard reception desk. I had counted on the Yard's interpreter being an Englishman who spoke Italian rather than vice-versa, and I was correct. Italian with a cockney accent. Almost broke me up.

I had shown my credentials to the officer at the reception desk; the Italian words discouraged him and after a quick, superficial glance, he handed it back to me. The cockney interpreter and I sat across from Inspector C. O. R. McDermott and waited while he went through the contents of the file.

"Well, now, tell Lieutenant Auri that the source was the Italian-speaking confessional booth at Our Lady of Lourdes Cathedral in Chelsea. This information comes from the priest who was receiving confession in that booth. It seems that an Italian, here on holiday, came to confess that he had known for many years the whereabouts of a part of the treasure that Benito Mussolini had with him when he fled Milan. He said that he knew that this treasure rightfully belonged to the Italian people and that it was a sin not to have spoken up, but that he feared for his life and he was ashamed of this fear."

The interpreter translated this information and I diligently took notes.

"He then identified the location of the treasure as two kilometers southeast from the house in which Mussolini's widow, Rachele, now lives in a town called Carpignano. But this is the information we sent to your Milan bureau . . ."

I almost fell into the trap of responding to his English, but caught myself and dutifully waited for the translation. "Yes," I said in Italian, "we received that information but the location indicated is a farm that yielded nothing. We were hoping that there might be something additional in the files that would pinpoint the treasure more exactly." Translation.

"No, that's all, that's the whole thing. The Italian, according to this report, was very nervous, and broke off the confession mid-sentence." Translation.

"He gave no clue as to his identity—his home town or parish, or anything like that?" Translation.

"No, and even if he had, the priest who took the confession would not have divulged it. Very strict about that." Translation.

"Did he indicate that Signora Mussolini was in any way involved with this buried treasure?" Translation.

"No—no indication of that." Translation.

"What about his accent—was your priest an Italian?" Translation.

"Yes, and he reports that the confessor did have a slight accent but he was not able to identify it." Translation.

I thanked McDermott and my interpreter, who accompanied me to the entrance hall and, on parting, cockneyed *"Arrivederci,"* which came out "Uh-ryva-duchy."

The guest room in the Middlekey house was on the second floor, next to the library. I awoke late the next morning to the sound of voices in the library. After a moment I identified one of them as Susanna Middlekey's.

"I assured you, Hines"—rising inflection—"that as soon as Mr. Middlekey arrives this evening I shall have him straighten it out."

"But, madam, he was to straighten it out forthwith when I spoke to him six days ago."

"He has a lot on his mind."

"Nothing I should think that would impede writing out a check for five weeks' back wages."

"Let's not descend to impudence, Hines."

"I don't wish to descend anywhere, madam. I just wish me back pay."

"You shall have it, Hines."

"I mean this evening, madam, or I shan't be able to remove the car from the garage in the morning."

I met Ted at the Royal Automobile Club at five o'clock. We were ensconced in the same hot alcove of the previous day, cleansing out our digestive poisons, as Ted put it, to enhance the night's revels, when I confronted him with the incident; he made no attempt to minimize it. "Overextended. That's the whole explanation. All this bloody capital and not a fucking shilling to spend. You understand? No way to liquidate anything without setting off alarums about the bad straits of PR, Ltd. But to keep up, PR, Ltd., must devour its young and suck its own blood. So there you have it. Ted Middlekey, the richest man on the poor farm."

"Then why are you dragging your feet about coming in on the treasure?"

"I had hoped to talk you out of it. I had hoped that if you decided not to face the danger, I wouldn't have to. Luxury has made me a coward. But God knows that the dangers of British bankruptcy are just about on a par with what might lie in wait at Dongo. Has it ever occurred to you that if Bis and I should show up in Dongo as part of your archaeological masquerade, it's quite possible that we will be recognized by certain people there as the former military investigators of the treasure?"

"Yes, it did occur to me, and I look at it this way: if you are recognized, then anyone made uneasy by the recognition must speculate whether you are truly archaeologists who, by coincidence, are back in Dongo on this project, or whether your presence really has some connection with the treasure you once investigated. I think this would be a psychological plus for us. It might create some tensions, jitter some nerves, start the pressure building. What do you think?"

"Yes—might. But I would feel better if I could talk you out of all this—even though I do agree that there is a strong possibility that some of that treasure is still somewhere in that area."

"Have you had time to think back on the leads you were pursuing?"

"I've thought about it but it's simply too far back for me to be helpful. But as I remember, Bis had something going about the River Mera. And he was also following some lead he had picked up on the whereabouts of that Swiss who had owned the villa with the hokus-pokus wine rack . . ."

"Luigi Hoffmann."

"That's the one. I'm sure he can fill you in. But, Jesus—1945 is a hell of a way back, Paul!"

"Not as far as you think. We're dealing with little mountain villages where there isn't a lot of coming and going.

Will you join up for the salvation of PR, Ltd., and Ted Middlekey, Unlimited?"

"Well . . . if Bis goes in, I will. But there's a factor I haven't mentioned—we have rather contrary matrimonial motivations. Bis is married to a woman from whom occasional escape is an absolute necessity—she is a gassy shrew who'd make commandos cringe—whereas my wife requires constant care and surveillance, as you can imagine. But I'll risk it if Bis declares in. Good old Bis."

"If Bis agrees, how soon could you leave?"

"Soon enough, I imagine. How many cuts to the pie, presuming there will be a pie?"

"The money man, you, Bis, Lefevre, me, and some small participations for two of my friends whom we'll need."

"You can forget Lefevre. He's a more than ordinarily ornery Frenchman. But what about Arnoldo's family?"

"I hadn't thought about that."

"They should have something."

"Agreed."

chapter nine

Ornery was not the word for him. A new word (new to me) that I had just heard in a shop in King's Road was more apt: gross. Louis Lefevre was gross.

The Lefevre Citroën-Peugeot Agency was on the Boulevard Raspail. I hadn't phoned or written, just walked in cold, and a salesman took me back to Lefevre's office. His face showed no recognition of my face or my name, and too much prodding was needed to resurrect his memory.

"I've just come from London, where I saw Middlekey, and I'm on my way to Stockholm to talk to de Jong. I'm organizing a project about that Mussolini treasure that all of us were investigating—a project to try to track it down—and I'd like to tell you about it and see if you want in."

"I do not wish to hear about it."

"Ted was reticent, too, in the beginning, but now he's . . ."

"Ted Middlekey's reaction does not affect me one way or the other. I repeat, I am positively not interested in any project about that treasure, and I do not wish to hear about it. Now, if you will excuse me . . ."

Gross.

But why so acerbic? At the moment he heard "Middle-key," and then "treasure," his lips twitched and his back seemed to straighten. My immediate reaction was that black blood had flowed between them back in 1945, and that the filtering years had not been able to purify it. I planned to ask Ted about that, although it might simply have been the result of a head-on collision between a supercilious Jaguar and a contemptuous Facel Vega. But then, again, it might even have been something that might lead to something else.

chapter ten

Bis de Jong had lived in Stockholm for ten years. Before that he had based his company in Amsterdam but the products he dealt in were power machines—turbines, generators and the like—and these were all manufactured in Sweden. The Holland Importing Company in Amsterdam became the Holland Export-Import Company in Stockholm, and prospered. Bis came from a long-line, affluent Amsterdam family that during the war had been wiped out by the Nazis. Bis's mother, father, brothers, sisters, relatives, were fed into Nazi ovens. At first Bis had been spared because he was married to a gentile, but when that protection was threatened, Bis escaped and eventually became attached to British intelligence and compiled a brilliant war record as a leader in the Dutch underground.

The day I arrived was the day of the annual trade fair, so Bis could not meet me himself but sent his company's publicity director, a young woman named Keva Olsberg. She took me to the fair, where at his impressive exhibit Bis was engaged in sales conferences with potential buyers. When he saw me, he immediately excused himself and came over.

"I am so sorry to be tied up today but it is nearly finished. Very busy sales. Very busy ulcer. Meanwhile, Keva, show Mr. Selwyn around the exhibition hall . . . oh, but wait, where are my manners? Not even a million-dollar sale . . ."

He opened a small cabinet-like refrigerator and took out a bottle of akvavit that had patches of snowy ice on its sides, and three bottles of Carlsberg beer. Keva poured the beer while Bis filled three little crystal glasses with the icy akvavit. He raised his glass.

"Welcome, Paul." We tilted down the akvavits, which we followed with a healthy quaff of the beer. My insides felt suddenly sunburned. "We have a very nice evening arranged, Paul. Keva, show him the American exhibit. Watch out for the akvavit, Paul. Keva, not too many toasts, now."

It was certainly unlikely, I thought, that anyone in Zonico or Dongo would connect this Bis de Jong with the tall, thin, heavy-haired young officer who was among them in 1945. It was not just that Bis had put on considerable weight and wore glasses and had lost most of his shock of wheat-colored hair. No, it was something total: as if he had been aged by a clumsy makeup man to play a character too old for him: he had a curious patina of underscored wrinkles, gray-colored skin and hair, dark circled eyes, over a rather youthful base, and the net effect was that you expected him to take off his disguise and reveal his younger self. Perhaps this premature aging—Bis looked at least ten years older than he was— could be attributed to the shrewish wife Ted had mentioned; and perhaps Ted's young cleavaged wife is what accounted for his lack of aging, as if the glands either measure up or don't, depending on demand.

Bis lived in the suburbs, so he had booked a room for me at the Grand Hôtel, on the harbor directly across from the Royal Palace. The room had a small balcony that afforded a sweeping view of the wide, many-bridged Strömmen River and the government buildings that stretched along it. Standing on that little balcony, sipping a Pimm's Cup that had been brought by a young blond barmaid, with the sunset-goldened water bowed around me, I had an inexplicable feeling of having mastered something. By something, I guess I meant my own destiny, a crazy surge of confidence that I had it made, negative evidence not withstanding, a euphoria more golden than the sunstreak that cut the water.

But the euphoria only lasted until I descended to the lobby to meet up with Bis and his wife, Malla. Malla was a Finn, and her disposition was that of the Finnish winter, which is six months of gloom without daylight. Instead of brooding and glowering, which I always understood were Finn characteristics, she emitted a perpetual nasal carp in a whine as penetrating as a jet engine's before takeoff. She either scathingly contradicted Bis or picked up his sentences after the first few words and finished them off. She never looked at him and spoke about him as if he were not present. There was a faint mustache on her upper lip; her face was dominated, however, by large rather frightening black eyes that moved constantly when she talked.

Keva Olsberg, supposed to join us for dinner, was a few minutes late, but Malla de Jong refused to wait for her. "These Swedish girls don't have any sense of proper and improper. And she an employee! Why, she should have been here to greet us. The table is reserved and we won't keep the maître d' waiting."

Keva appeared before we were seated. Her transformation from efficient public relations woman by day, to dinner companion for the boss's friend by night, was remarkable. She wore a stark black dress with a plunging neckline that dramatically accentuated her blondeness. At the fair, she had had her hair tightly up; now it hung down to her shoulders and loose, the white-yellow color and texture of corn tassels when they first appear. Her eyes were a chameleon blue, infinitely changing shades, her nose was too fleshy and her face too round, but the combination with her hair and eyes and graceful neck was striking.

The Winter Garden, where we were having dinner, was the main dining hall of the Grand Hôtel, done in the style of an overpowering Spanish garden, with fake rococo Spanish windows and balconies towering above the diners, reminding me very much of the Moorish lobby of the Fox Theatre in St. Louis. The members of the orchestra, in winged collars, played fox trots, with an occasional rumba or samba, and there wasn't a miniskirt in the house.

From the time we sat down, Malla de Jong didn't shut up. She insisted on describing every dish on the menu for me, even though there was a section in English; her opinion of the Swedish dishes was invariably hostile and she left me no alternative but to order *canard aux cerises,* which was what she was ordering, and which was the last thing I wanted to eat on my first trip to Sweden. And *foie gras* to start with, in the land of the herring.

While Malla's nasal whine was momentarily directed at Bis, berating him for some household forgetfulness, Keva, who was sitting beside me, said, "Would you like to dance? That's the way it is in Sweden, the girls can ask the boys."

She put her body completely against mine the moment we started to dance, and she held her left hand against the back of my neck. It was a very direct and exciting communication. "Do not make fun of my English. It is all taught to myself. Oh, yes, a little in school. But I did not go on very far. Neither with my English or with school. The de Jongs speak so perfect, it is an embarrassment for me."

"Your English is fine."

"This is rarely occurred, that I go out like this for Mr. de Jong. It was understood from the incept of my job that I

would not have to be the social date of businessmen, especially Swedish."

"Why especially Swedish?"

"In my own life I do not go out with Swedish men. I am
divorce with two small boys but I do not go out with Swedish.
Place your mind on . . . the thing is, the Swedish girls with
their baby pills make it very hard to be a woman in Stockholm. You cannot go to dinner with a man without including
going to bed. So you sit home and read and leave the men.
When you want a man, better to phone a friend and say come
and make love to me. But it is the Swedish girls, they are so
terrible. Everything you have heard is more true than you
have heard it. I have this young Italian friend goes to the
university—he is most handsome and Italian dark of the
skin. Swedish girls are crazy over dark skin, so my poor
Italian friend, who wants to study engineering and make
good marks and go back to Naples to be this engineer—oh,
that is not to say he does not want to have girls, too, he is a
very normal fellow—but what happens? The girls come into
his room, beautiful young university girls, they just come
in, in the afternoon after classes, in the evenings during
study, and they talk to him a little and they undress and they
want to make love with the dark Italian . . ."

"How is your friend doing in school with all this going
on?"

"Awful, he is doing awful, he is always so tired, he falls
asleep instead of study, or he has just put his mind to write
a paper or something, and here is some luscious piece come
to sample him. Oh, no, the Swedish girls are of a terribleness! I will show you the newspapers. There are whole
columns like, 'Miss Inger Smorga proudly announces the
birth of her son, Rolf.' "

"But why is Miss Inger Smorga mothering a little bastard
in this time of the pill?"

"I don't know. I don't know what goes on. I will have zero

to do with the pills. I am funny about my insides. If I want a man, I prepare myself for him . . . oh-oh—Mrs. de Jong is making gestures. Like a traffic policeman. We better go before she starts throwing rolls at us." As she pulled back her cheek and started away, her lips lightly brushed against mine.

"I was just saying to Bis," Malla had started her whiner going before we actually reached the table, "that I don't approve of eating in restaurants that have music for dancing. It's one or the other. If you have come to eat, then the concentration should be on the stomach, not the feet, and jumping all around in between the food, God knows what it does to the digestion. But at least it is not this insane crazy dancing. Did you see the reports? The young people are all going deaf from the terrible noises of the rock and roll. Did you see that, Bis? The next generation will be deaf."

"I should buy stock in hearing aids."

Keva got us back on the dance floor after the overly cherried duck. Her body seemed even closer. This time she didn't say a word, just placed her cheek against mine in such a way that the corner of her lips touched the corner of mine, and she imperceptibly moved her body against me in a way that had nothing to do with the music. She danced only one dance and then abruptly led me back to the table.

To my unbelieving delight, Malla de Jong was getting ready to leave. "It is the price of living in the suburbs," Bis said.

"The price of the suburbs and a twelve-year-old boy who still needs a babysitter. The suburbs! It is for the boy, Bis says, but what about me? It's a convenient way to keep me prisoner in the country while you are living it up in the city."

"Now, Malla, you know I take the 6:10 every . . ."

"The suburbs! You have no idea of the horror of the

trains. Bis has the car, but I simply will not drive with him. He drives a car like a milk horse, dreaming along, hoping that it will find its way. I told him when he gets a chauffeur I'll drive with him, not before, but he still insists on driving— you might think he *wants* to drive without me. Well, I must fly. The train station is just two minutes from here. Now Bis will stay on to be your apron until eleven, but he must leave by eleven. It was very nice meeting you, Mr. Selwyn. Bis has told me about your ore strike in Italy. Just exactly what kind of ore is it?"

I went cold. What ore strike? "Now, Malla, you're going to miss that train," Bis said, rising. I also rose, hurriedly, and extended my hand. Bis took her out to find a cab.

"You know how it is when they are drilling the street outside your window all day long and suddenly they stop," Keva said, and she giggled at her image of Malla de Jong as a pneumatic drill.

"What's an apron?"

"Well, you call it chaperon, we call it apron. You see, that is the old-time way in Sweden, the first date there must always be an apron."

"I guess 'apron' because it's something that covers the girl's private area."

We had strong coffee and weak liqueurs and Keva danced every other dance with Bis, who began to smile and perspire and tell us jokes that he had heard at the fair that day.

He left promptly at eleven o'clock, making a luncheon date with me for the following day. Keva took my arm and we walked along the quai, now slightly misted, and crossed the Strombron bridge into the old city. It had the look and feel of the Grenelle Quartier of Paris. Keva searched along the old, narrow, winding streets for a cellar she knew, Frati's Källare, but it was difficult to find it in the thickening mist. It turned out to be a series of rooms at the bottom of a long, narrow, precipitous stairwell in what were sections of an old cave. We ordered beer.

"What did you do before you worked for Mr. de Jong?" I asked her.

"I used to interview for television but too much was expected of you that had nothing to do with TV. So there we are back to the Swedish men. You probably suspect by now I do not like them very much. This is unusual for me, to be out in the evening like this."

"You mean you don't go out to dinner?"

"No, I only eat lunch because I do not like to eat alone and there are always people at work to eat lunch with. But I will not dinner with Swedish men with me as compulsory dessert."

"What about other men? Have you traveled and met other men?"

"Oh, I have met other men. But not many. There was this Michael Bamberg. He brought me to the United States but had to be very careful because of his wife who he loved. We did have three days together in a hotel called The Fairmount in San Francisco. I loved San Francisco. I think I would like to live in America, but better Rome. But, if America, I could have a dressing table full of bottles and rub lovely things all over me and attend to my face. Now it's just soap and water and a jar of cold cream that smells like herring."

She held up her glass. "These are my first drinks, what do you think of that?"

"You mean your first drinks ever?"

"Oh, no, not *ever*, but weeks and weeks I had this kidney infection and I could not drink. The doctor gave me medicine for it, but I could not use it. It was in a little tube to put up, he said, where I made pee-pee. I was flabbergasted—is that a word? I say, 'You mean I have a separate place to make pee-pee?' I am thirty years old and never knew I had this special place. Well, I have never taken the medicine because I tried very much but I could not find the place to put it. You can only spend so much time looking for a place like that and then you must give up."

Keva's apartment was four rooms and a bathroom, a strange bathroom that contained only a sink and no facilities for bathing. Most of the room was filled with large red plastic cans that contained heating oil. The toilet was in a separate closet.

Both the living room and Keva's bedroom were dominated by huge *kakelugns,* white porcelain stoves of great beauty that filled half a wall and ran their aged, cracked porcelain to the top of the high ceiling. The furnishings had an improvised quality but Keva's ingenuity had cleverly compensated for her obvious lack of funds. Beyond her bedroom, which contained little more than a large square bed, the *kakelugn,* a bookcase and a record player, there was a bright red kitchen, and beyond that her sons' room with its double-decker bed.

Keva lit a large squat candle on the table next to the record player, and another on the little table at the head of her bed, explaining that she did not like electric lights.

"Do you mind that I play some discs? That is one of my things, to always have something on. Chopin for me is like an appetite—I mean, like hunger, thirst. I must every day have some Chopin." She came over to me and smiled up at me; she unbuttoned my coat and took it off and adroitly untied my tie and unbuttoned my collar. Then she kissed me.

"I know what I play for you—your Tom Lehrer. He is a hero here, you know. Oh, that Tom Lehrer comes to Stockholm the girls will never let him go."

"Who is Tom Lehrer?"

"Who is Tom Lehrer?" She looked at me as if I had slapped her. "Who is . . . you're joking me!"

"No. I really don't know."

"Just the greatest, funniest, well . . . I don't know! Who is Tom Lehrer! I will play you my favorite. Then you will know. Alma. This Alma, she was a Vienna beauty who had many love affairs and also managed three marriages—to Gustav Mahler, Walter Gropius and Franz Werfel. So Tom Lehrer wrote this song." She placed the needle on the record two or three times before she found the band she was looking for. A young, light voice, Tom Lehrer's I presumed, was saying, "When Mozart was my age he was already dead for two years." There was a long paean of laughter and applause from what sounded like a huge audience. Then Tom Lehrer began to sing to piano accompaniment and Keva sang along with him.

> "Alma, tell us,
> All modern women are jealous,
> Which of your magical wands
> Got you Gustav and Walter and Franz?"

Keva began to undress, both of us, taking turns, her shoes, then my shoes, her stockings, mine, her dress, then slowly undoing my shirt buttons, unzipping my pants. "I use to wear a girdle and I did not mind it but I did mind the ignomy of jiggling around to get it on. That a good word, isn't it? Ignomy. Michael Bamberg taught me that. It is one of my best. Also flabbergasted." Tom Lehrer had come to another refrain and she joined him:

> "Alma, tell us,
> All modern women are jealous,
> You should have a statue in bronze
> For bagging Gustav and Walter and Franz."

She was naked now, and she came over and held me for a moment and ran the soft flats of her hands along my back; then she left for the bathroom. Her voice carried back into the room, over the sound of running water:

"Though you didn't even use Pond's,
You got Gustav and Walter and Franz."

I had been trying very hard, ever since I had hesitated when the taxi stopped but she had taken my hand and pulled me out after her, not to think in any way about what was happening. That was going to be the way, not to think at all, just go along with it, but now with Keva preparing herself and the room empty, I began to feel disturbed; I forced myself to concentrate on Tom Lehrer. I took off my shorts and crushed them up and flung them as hard as I could against the back of a chair. Listen to the record. Don't think of a thing. It's all right.

Keva returned by way of the kitchen, bringing with her a blue bowl with bright red apples in it. She put the bowl next to the bed candle, selected one of the apples from which she took a hearty bite, then put it to my lips and held it while I bit further into her bite.

"I wish I had nice big breasts for you. I know American men like big, floppy breasts. When I was young, at home, growing up, I used to have a big thing about my breasts. I sent away for stuff I rubbed on them, and tried exercises and all sorts of things, and then I would run up and down the stairs to see if they would jiggle. That's what my goal was— to make them big enough to jiggle. But they never did. Sometimes I would *imagine* they did, running up and down the stairs holding a mirror before me. Oh . . . oh, I suddenly want to be in bed with you!"

Her breath smelled of the apple and the juice had made her lips a little sticky. "I am hungry. I am very hungry. Oh, you're delicious. You smell delicious. Now that's the way a man should smell. Oh, yes, oh, yes, that's the way." Ted Middlekey obviously knew the right perfumer.

Keva rubbed her nose across my shoulders, then slowly down my back, making little sounds of approval. Then she started to kiss my body, kissing in some kind of pattern, a rhythm of kissing, and I tried to respond to the rhythm, thinking only of that, but I could feel my body getting moist. Far away now, my ears filled with the hum of rising sensations, Tom Lehrer was building Alma to her sendoff:

"Alma, tell us,
How can they help being jealous,
Ducks always envy the swans . . ."

As the moisture increased I could feel the mounting arousal bank itself and I strained against it, trying to force myself back up to where I had been.

"Who get Gustav and Walter,
You never did falter
With Gustav and Walter and Franz!"

But it was beginning to drain off; the flow of the current reversing, the perspiration rising, the feeling of emptying out, of succumbing. That's when I heard the little boy crying. At first I thought it was part of the Tom Lehrer record which had moved on to another song, but then it became part of the room and Keva rolled away from me and the little boy was in bed with us, sobbing, only half awake from his bad dream and his asthma. Keva took two pills from a bottle on the bedside table and the little boy swallowed them dutifully, gagging a little because of the asthma. Keva then held him in her arms, his little pajamaed body quivering, but Keva held him tenderly and spoke to him soothingly in soft sing-song Swedish. I had pulled the coverlet over me and frozen myself on the edge of the bed against the wall, apprehensive that the little boy would become aware of my presence; but Keva seemed not at all concerned about that as she gently rocked the boy. Once she reached out an arm and touched me, as if to comfort me too. I desperately wanted to escape from the bed but I was obviously trapped. The candle burned low. The record player had shut itself off.

* * *

When I awoke, Keva and her son were asleep in each other's arms and the candle had burned itself out. Very carefully I eased myself out of the bed, dressed by the light of a street lamp outside the window, and noiselessly let myself out of the apartment.

Bis's club, one of Victorian elegance which had obviously been modeled after White's in London, was only two blocks from my hotel. Bis had brought along a large manila envelope containing the dossier he had compiled in Zonico and Dongo twenty-four years before. I did not ask him how it happened to be in his possession rather than in the military archives where it belonged.

I read through it before lunch, sitting in the Tapestry Room, which was the bar, sipping Bloody Marys, Bis reading the newspaper while I read about the River Mera and what it had yielded and the testimony of several of the Nazi soldiers in the convoy that had crossed there. After reading the Mera section, I was sure that certain investigations were still in order, even at this late date.

The section on Luigi Hoffmann was even more provocative, but only if Hoffmann, who was in his forties at the time of the investigation, were still alive. The connections that Bis had unearthed between Hoffmann and the underground certainly indicated that he had been informed about, if not party to, much of the activity related to the recovery and disposition of the treasure. But finding Hoffmann, who had never been located, and, if found, getting him to talk, were certainly large orders.

The meal was straight Oxford Circus: pea soup, roast beef, potatoes, sprouts, cheddar and tinned fruit, with coffee and cigars in the Trophy Room. Bis apologized for not having alerted me to his Zonico ore story, but quite frankly discussed his perpetual need to remove himself for short periods from the Malla presence. "She has her virtues but her unrelenting intensity is hard to live with on an uninterrupted basis." I thought, How kind can a man be to a woman who grinds his balls for breakfast? "But I have always been intrigued with having another look around Zonico and Dongo. Surely by now all the traces of the important treasure are gone, but the challenge is, Where are the hiding places? I agree with you that some of that treasure was not disposed of. It was too distinct, perhaps too difficult. It is bound to be, in time. Ted phoned me just before you arrived here. He is less keen than I to get involved in this, but we agreed we would both go for the first two weeks, to help you get set; then one of us would go home and from then on we'd alternate being there. That way we could tend to our businesses, and our families, and at the same time keep in touch with you in Dongo. The only thing worries me is the fellow Giorgio whom Ted told me you want to make permanent staff. Can he really be trusted? An ex-convict . . ."

"So am I."

"Yes, yes, but you know what I mean."

"He can be trusted. Completely."

"Well, we will have to trust your judgment on that. But once there, we must form our own judgment, of course. You understand that. You are in charge, but the risk is mutual. Now, how was your evening? Did Keva show you all you wanted to see?"

Keva picked me up at the hotel in her little black Volvo. "I only have my license since January. The Volvo was second hand but I have a friend who knows about such things and he found it for me. I pay such a little a month. It is my outstanding pleasure." She drove to the Museum of Modern Art on Skeppsholmen, an island in the Strömmen adjacent to the promontory of the Old City. There was a special exhibition, on loan, of the works of the Norwegian artist Edvard Munch, whose paintings were a passion to Keva.

In the museum, on the way to the Munch exhibit, Keva led me to the permanent Picassos, not to see the pictures, it turned out, but to read a Picasso quotation that appeared on the wall at the entrance. She translated it for me: "There is no abstract art. You must always start with something. Afterward you can remove all traces of reality. There's no danger then, anyway, because the idea of the object will have left an indelible mark."

She looked at me intently, the blue of her eyes very dark. "I believe that. Do you believe that? I mean about life. It's a very important idea about living. You have a relation. It is gone. It seems to have disappeared. But no. The thing that caused it was real. It leaves an indelible mark on you. I am covered with indelible marks."

I liked some of the colors and forms of the Munch paintings, but I had been so long removed from the art world that I felt alien. Keva was especially enthusiastic about a painting of two lovers, titled *The Kiss*. She said, "The way the faces melt into one—that's us. I only like the delicate line things, not the big paintings. The big ones are anybody." There were reproductions on sale at a desk near the exit, and I bought a replica of *The Kiss* for Keva. She was delighted.

Near the museum was a music shop where Keva found a recording of a particular piano étude that she had been searching for. We went into a booth to listen to it. "What you listen for," she said, "are the little high runs, and then the falls. It is like flying. You listen and you feel you are in air."

We ate dinner in the Golden Peace Restaurant, where they had twelve kinds of fresh herring and uncooked unsmoked salmon marinated in a sauce covered with fresh dill.

"Can you imagine," Keva said, "that a night and a morning passed and we did not make love. Tonight, I promise you, everything will be placid. That is another of my good words. Placid."

"Michael Bamberg was very good for your vocabulary."

"That is not a Michael Bamberg word. I have other sources. Give me a word from you."

I thought. "Titillate."

"Is it dirty?"

"No. It means to excite or stimulate pleasurably."

"Oh, yes. I hope so. Tonight."

"Well, I'm afraid I wouldn't feel placid . . ."

"It was a rare thing, the boy waking like that."

"I would be too uneasy. I would feel . . . well . . . nervous."

"I would come with you to your hotel, but I have a terrible thing about hotels. Swedish hotels. Only Swedish hotels. Everyone seems to know you did not come with the key. In the elevator, you should see the eyes of the Swedish men, the way they look at you: when you finish with him, come to see me. And the concierge with his long Swedish nose. He gives it to you terrible. Especially in the morning. The lift boy makes a big racket with the gate when you are departing, and the concierge looks up and so does the mail clerk and the cashier and they turn their sour eyes on you so that everyone in the lobby looks at you. The Greek woman stoned in the pit by the villagers. Look, tomorrow is Saturday. I will send the boys to friends in the country. You come at noon, I will fix lunch and we can stay in bed until Sunday night. There! We will make up what we lost."

Bis came for breakfast the following morning and we discussed more details of the impending operation. He gave me his dossier to take along. I packed and made the eleven o'clock plane for Rome. I sent Keva a cashmere sweater from the airport, with a note apologizing for my unexpected departure; I thought about her all the way back to Italy, wondering if she had left an indelible mark on me.

POINT OF CONTACT

How does the fowler seek to catch his game
By divers means! all of which one cannot name;
His guns, his nets, his lime-twigs, light and bell;
He creeps, he goes, he stands; yea, who can tell
Of all his postures? Yet there's none of these
Will make him master of what fowls he please.
Yea, he must pipe and whistle to catch this;
Yet, if he does so, that bird he will miss.

The Pilgrim's Progress

chapter eleven

The expedition set out for Dongo on August 7. Ted and Bis drove the sand-colored van with a sedately lettered "Spedizione Internazionale" on its door, while I followed in a Volkswagen station wagon; we had had to purchase the van, but the station wagon had been rented for ninety days. We all wore khaki, not uniforms exactly and not matching but it gave us the right look.

We necessarily followed the Mussolini escape route, since that was the primary route to Dongo, starting at Como and passing through the lakeshore towns of Cernobbio, Moltrasio, Tremezzo, Menaggio—towns that figured prominently in the fits and starts of Mussolini's last three days.

Giorgio had gone ahead to scout for a headquarters, and we had delayed departure until he had notified us that he had found just what we were looking for—a large furnished villa in Zonico, high on a ridge of the steep-rising mountain foothills, with a great sweep of Lake Como before it. Giorgio had been impatiently waiting for me when I returned to Rome from Stockholm, and it had been cheerful and heartening to see him again. He was someone I could trust and he trusted me. The people I was now involved with, Dan included, were relative strangers; Giorgio was family. The friendship we had forged in prison was strong. I had many times discussed this treasure project with Giorgio, and I felt he knew more about it, and certainly was much more sanguine about its advisability and prospects, than were the others.

Giorgio was in his late thirties, ebullient, impatient and utterly unscrupulous. He had great talents for circumventing the law, or popping right through it unscathed, being especially proficient at forgery, picking locks and pockets, and various highly refined swindles. Sometimes he spoke English with a mock Italian accent, sometimes he laid on a British accent, and sometimes he handled it pretty straight, or with a hippie twist. His linguistic versatility was attributable to a two-year stay in London, where he was involved in a highly complicated swindle that almost worked, to the tune of two million pounds; but "almost," in the world of swindles, is not good enough and Giorgio was lucky to escape a few hours before the Scotland Yard noose was tightened.

He had planned his escape route well; he wound up in the United States, where, determined to repudiate the nefarious life he had always led, he got his first honest job, as a waiter at an "in" Italian restaurant called Gino's. In a very short time his fluent English had become Americanized, and his new contacts had landed him a captaincy at a glamor eatery, Orsini's. Unfortunately, in his position as captain, the contacts became too good. Giorgio was soon distracted from the straight and narrow, and with the dangled lure of a sure killing, he got involved with one of the restaurant's clients in a project that simply required him to bring a small but highly valuable package into Italy. Unfortunately the airport police were on hand to receive both Giorgio and his package and that's how he came to spend four years in my company.

When we first met in the exercise yard (on hearing that the yard contained an American, he had sought me out), he explained his dilemma succinctly: "I wanna get rich too quick."

Now, four days after I had explained our requirements for certificates, passports, university accreditations, diplomas and other forged needs, Giorgio produced perfect specimens of everything. I had been uneasy about Ted's and Bis's reactions to Giorgio, who always came on pretty strong, but whatever doubts they may have had were effectively dispelled by the dazzling quality of his forgeries. At one point Ted asked Giorgio if, after all these years, he really thought we could pick up the trail of the missing treasure.

"You speak spick?" Giorgio asked.

"You mean Spanish—no."

"Well, no matter—it's a very old Spanish proverb that loses nothing in translation: 'With patience and saliva, the elephant fucketh the ant.' "

From then on, whenever we ran into obstacles and frustrations, the hue and cry was: "Patience and saliva!" Giorgio suggested we print it on buttons.

Zonico and Dongo lie cheek to cheek, sharply pitched upward from the lakeshore. Dongo, the larger village in size and population, had two cinemas, Zonico, none. But Zonico had the one and only ambulance, operated by a wizened former *ufficiale* named Paulo Benfatto. The pitched streets of both villages were cobblestoned and too narrow for American cars. Dongo had a large well-proportioned piazza with cafés on two sides; its imposing City Hall faced toward the lake which formed the open, fourth side of the piazza's almost perfect square.

Zonico, on the other hand, had a very scraggly public square that was not a square at all but just an old café that stood beside the highway, with a cobblestone road that joined it to the old shed that housed the ambulance. At the upper limits of Dongo, where the mountain pitch became too steep to build on, there was a large, successful iron foundry that employed eight hundred workers who came from villages all around (it was a much smaller foundry with only fifty workers when Ted and Bis had been there in 1945). But the most surprising development was the huge ore-processing, cement-producing complex at Zonico's upper limits, a complex that had been nonexistent in 1945 and now employed thirteen hundred workers from as far away as Cernobbio. It naturally occurred to us, that some of the Mussolini treasure could have financed this factory, which was owned by a Benno Barbelli, who had operated a three-man pottery kiln back in 1945.

Dongo had a church, St. Anthony's, just off the piazza; its other religious establishment, far up the mountain, was the Santuario Madonna della Lacrime. Zonico had no church, but in an even more remote mountain position than Dongo's Santuario, there existed the Monasterio di Santo Zacharia, which housed an order of monks who were committed to a vow of eternal silence.

Soon after arriving and installing ourselves in the Villa di Cielo, I arranged a meeting with the mayors of both villages and presented our credentials. Explaining that our project would affect the villages, we said we wished to sponsor a public reception to introduce ourselves and establish good will. Public events in these remote mountain villages were few and far between; the mayors happily endorsed my suggestion and proclamations were posted immediately.

During the first week our expedition went through the motions of surveying and staking out the shore area where the excavations would take place. The Dongo police warden, who wore a battered blue uniform and circulated on his bicycle despite one leg frozen crooked at the knee, kept away the curious, but we played the possibility of recognition doubly safe by keeping Bis and Ted, especially Ted, pretty much out of sight for the time being.

Dan and Natalie arrived with two servants whom they brought us for the villa. We could not, of course, risk any local servants in the intimate confines of our operation; hence, these two women, who had worked for Natalie for more than five years. We had to hire local workers for our excavation crew but their only contact with us would be at the excavation site, which was well removed from the villa.

Dan and Natalie were glowing from the sexual sunburst of a weekend in Siena, about which they issued a number of uninhibited bulletins.

"Dan and I are like the tides," Natalie confided to me as we took an after-dinner turn around the villa's rose garden. "My work as a creative artist carries me in one direction, and Dan's work carries him in another. Of course, I know about his sexing around, but there isn't any substance to it. I flip out once in a while the same way. That's how I know about substance and the lack of it. What always happens is eventually the tides change and wash us back together again and we discover the Wagnerian sex thing we have and fall madly in love all over again.

"And it happened last week in Siena. We went to see the Palio—you know, the big pageant that winds up with a wild horse race in the Piazza del Campo. Well, we had booked a hotel room that had a balcony that overlooked the piazza, and we were out there watching the marvelous pageant that precedes the race—when standard-bearers from the seventeen *contrade* in their fifteenth-century costumes parade around with their flags, waving them high, spinning them, twirling them around their bodies, then tossing them up through the air, the flags swiftly plummeting back, the bright silk dancing in the sunlight. It's one of the sights of the world, unpaintable, unphotographable, too much, too complicated, too personal. There we were on our little balcony watching and we began to get very sexy, and suddenly we couldn't wait for the horses, so in we went and threw ourselves into bed in a white heat and while we screwed, outside the horse race started and the frenzy of the crowd and our frenzy and nobody in the history of the world ever screwed like that and Dan and I both came at the very moment the winning horse crossed the finish line and the roar of the crowd and our roar came together." She paused dramatically, breathing heavily, reliving the moment. "That's how it is with Dan and me. Every once in a while we fall insanely in love, as we are now. We'll probably be in love now for weeks."

Distracted by the activity of the move to Dongo, I had been able not to think too much about Iris or Keva, but Natalie's Palio paean caused this submergence to surface, and black night thoughts ruined my sleep again. I also had the uneasy feeling, during the four days she stayed, that the real purpose of her confidences to me about her sex life with Dan was seductive; she had a way of putting her hand on my arm while she described her ecstasies with Dan. Maybe I wasn't reading her correctly, but *something* was coming through my sleeve that was meant for me.

High on my priority list was an investigation of the 1957 trial in Padua which had been officially convened to try those people who had been involved in the disappearance of the treasure. After twelve years of detective work, the Italian government finally named thirty-five defendants to stand trial; three hundred witnesses were subpoenaed to testify. The trial was supposed to last six or eight months, but it had barely got under way when it was abruptly and mysteriously halted by the trial judge, and it was never reconvened. All the defendants and witnesses dispersed, and from that day to this the government made no further inquiry into what happened to its treasure.

During the weeks that the trial was in progress, several important witnesses did give testimony and my objective in going to Padua was to read the trial transcript with an eye to uncovering any leads that we might pursue.

The run to Padua from Dongo is only a few hours, no-speed-limit super-highway most of the way. The archives of the Assize Court were orderly and it only took two days to read the transcript of the 1957 trial. Among the three hundred witnesses who had been scheduled to be called were Rachele Mussolini and her children, Romano and Anna-maria, but only twenty-six people were actually interrogated. The most important defendant was Dante Gorreri, who was at that time a Communist deputy in the legislature, and who was charged with having received, in 1945, 400,000,000 lire (1945 value, $32,000,000) which he had fed into the coffers of his party.

On the witness stand Gorreri swore that all he had received were 15,000 Swiss francs which were used to finance anti-German partisan activity. He specifically denied ever receiving a gold watch and an alarm clock (the only items actually found in his flat) that belonged to Mussolini. In the proceedings, Gorreri was also charged with ordering the murder of the two partisan women, Gianna and Anna Bianchi, but the Public Prosecutor did not go into that in his questioning. Most of the accused simply denied having received whatever they were charged with. Remo Mentasti, accused of receiving a box of jewels and other objects belonging to members of the Mussolini entourage, said he knew nothing whatever of the matter. I quickly skimmed all this testimony, but I did find a few statements which I took careful note of:

1. Twin brothers from Milan, Paolo and Giocanni Zatta, stated that they had taken temporary work on a farm near Lodi where they met a young woman who showed them a picture of a former German SS officer who, before he was killed, told her of a box containing gold and jewelry that was buried on the right bank of the Mera River.

2. A witness named Bianca Calli, the mayor's daughter, who helped the partisan Gianna prepare a written inventory when the treasure was brought to the Dongo City Hall, testified that when it came time to have the inventory typed up, Gianna took it over to the school house "where she got assistance."

3. Carlo Maderna, a partisan who had driven one of the lorries that transported some of the treasure from the City Hall after it had been inventoried, replied to the question of whether the Communist partisans made off with his cargo: "You know, there weren't just partisans—there were some foreigners around too. Not at the moment when Mussolini was captured, but certainly while the booty was still in the area." As I read this, I thought about Luigi Hoffmann, who seemed to have cropped up again, although unnamed.

4. A lawyer, Luigi Grassi, who in 1945 was Como's chief of police, in testifying about some jewels which had turned up in Como, said that an informant had referred to them as the Squassoni delivery for Dongo. In none of my notes and research memos was there anyone named Squassoni.

5. A witness named Terzi, a Communist, being harassed on the stand by the Public Prosecutor, blurted out: "Maybe a lot of the stuff just passed *through* our hands, and not *into* them. And maybe some of that stuff did, in a way, get back to the people."

While I was in the courthouse reading the trial transcript, Giorgio, who had driven with me, was spending his time talking to people around the court who had been there in 1957 and who might throw light on the dark subject of why the trial was abruptly halted, never to resume.

"Nobody wantsa talk much. I'm put on this pose of American journalist. I talk it New York eye-tal or Georgia cracker eye-tal. You wanna demonstrations?"

"Not now, Giorgio. What I want now is what the hell did you find out, if anything? And not in dialect!"

"Ah-ah, Massa get cranky. Okay. Business. Well, these are very shut-up pussy cats around here, let me tell you. Except one guy. He's boiled because only yesterday he expected to be promote to Chief Clerk but somebody else get it and he's scorched. So we go in and load some vino at the friendly courthouse bar—that one where you and me had lunch—and he gets into the chianti and pretty soon he's talking about this judge, that judge, I'm leading him on, of course, and then he mentions this one Judge Rambellini . . ."

"But he wasn't the trial judge."

"No, that's it—he was the Chief Administrative Judge. Above the trial judge. He ordered the perjury hearing that stopped the trial. And he never reinslated—"

". . . slated."

". . . stated it. But get this—it's too floody buckin' much—one year later, 1958, Judge Rambellini, big life-time judge, resignates, and since then lives very poshy—buys big, plenty expensive villa in Florence, summer villa Capri, owns this and that, has a big thing in London. My fellow does not know exactly but the judge has a fancy flat there and owns the race horses—that much he know. This Judge Rambellini is a money swinger, all right. And it all popped off one year after he cut that trial dead."

chapter twelve

The reception party which we gave for the Zonico-Dongo
citizenry was held in the Sala d'Oro of the Dongo City Hall,
the baroque, ceiling-frescoed ball room which appears on all
the Dongo postcards and is a last reminder of its nineteenth-
century glory. Both mayors wore their ceremonial sashes,
the ladies prominently displayed what jewels they could
muster, all military medals were on lapels, those who pos-
sessed old military dress uniforms wore them, others wore
evening clothes of various styles and vintages, and the ones
who did not own evening clothes simply wore winged collars and black ties with their black Sunday church suits. The
whole gathering had the air of being a set for a rather
carelessly mounted period movie. We had hired a group of
musicians from Gravedona who played a monotony of
waltzes.

The afternoon of the party we had had a boiling argument
over whether we should unveil Ted and Bis, and with their
recognition deliberately create suspicion as to our real mission and cause the tensions to rise; or whether we should,
for the time being, play it safe and as much as possible keep
our treasure inquiry to ourselves. Bis and Ted were staunchly

and vociferously for the latter course but Dan, Giorgio and I eventually prevailed.

When the time came to speak on behalf of the expedition, after explaining what we hoped our excavations would uncover, I introduced all the members of our group; I half-expected an immediate stir when Ted stood up and took his bow, but he received the same kind of distant, polite reception that Giorgio had received. Same for Bis. I did not present Dan since he planned only to appear sporadically and to keep his actual involvement to a minimum.

When the formal part of the evening was over—speeches by the two mayors, and by Father Ammasso of Dongo's St. Anthony and Father Donato Piccionastro of the Monastery of St. Zacharia—food and wine was placed on the tables and some of the people began to dance to the stolid music.

But it did not take long for the seeds of recognition to sprout. Paulo Benfatto, the ambulance driver, wearing his frayed *ufficiale* uniform, soon sought me out.

"The gentleman you introduced who stands over there, yes, that one, he looks so much like an Allied officer who was here years ago, as the war was ending . . . I don't suppose it could possibly be the same?"

"Well, yes, as a matter of fact Mr. Middlekey *was* an officer with the British army. He had been an archaeologist before the war and, of course, went back to his profession afterward."

"As I recall, he was here about the valuables that disappeared when Benito Mussolini was captured in Dongo."

"Yes, you have a good memory. And now he's returned here in his real profession to see if he'll have better luck locating the Roman spa that disappeared a long time before the Mussolini treasure. But it's quite a coincidence, isn't it? I mean, two such events happening in a little place like this?"

"That's what I was thinking. Did he ever find any of that Mussolini treasure?"

"I don't know. A lot of it is still missing, isn't it?"

"So they say."

But not a word about Bis. Age had disguised him too well.

Giorgio sidled up with the brilliant notion, confided sotto voce out of the corner of his mouth, that perhaps some of the missing gold had been distributed among the gold trappings of this room; he was especially intrigued by two gold griffins that supported an ornate sideboard. I congratulated him on having achieved a state of pure lunacy and reminded him that he was supposed to be casing the jewels.

"I have, I have! All paste, or out of the ancestral closet."

"Well, keep looking. Some heaving breast is going to hang it right out there for you."

Father Donato Piccionastro was the administrative head of the St. Zacharia Monastery, which meant that he was one of the few in the order permitted to speak, and was, in fact, the monastery's voice with the outside world; his loquaciousness certainly compensated for the pervasive vows of his silent brethren. He chain-smoked cigarettes and spoke English effortlessly.

Out of his introductory small talk there emerged the rather alarming fact that he himself was an amateur archaeologist, that he had been on digs in Palermo and Catania, and would we be receptive to his joining us on those days when he could be spared at the monastery?

"Of course—glad to have an extra pair of hands."

"It's hard to believe that the Romans situated a spa here —at Sirmione there was the phenomenon of the hot sulphur springs . . ."

"There is evidence that there were also hot baths here, but that the sulphur springs dried up long ago."

"You don't say? Well, it will be very interesting to see

your research and diagrams, and you are most kind to let me join your little group." He then launched into a detailed account of a particular find at Palermo, and as I pretended to listen to him I thought our little group had better watch its step.

Giorgio had to wait patiently until Father Donato had finished to bring me his good news; he simply handed it to me, an opal and diamond locket. On its reverse side, engraved on the gold, was the inscription, "Clara, I am you— you are me, Ben," and two dates: 24.4.32/24.4.41. With his head Giorgio indicated the tall, gray-haired woman from whose neck he had adroitly lifted the locket. I gave it back to him, so that he could restore it before it was missed. The woman, it developed, was the wife of Bernardo Gattamelata, who owned Dongo's one auto-repair garage. He had operated his garage all through the war and somehow had escaped military involvement in any form. He was not at the party. The explanation was that he was in Milan on business.

A few days after the party, the dig officially got under way. Our staff of local diggers had been hired and briefed, and stakes and string lines had been laid down after elaborate surveying with instruments we had used in pretense. Father Donato came to the excavation site for about an hour one afternoon, but that was insufficient time to poke about much.

Once the dig started (very cautiously and slowly, to consume as much time as possible), Ted and Bis slipped away to the north to investigate the River Mera, at least that part of it immediately adjacent to the lake road from Dongo. They were skeptical of the information I had turned up from the Padua trial transcript (the testimony of the Zatta twins that a German SS officer had buried a box containing gold and jewels somewhere along the right bank of the river), but still, it was the kind of information that could not be totally ignored. But, Ted had pointed out, someone surely had made a search back in 1957 when the Zattas testified. Bis, however, had always expected a yield from the Mera based on his 1945 investigation—not this German SS box, necessarily, but he had felt that since the German convoy, on leaving Mussolini to his captors in Dongo (some of the treasure in their lorries must have escaped detection), had passed this route, and since the Germans would have had to secrete that treasure before reaching the guards just beyond at the Swiss border, where better than the Mera, which was just about the only accessible place between Dongo and the heavily guarded border.

Paulo Benfatto spent most of his time sitting beside his ambulance which he kept parked outside its shed, ready for a quick (but highly infrequent) getaway. He was very proud of the old ambulance that glistened in the sunlight. I effused over its beautiful condition and Benfatto toured me through and around it as a guide might lead a tourist through St. Peter's. That over, I sat down beside him and we chatted for a while about the two towns and some of the people.

"By the way, I asked Ted Middlekey about the treasure—you know, what we talked about at the reception. It's too bad he doesn't speak Italian so you could discuss it with him. Anyway, he said, no, none of the treasure was recovered by his group. You were here all through that period, weren't you?"

"Yes, including the capture and the executions. I was as near to the Duce as you are to me when they took him down from that truck and he removed the Nazi coat he was wearing."

"Were you around when they started to take all the gold and jewels and everything else from the cars?"

"Part of the time. They tried to clear us out—get us out of the square."

"They?"

"The partisan group. The ones that made the capture. But it was easy to see what was going on—the streets all run steep uphill and you get a pretty good view of the square from almost anywhere."

"I guess they took an inventory of all the stuff they carried into the City Hall?"

"I hear they did."

"Do you suppose anybody around might still have a copy of it?"

"Can't say yes and can't say no, but one thing I can tell you, nobody around will say much about it. I'll bet I haven't heard the subject of that treasure come up more than once or twice over the past twenty years."

"Why's that?"

"Well, right after the war, a lot of the people who had to do with that inventory began to disappear or wind up dead —floating in the lake. A nice couple I knew, both partisans, good people, very brave, both murdered. Why, hell, the mayor of Zonico disappeared one day going from his office to his house and they never found a trace of him. We have a street named after him. Well, enough people wind up dead or wiped away and other people get the message pretty good. No, not many people around here have much to say about all that."

"How about you?"

"Including me. But I'll tell you something about the execution that always bothered me. You know, the cabinet ministers who were with Mussolini who were lined up in the Dongo square and executed? . . . Well, they lined them up right at the edge of the lake where there's an iron railing, with their backs to the lake, the piazza jammed with spectators. Marcello Petacci, Claretta's brother, was supposed to be shot along with the others, but the ministers made a big stink about it—they didn't like him and they didn't want him executed in their company, so the partisans agreed, and Petacci was kept to one side while the ministers got theirs first. It was a terrible mess, though. The firing squad must have been drunk because half of the ministers were just wounded, and some of them began to run around the square and people in the crowd who had guns began to fire at them, and in all the confusion Marcello Petacci dived in the water and began to swim to where there's a breakwater not very far from shore. The two partisan guards who were supposed to be watching him fired into the water and he disappeared, but they never found his body. The water's not very deep just off shore there and they dragged all around for him—they never found him and the body should have surfaced."

"What do you think might have happened?"

"My personal opinion—you understand, it's just something occurred to me and I've got no proof or anything like that—but, you see, when he heard the shots he could have gone under and swum underwater to the breakwater, which is high enough so that people on shore can't see what's happening on its other side. What if there had been a boat there that he could have used? Or what if he just swam close to the breakwater all the way along it? Either way he could have escaped. I'm not saying he did. But he could have."

The following day, an old woman from Dongo came to see me. She must have been ninety but she was straight and clear-eyed and her hands were strong. She invited me to have a coffee with her, carefully writing her name and address on a piece of paper.

"I want to show you something," she said. "It's time I told somebody about it."

"Is it about our . . . excavation?"

"No. My friend, Paulo Benfatto, told me about speaking with you—it's about that."

"Fine. I shall certainly be happy to have coffee."

So this would be the beginning, the old ones whose lives had run and their risks so little now. As the afternoon moved on my anticipation of the old lady's revelation mounted, but I did not tell the others.

The old lady lived alone in three rooms at the top of a street as narrow as a cart. The rooms were clean and simple, and framed memorabilia of joyful events decorated the living room where she served us thick black coffee in earthenware mugs. She showed me some interesting photos taken in and around Dongo during World War I, and some pictures of her four sons, all of whom had been killed in various military engagements. Her husband, too, was dead, killed by a personnel mine that exploded in a field two years after the war had ended.

"I am so glad you came. It is a heavy burden to carry a secret for as long as I have. But I know you are interested in what happened here when Mussolini was captured."

I could feel the blood in my temples as she went over to a large old cabinet in the corner. She took out the bottom shelf and reached her hand behind a false back at the bottom, bringing forth a square cardboard box tied with twine.

"I was in the Dongo piazza that day when they began to unload the vehicles and take away the Duce's things and I . . . well . . . I helped myself . . . as did others, but that's no excuse. I am a righteous woman and I have never stolen nor coveted nor even borrowed except for this one time. And I must tell you that all these years I have not even been able to speak of it in confession. But there is something about you, the way you spoke to us at the reception, I felt I could tell you, and could trust you."

"I assure you, signora, you can. Your secret can be shared with me and go no further."

I tried to be steady and unhurried in untying the twine and opening the box but my fingers trembled. Now the lid was off and the old lady lifted away a top layer of tissue paper and then she brought it forth—a German helmet. "This is the actual one the Duce was wearing. He first took off his German coat and then this helmet which he dropped to the pavement. It rolled a ways and wound up at my feet. I could not resist. Everybody was watching Mussolini, so when I picked it up and put it under my coat no one saw. Would you like to try it on? I have had it out many, many times but I have never shown it to anyone. I would like to see how it looks. Would you like to try it on?"

Days passed. Constant expectancy. Townspeople came, curious about the excavation. Father Donato came with sophisticated archaeological tools—and questions. The mayor of Zonico came with a newspaperman from Menaggio.

But no one came about the treasure. If we had succeeded in creating tension and suspicion, it had produced no results. Ted and Bis reported that their search of the banks of the Mera had also been fruitless.

It was apparent that if we were to move forward, we would have to move ourselves and not wait for a boost from some unknown but accommodating person. Paulo Benfatto had given me the word: fear. "Not many people around here have much to say about all that." He did not say that they did not *know* about all that—only that no one would talk about it. So it would be necessary to evaluate carefully every lead we had, no matter how seemingly insignificant. We had so few that we certainly could not be choosy. If we could pry up the Dongo lid, just a corner of it, information might begin to leak out. But how to penetrate the impenetrable? Fear is a seamless seal, one thing you observe if you have spent many years in prison: men become absolutely loyal to silence, willing to trade away a chunk of their lives rather than risk reprisal.

Dan and I talked about this on our way to the Mera. Although Ted and Bis had reported negative treasure findings, they had mentioned the burgeoning state of the Mera's underwater life, and Dan, who was a fishing nut, had convinced me that an afternoon away from the non-bubbling Dongo cauldron might be a good thing.

"So what specific leads are there?" Dan was driving, I was talking. "Mrs. Gattamelata and her Claretta Petacci jewel. Giorgio has gone over every inch of her house, and when he says there's nothing else there, we better believe it. And as you know, there's no such thing as vaults or safety deposit boxes around here."

"Where does Gattamelata keep his valuables?"

"There's a safe in his garage and Giorgio has been through it. Nothing."

"Why don't you hit her right on with it? Beautiful jewel, where did you get it?"

"Yes, that's all there's to do—but the timing—it's got to come at just the right time."

"Oh, hell, I don't know about that—a little flattery, tickle her ass. With a woman any time can be the right time. And it doesn't matter how old they are. In fact, the older they are, the more susceptible they are."

"You want to tackle her?"

"No—but I will."

"Okay—so what else is there? The few leads I picked up out of the Padua transcript. Like the testimony of the Zatta twins about the Mera River box—which we can forget about."

"It's possible Ted and Bis missed it."

"Possible, but for the time being, let's say it has checked out negative. But there are two leads which have not been followed at all. Not that I haven't thought about them. I certainly have, it's just that they're wet soap to pick up. First, that witness who testified that Gianna, who helped compile the inventory, took it over to the schoolhouse to get it typed up with someone's assistance."

"Now you don't really mean to say you find that information reeking with possibilities?"

"Not reeking, but maybe a slight redolence, an aroma from far off that just barely reaches the nostrils."

"You've got twice the nose I have."

"Well, how about the second lead. At the time those jewels were passed, it was said, 'This is the Squassoni delivery for Dongo.' Why can't we turn up, then or now, any one named Squassoni?"

"I admit that's more of a lead, but I don't think it merits alerting the bloodhounds. Twenty-four years ago someone mentioned the name Squassoni. Big deal."

"Are you just as cynical about the testimony of the partisan who said that when the treasure was still in the area, being moved around, there were foreigners here, and not just partisans?"

"Undoubtedly referring to Luigi Hoffmann. Which puts us back on *that* dead-end street, because we don't have clue number one as to where to look for Hoffmann—or the three bags of wedding-ring gold or the box with twenty-two crown jewels or the crates with thirty-three million lire—all the stuff that was snatched from the organ pit of your Como villa."

"You're too fucking cynical, Dan."

"I'm fucking realistic, that's what I am."

"What about Judge Rambellini and his sudden wealth?"

"Hey you, Judge Rambellini, tell us why you stopped that trial and how come you suddenly got race horses in London and villas in Florence and a hotel in Capri and you give up a lifetime judgeship, just like that? Tell us that, Judge."

"Okay, clown, you know as well as I do that for a price there are people willing to talk about anyone or anything. Maybe not in a closed town like this where everyone knows the thump of everybody else's pulse. But Ted is poking around in London and if anyone can, he'll find the little place in the judge's hump where he can run in the killing sword."

"If the judge doesn't get him with one of his horns before that. It's not like fighting the bull—only two horns. I'll bet the judge has twenty or thirty horns and you know the odds against going into the ring with a beast like that."

Like the leads, the fish were there but they were elusive and not biting. The speckled sun, filtered through the dense leaves, was warm but not oppressive, and after a while we propped our poles with rocks across the butts and stretched out on the grassy bank.

I thought Dan had fallen asleep, but with his eyes closed he began to ruminate. "You know, back there—I was just thinking—when we first met and the war was ending, I knew precisely what I was going to do and who I was going to be. Only time of my life I felt I had a direct line on myself. I was very serious about writing. I used to say that America has produced only two writers, Melville and Twain, and I used to carry on about why they were the only authentic geniuses, and on and on, and how now, finally, there was going to be a third, Dan H. Reeder. Then I'd really give it to all the phonies: Hemingway and Faulkner and F. Scott and Steinbeck and all the rest, tearing into them, putting down their stuff as bullshit. I was secure, man, I was rock. I went civilian all beefed up. I had that direct line and all my illusions intact and an ego like skyscrapers. But I blew it. I didn't give it a hot chance in hell. I fucked up and ran for cover—grabbed a wife, put myself in the dog-run straight jacket every man wears and gave up hitting in the three slot behind Melville and Twain.

"So I run, run, run. Commotion instead of motion. Just move. Up, down, back, sideways. What's the difference? See Dan. See Dan run. See Dan run fast, fast, so everything's a passing blur and Dan can't see where he's been, where he is or where he's going. Run with the television cameras, run with the beautiful people, run after all the cunning cunt. I guess you'd have to say it's my insecurity. I guess I *need* to produce all that TV shit—they use more of my stuff than anyone else's—to prove I'm an electronic hot-shot. Never mind quality—of course it's all dribble. Quantity. That's the gold star. And the snatch too. Do you know I've never had a real affair? It's draw a bead on a flashy quail, stalk it, flush it, shoot it down, hang it on the game belt and stalk on. Natalie knows. She says it right out—she's some great piece of woman, that Natalie. She says it: Dan's got to have his security nooky."

"But what does it prove, Dan? I mean endlessly chasing tail to the point where, well, maybe it's your own tail you're chasing."

"Because listen, man, when a really attractive piece gives it to you, you know you've still got it. The excitement of the hunt—it does prove something. But sometimes, like now, I slow down for a second and really look at myself hanging up there in that open sky, and I know it's not a way of life; it's not even *life*. It's a fucking fantasy and one of these days I'll wake up to the reality—the reality of a hanging shed full of dead quail and forty miles of old TV tapes."

One of the lines snapped forward and bobbled but it was only a perch. We packed up our gear and had started to climb to the top of the embankment when we saw the wooden box resting against the trunk of a tree. It was heavily encrusted with mud and had obviously been opened recently. The wood inside was clean. It was empty. Dan took his fish knife and carefully scraped away the mud. It wasn't an ordinary wooden box, and as Dan scraped we could see that it was a small cask with a fitted top. When he finally uncovered them, the markings were faded but unmistakable: a series of numbers and a military designation.

"I think we should hit them separately," I said, "but at the same time. Why don't you take Bis?"

"Shall we try to be devious?"

"No, let's put it to them straight: 'Why didn't you mention finding the box? What was in it?' "

As we passed through the Dongo piazza on our way back, there was Signora Gattamelata sitting alone at a table in front of the café, having a coffee and reading *Epoca*. Dan slipped out of the car, and I drove on to Zonico alone.

chapter thirteen

Ted and Bis independently told pretty much the same story—it was just an old empty box, why would they mention it? They had located many worthless objects in the low part of the river bank where the earth was soft and muddy. No, they didn't know it had military markings—the thick coating of mud covered everything.

Signora Gattamelata was more illuminating but less believable. A long time ago—the war had just ended—while eating in the Fagiano, Dongo's only restaurant, the signora's fork had mysteriously collided with something nonedible which, to her amazement, turned out to be the exquisite pendant we had seen at the reception. Yes, of course, the inscription was obvious. No, she never gave a thought to turning it over to the authorities. Why should she? Didn't everything else disappear? When others turned in theirs, she would turn in hers.

My nights alone were a catalogue of despairs. After we disbanded to our respective rooms, and behind my closed door, I lay sleepless in the brass bed and reality passed in review. The reality of Iris; the reality of Keva; the reality of how much time had passed, and how little, if anything, I had to show for it.

So on this night, my sleep fouled by the realities, not even able to read, I had gone to the table I used as a desk and had started to shuffle through the few meager leads we had; I came to the Padua trial statement by Bianca Calli and for the hundredth time reread her words: "When the time came to have the inventory typed up, Gianna took it over to the schoolhouse where she got assistance." But on this night, this particular rereading suddenly brought forth a question: Who gives assistance at a schoolhouse? Obvious answer, you lout: a schoolteacher. What likelier person to be the typist who Gianna sought for assistance? The more I thought about it, the more anxious I became to visit Dongo's schoolhouse; impatience for the day makes for a very long night.

Elenora Campisi was the only teacher still on the staff who had taught there in 1945. She was quite old but vigorous and alert. I dropped in on her at the end of the school day just as her last students were leaving the classroom. She had been at the reception so she knew who I was.

"I came to see you about a matter which, of course, I shall keep in strictest confidence. I understand that you have a copy of the inventory of the Mussolini treasure, which you typed up back in 1945 when it was assembled. I would like very much to look at it. Of course, I would never divulge its contents or reveal its source."

She sat back in her chair, her eyes wide, her lips apart; the fingers of her right hand fluttered up and pressed against her chin. Her lips moved a few times soundlessly; she turned her eyes away briefly, then turned them back to me, and this time amazement had given way to fear. I had my answer; the long-shot gamble had worked; the schoolteacher had given assistance and she had not been able to resist keeping a secret copy of her handiwork.

"The inventory is a valuable thing. I would expect to pay you very well for your cooperation."

"No, signor, no payment." Her voice was tired; she took off her steel-framed eyeglasses, wiped them, carefully reset them on her nose. "Actually it would be a relief—finally, after all these years, to talk about it. I was for the longest time afraid. And with good reason. But now I am old. And perhaps those who created the fear have subsided, one way or another. At any rate, I have little to lose. But I do not understand your involvement . . . I mean, what has this to do with your archaeology?"

"Our expedition has a variety of purposes."

"It makes no difference. In fact, I prefer not to know, not to be involved by knowing. Just to divest myself of . . . all that. So, if you would like, you may come to my address this evening . . ."

"Would you object if I came now?" I did not want to give her thinking time in which to change her mind. "I would come, say, in half an hour."

"All right. I live very near. A half-hour would be fine."

What she had was not the entire inventory but only a carbon copy of one page of it. She explained that the typed inventory had consisted of an original and five carbon copies but that when she had assembled the sets, she found that inexplicably an extra copy had been made of the last page. There were no surprises in the items listed on the page: foreign currencies, various gold listings that indicated the form the gold was in—ingots, scrap, coins, etc., singly listed jewels; altogether fifty-two items on the page.

As I said, the items themselves were as expected, but

unexpected were symbols that appeared before each item in the margin. There were three symbols: +, C, S.

"What do these symbols stand for, signorina?"

"I don't know. The first inventory did not have them. But several days after we finished typing that first inventory, Gianna brought it back with many new listings added and these markings in the margin and I retyped it."

"Did you ask her about them?"

"No. I asked nothing. I am not curious. And besides, there was an atmosphere of guns and terror and executions in the public square, and since I am fearful by nature even in the best of times . . . well, you can imagine."

"Was there any discussion about this inventory that you overheard—for instance, I mean, where these items were to be taken, anything like that?"

"No. Whatever happened about the inventory was Gianna's concern. No one came to the schoolhouse. Just Gianna. I would type and she would carefully check my typing, then she would go somewhere with the inventory."

"May I copy down these items?"

"Take the sheet. I want to be rid of it. I want to be rid of all of it. It is something I'm ashamed of, all these years."

"Ashamed? Of having this inventory?"

"Well, not only the inventory. There's more. A few days after I typed the second inventory, I received a visit from a gentleman who thanked me for my cooperation and said that the Central Committee of the Resistance would be especially appreciative if I were never to remember anything of what I had typed. As a token of their appreciation, he left with me a parcel wrapped in newspapers which he said I was not to open until after he had left. I urged him not to give me anything, that I did not want to be compensated for what I had done, but he said that he *had* to leave the parcel because my possession of it would involve me in such a way as to insure my forgetfulness of the contents of the inventory. I was too frightened to open the parcel that night. More frightened of that man than I was of the parcel, really."

"What did he look like?"

"He was a very tall, angular man with splendid manners, and very handsome, actually—I was young then and observed such things in men—but there was an air about him of . . . of . . . how can I describe it? Mystic. Yes—a mystic. He seemed so terribly in control, not just of himself, but of me too. The way he looked right at me and talked right into my eyes, I responded to him, as if hypnotized."

"Perhaps you were hypnotized."

"I don't know. I have actually never been hypnotized. But from having read *Trilby* I could recognize elements of what is described there."

"Perhaps you had been hypnotized not to open the package until the following morning. And perhaps you had been conditioned not to reveal the contents of the inventory because of possession of the contents of the package."

"You think that's possible? That I had been hypnotized and didn't know it?"

"I don't really know. I'm only guessing."

"Well, it's possible . . . it just never occurred to me."

"Do you still have the contents of that package?"

"I have the package. Of course I opened it, but afterward I re-did it and I have kept it hidden ever since."

She disappeared into her bedroom. I wondered if this was going to be a repeat of the old lady going to her cupboard for Mussolini's helmet. When she returned she was carrying a package wrapped in newspaper. As I untied the twine around it, I checked the dates on the newspapers. Inside the newspapers there was a cardboard box and inside that were two small white drawstring bags, each

with a tag attached to the end of the drawstring. One said
"L. Rosetta, Via Massi, Perugia"; the other, "P. Umbra, 17
Via Frate, Assisi."

Each was filled with small ingots of gold.

"I want you to take them. I do not want to be compensated for them. But you must give your word never to
say where they came from."

I gave my word. I put a bag in each of my side pockets,
dead weights that felt like they would rip through the
seams.

"I am certainly indebted to you, signorina."

"No, no. Don't be. I cannot tell you what a weight you
take from me." About ten kilos. She walked me to the
door.

"This man, your Svengali—did he tell you his name?"

"Yes. When he introduced himself. Luigi Hoffmann. I
never saw him again."

It was easy to identify the bags of gold: in our 1945
investigation we had obtained a deposition from the former
cashier for the Fascist chief of police who testified that the
Mussolini government had used the chief of police's secret
fund to buy gold from various jewelry shops in central
Italy. Some of the gold, he had told us, was transformed into
ingots, the rest put in small bags with tags that indicated the
quantity and the name and address of the jeweler from
whom it had been purchased. That was the source, then, of
these two bags.

All that evening I thought about the two bags of gold,
which, for the time being, were nestled behind a section of
the broad molding which framed the closet door in my
room. What I also thought about was that empty box on
the bank of the Mera. "Full disclosure" was a phrase I was
familiar with from my law school days, but what about
"reciprocity"? I must confess that ever since the discovery

of the empty box, despite their explanations, I had narrowed my eyes a little every time I saw Bis or Ted. There are waiters who, having agreed to pool tips, nevertheless palm what they can get away with. These two bags could well be the only treasure recovered—unless Bis and Ted had foraged something from that wooden box that they were keeping to themselves.

The following day I called Bis, Ted and Giorgio into the library and showed them the inventory sheet. We spent a good deal of time discussing the three symbols. Giorgio suggested that "C" might indicate *Communisti,* which we all thought was a sensible suggestion, but no one turned up anything believable for "S"; as for +, there were no suggestions at all.

That night I took one of the bags from behind the molding and transferred it into the bottom of a high-backed upholstered arm chair. I had learned not to keep all my eggs in one basket—learned it the hard way.

chapter fourteen

A few days later the workmen at the digs, under Ted's supervision, made an electrifying uncovery—a dazzling lode of Roman artifacts. In no time, a crowd of villagers had appeared to witness the careful exhumation of broken pottery, funeral urns, jewelry, coins, a piece of wheel, statuary (fragments, broken-nosed heads, torsos), pieces of columns, bricks, glass, mosaic bits, metal tools, a charioteer's helmet, inscribed stone, and other Roman vestiges.

When we were mounting the expedition, it had been Ted's brilliant notion to purchase a variety of Roman artifacts from Milanese antique shops and bring them to Zonico, surreptitiously bury them in our dig area, and then at a propitious time, direct the excavation to that location and "discover" them, thus authenticating our archaeological presence. It couldn't have worked better.

I had been putting it off and putting it off, but after Giorgio's return from his Bellagio scouting trip, I could put it off no longer. Giorgio had reported that the Disio house was closed up and had not been used for a long time. He had learned from neighbors that Arnoldo's mother and wife had both died years ago; his brother, Pietro, was a permanent resident of Stuttgart in West Germany, and his daughter, Julietta, was a designer for a fabric concern in Como.

So it was Julietta whom I would have to face. I remembered her as a plump, one-long-pigtailed child, hair the color of beeswax, withdrawn, serious, with glasses, and not easy to talk to.

"I'm terribly nervous about this, Ted. The minute she knows who I am . . . who knows what she'll do? But you can bet it will be hostile. And why not?"

"Well, start out this way: 'Signorina, the minute you hear my name you won't want to listen to me . . .' "

"And then what?"

"Then start talking."

"And if she won't listen? Why should she listen?"

"She'll listen. Woman's curiosity. She may not be a friendly audience, but she'll listen." Bis disagreed. He thought I was wasting my time.

The name of her fabric house was Nuvola, and I sent her a note there on the stationery of the San Gottardo Hotel, where I had checked in, to the effect that I had been a friend of her father's during the war and would she please meet me after work in the café across the street from the Nuvola building. I did not sign my name. Ted's brisk assurance failed to allay my apprehension, but I felt that meeting in an open café might ease things. I came early and tried to shore up my sagging confidence with a double scotch. I should have brought Ted along to act as a buffer, but he and Bis had gone on a rather delicate mission to the St. Zachary Monastery. They were both staunch Catholics, in fact Bis was a Papal Knight, and with this as their wedge, plus our archaeological kinship with Father Donato Piccionastro, they were going to try to find out if any of the

Fraters (I don't know how they planned to circumvent the vow of silence) who were in Dongo in 1945 had received any information that related to the treasure. In my view it was a rather hopeless mission, but no more hopeless than our entire project at that point.

Here again I was faced with the bizarre process of thawing time. Just as my life had congealed at the moment I had entered the deep-freeze of prison, I had expected that on leaving, it would by itself uncongeal; that slowly the heat of the real world would penetrate the gelidity, as automatic and natural a process as occurs when, in the morning, a steak or a chicken is removed from the freezer and put on the kitchen table so that by evening it will be ready for the skillet.

But over and over again I had found that there was nothing automatic or natural about my defrostment. Just as now, waiting for Julietta Disio, I was still frozen into life as it had been the last time I saw her: a little girl on a swing outside the trim white house in Bellagio, silk streamers of her dress fluttering in the wash of the rising swing. Then her face suddenly ajoy with sight of her papa, running up the walk to his arms, "Papa, Papa!"

That was yesterday, for nothing changes or grows in the sunless cement of prison years. How could I imagine that that little girl is a woman of twenty-nine, for I am still the age of her father when I knew him. Not precisely, for Arnoldo was ten years older than I.

To her, I must be the villain who took him from her, the grownup blur whom she may remember sitting at the big round table sharing pasta from the white pass-around bowl, in front of the fire, sipping espresso and Stock, talking and laughing with her father, and once, sitting on the steps outside the door, telling her a story about a snowy owl whom I trained to play "Frère Jacque" on a set of bells.

* * *

At five o'clock clusters of workers began to emerge from the Nuvola portals, and when one woman stood uncertainly for a moment and studied the café, before crossing the street, I presumed it was Julietta. She was tall, her long, light-brown hair caught at the back in an arch that brushed against her neck. She held her body rather stiffly as she moved, but she stepped lightly and gracefully. In fact, that was my overriding impression of her—gracefulness; as she came closer I could see that was especially true of her features: graceful, all of a delicate piece, dominated by wide-set eyes, upturned at the outer edges but less round than the doe's, not near enough yet to see their color but guessing they were gray or gray-green, a complement for her skin which was darker than her hair would suggest, characteristic of a genre of Lombardians who preserve the fair-darkness of their Renaissance ancestors.

Now she stood in the entrance to the café, and her twentieth-century–Renaissance face held me motionless. It was a struggle to get to my feet and approach her.

"Signorina Disio?"

I escorted her to the little round table. She ordered a negroni. She was wearing a green silk dress with a subdued Pucci-like design, perhaps her own, but no jewelry except for an old-fashioned ring (incongruous with her dress), little diamonds in a platinum mounting, on her right hand. She looked at me expectantly. In my stomach I felt a great gnaw of apprehension.

"When you find out who I am, signorina, you will not want to talk to me—but I hope you will make yourself listen to what I have to say."

"You said you had been a friend of my father's . . ."

"I was. Although you have been made to think otherwise, we were good friends and no matter what you may think happened, I didn't harm him. I have had a long and cruel punishment—without crime."

She looked straight at me, her eyes unblinking, her face showing nothing. She looked at me like that for a long time, then she turned her head and looked out at the street. "I've forgotten your name," she said, her eyes on the street. She spoke English now, perfectly, with an English accent.

"Paul Selwyn."

"Yes."

She looked out at the street for quite a while. I wanted to start talking, but I couldn't. Her negroni arrived but she did not touch it. Her profile against the soft light of the early dusk was virtually unbearable; to escape it, I looked down at her hands; they were narrow hands, fingers fragile but not long, skin translucent.

"The main reason I want to talk to you is because all these years I've had such guilt about Arnoldo—not the guilt of killing him—I didn't kill him—I never saw him again after he left our villa that evening; but *that* is my guilt, that I let him go alone on a mission obviously full of risk. I tried to stop him from going. I was against it. But when he remained adamant about going, I should have gone with him. We were a team—and I was his friend. I was afraid, though, that the rendezvous was a trick, an ambush, so out of that fear, I let him go alone. That's my guilt. That's what I thought about and thought about those long years in prison —if I had gone with Arnoldo that night, perhaps he wouldn't have been murdered. Of course, we might *both* have been killed. But the point is: I should have gone. I was a coward not to have gone. That's why I want to tell you what really happened. You are the part of him that survives and I want you to know the truth about me—so that in that way I can try to account for . . . well, how I failed him."

"Why should I want to hear about all that? What has it to do with me?"

"I thought . . . doesn't it interest you—the truth?"

"No."

"But you must have thought about what really happened to your father."

"The court said you killed him. You told your story—this story that you now want to tell me, I presume—but the court didn't believe you. So that's truth enough for me."

"But I'm telling you it's not the truth. Courts are not infallible . . ."

"What do I care? My father is long dead. So many men died in the war. How can it possibly matter to me whether my father was a hero leading troops into battle when he was shot or whether he was shot in the back by a treacherous ally. His death is the only truth I care about. It is all that mattered."

"But how do you know what matters until you hear . . ."

"I do not want to hear. I do not want all that which has settled to the bottom stirred up again. Why? For what?"

"I was your father's friend. I am up here on something . . . that I want you to benefit from. Arnoldo's share. They owe both of us something. Perhaps you know some things that can help. Whether you do or don't makes no difference. It's due you as his daughter."

"What are you talking about? What thing are you here about?"

"Not here. Not Como. I am only here to see you. Where I am is in Dongo. What I am after is the missing treasure that did us in. Just as I cannot possibly be materially compensated for my years in prison, so you, too, can't be given anything that will assuage your father's death. But why shouldn't your life be easier? You're not married. You have to make your own way. At least this could remove that burden."

"So it comes out. After all the nonsense about your guilt and all that, it develops that why you are really here is to find out if I know anything that might help you locate that damn treasure."

"No, I assure you . . ."

"That treasure which has cursed my life—why do you think my mother died, so young? Grief over my father's death. The sudden horribleness of it. And now you want me to involve my own life in it." She rose quickly from the table, knocking over her untouched drink which spilled forward onto me. I made no move toward wiping it off, nor did she apologize. Her face was flushed and she clenched the handle of her handbag with both hands.

"Guilt is not the word for you, Mr. Selwyn. It's greed. You didn't get it all the first time and now you have come back to find the rest of it. And you'd like me to help you. The man who murdered my father." She was gone. The waiter came and mopped the negroni off the top of the table. I ordered another scotch. I drained the last of my drink and waited impatiently for the new drink to arrive. I did not want to think. I had told her the truth about my feelings of guilt toward her father. I had tried to be honest. I had wanted so desperately to reach something in her that would have made a connection, a cable strand that I could have used as beginning strength toward a bridge. Not just for the project; it was a long shot to have expected her to have any remembered helpfulness. But a bridge to *her*. Arnoldo's daughter. The daughter of the man I was convicted of murdering. As if I wanted to be very sure that I would not have to face a real challenge to my already proven inability to function as a man. What if I tried to make love to a woman who really counted? Don't think about that. Think about what she might have been able to tell you. I can't concentrate on that. Why do I feel that she is as alone in the world as I am? How do I know that? She probably has a man she lives with. Or a married man whose mistress she is. That's how it is in Italy. Anyone that damn beautiful with a body like that who moves that way is not alone in the world. But I did feel it. Very strong. How do you explain that?

It was a pleasant café, unhurried, uncrowded, the waiter there only when you wanted him to bring another drink. The night was warm and the street, a commercial street, quiet at night. I took off my coat and put it on the back of my chair, loosened my tie, and borrowed a pad of paper from the waiter. Tomorrow morning I would return to Dongo and I thought I might list all possible leads we now had to explore. It would be a meager list. But it might help get my mind off Julietta. Sitting there in the pleasant café, drinking scotch and writing a therapeutic list would do all right for now—but later, in my airless room at the San Gottardo . . . God damn it, I don't want to think about that. I know what it will be—another night of tossing from belly to side to back to toilet to book to window to mirror to window to street—walking the echoing, deserted street. I had had, by now, many such nights. But that did not make another night any easier.

I was now on my third drink. I started to write the Dongo entries but what my mind went to was her face and the way the cheeks sculptured up to the high-set cheekbones which were Arnoldo's.

She sat down without saying a word. I had not seen her approach. Her eyes showed that she had been crying. The waiter came over and I reordered her negroni.

She sat for a while, looking down at the table top, chewing gently on the left side of her lower lip. She took a sip of her negroni, put it down, then took another sip. "My mother once said—the only time she ever talked about you—that she did not believe you killed my father. That is why I've come back. I think you should have a chance to say what you have to say."

"Your mother said that? She thought I did *not* kill your father?"

"Yes."

"Did you ask her how she knew?"

"No. She was very upset. She was always very upset after my father's death. She talked a lot about him. About what had happened. I would just listen. I was too frightened to ask questions. My father dead, my mother always crying and her hair suddenly gray, and my uncle, Pietro—my father's brother—so strange to me, so distant to me; I guess I wanted him to take my father's place, but he resented me so, and I became frightened of him, of everything."

She had not looked at me directly since she sat down. Now her eyes were on her glass, her forefinger circling its lip. "My mother said that about you because she saw how you were with my father—what friends you were—those few times you came to visit."

"Do you remember those visits?"

She lifted her eyes and again I felt a strong wave of reaction.

"Yes. Of course. I only saw my father two times during the war. And then those few times just after the war when he came with you. I was born in 1940 and he was in the war, one way or another, from 1939 on. So—yes. Oh, yes, I remember those times he came with you very well."

"It seems strange to me—this metamorphosis from that little pig-tailed girl to the woman you are. Do you realize you bear absolutely no resemblance to yourself as a child?"

Her eyes flicked away. The remark seemed to irritate her. "I will hear what you have to say. But tonight, I'm too upset. Perhaps tomorrow."

"Okay. I'm pretty upset myself tonight."

"Shall we again meet here?"

"Fine. May I escort you home?"

"No—thanks." She got up to go. "I'm sorry about spilling the drink on you."

"I don't mind."

She smiled. "Because I am willing to hear you out does not mean that I necessarily share my mother's point of view."

That night I slept well. I had been having a recurring dream that took place in various public places—a theater balcony, a hotel lobby, in the center ring of a circus, the back platform of a bus—always with some of my clothes missing (usually my pants and shoes, but in one dream I discovered I wore only the front half of my clothes, and my back and ass were stark naked), but this was the first night I could remember when I had no dreams at all.

The following day was interminable, waiting for her and rehearsing over and over again what I would tell her—not so much what as how.

She arrived at exactly the same time; she wore a bright turquoise dress and she had done something different to her hair. She looked sad, I thought, but the sadness seemed a quality of her face, not an expression of mood.

She was as aloof as she had been the day before but she listened intently and without rejection as I told her in detail everything that had happened, and it came out of me so straight, so exactly how it had been, that I felt she couldn't help but know that it was the truth. When I finished, I just took it for granted that she believed me. I did not pause for her reaction, to hear what she had to say, but I just took it for granted that the guilty had, if not proved his innocence, at least demonstrated that there was reasonable doubt of his guilt. I then told her about our operation in Dongo, what we had discovered, what we hoped to discover, the nature of my associates—all that. I apologized for talking so much.

"Do you have any family in the States?"

"No. What small family I had—everyone is dead."

"Friends?"

"Not any more."

"Where will you live?"

"I don't know. Depends on how well I do in Dongo, I suppose. I haven't really thought about it. If I succeed in Dongo, I can live anywhere—and I mean *live*. If I fail, then what the hell?"

"Money means a lot to you."

"After all I've been through, I want to start from *something*. Yes, it does mean a lot to me. Yes. And it means nothing to you?"

"Not nothing, there is something I would like to achieve with the help of money. Not for myself. As far as I am concerned, money has little meaning. But then I have not suffered as you have suffered."

"May I ask you a few things about your family? I'd like to know about your Uncle Pietro. He had been a novitiate at St. Zachary's during the war, hadn't he?"

"Yes, but rather briefly. He never got to the point of taking vows."

"When did he leave?"

"When the partisan underground began to make itself felt. He only fought with the partisans. My father had first been an officer with Mussolini's Black Shirts and later defected and became a partisan."

"Tell me about your uncle after the war."

"He lived with us for a few years. Then one day he announced he was going to Germany. I was in school in Switzerland by then—so I was pretty much out of touch with the family—but I heard that he had settled in Stuttgart and gone into the construction business. His company became very prosperous—it's called the Rex Company—and today it's the biggest producer of prefabricated housing in Germany."

"Where did he get the money to start such a business? Was he a wealthy man?"

"You mean when he lived with us? I should say not. I remember how they quarreled, my mother and him, over the fact that he never bought anything, or contributed anything to the household. At that time it was hard for us— my father had left very little. Certainly Uncle Pietro was quite poor."

"Then what could have happened when he went to Germany?"

"I have no idea."

"Do you know why he went? Why Germany? Did he meet someone? Or have friends there?"

"I don't think so. My mother was very surprised. Uncle Pietro had always been so anti-German, so violent about the Nazis. Oh—I see what you're thinking: the Mussolini money."

"Was it possible? Did you ever hear anything that . . ."

"No, just the opposite. He was so violent about my father's death . . . Pietro was a violent man, fierce temper, terrible stories I heard about what he had done as a partisan—and about you. I remember his explosions when you were being held in jail those years before your trial— how he was going to get to you in the jail and kill you with his own hands. No, all I ever heard about Pietro and the treasure was like that."

"Did he send money to your mother once he became successful?"

"Never. Not a thing."

"How did you manage?"

"Sometime after my father's death my mother discovered that he owned quite a lot of land along the shore in Bellagio. It's value had increased enormously and my mother sold it off and we were able to live on that until she died. That's how she managed to send me to school in Switzerland."

"Which explains your excellent English."

"Yes. It was a lovely school."

"I'm going to suggest something that may shock you—
your Uncle Pietro was one of the few people who knew
about what went on in the villa I shared with your father—
what we were after, our movements. Your father and
Pietro were in constant touch with each other because
Pietro and his partisan group were helping us. I told you
about the things that were taken from the organ pit in the
villa—they would have financed a construction business
very nicely."

She thought about that. "No, I don't think that was
Uncle Pietro. I don't think he could have."

"Well, think some more about it. Maybe some little
incidents, insignificant at the time, will come back to you.
All I ask is that you think about it. If I wanted to meet your
uncle, would you help me?"

"You mean to go to Stuttgart?"

"Yes, I suppose."

"Mr. Selwyn, I have not made up my mind about you.
You tell your story very convincingly, but I would probably
be as swayed the other way if I were to hear the prosecutor's
side of it. But, besides that, why should I get involved in all
this? I don't know why . . ."

"You said you had some use for money . . ."

"Not for myself."

"Granted—but use for it. What if I told you, in strictest
confidence, that I had already recovered a little of it, and
that if you were willing to cooperate, however you could,
you would already be a participator in what I have."

"No, I don't think I could justify . . . no . . . I really
must be going." She started to rise but I put my hand on
her arm.

"Please. A few minutes more."

"I do think I believe you about my father, Mr. Selwyn,

if that's any comfort to you. But this is not a time for me to . . . not a good time for me to be involved in . . . in anything."

"I don't know how to say this . . . but, well, it's all so damn difficult and I'm afraid to trust anyone. I've been so long out of this bloody hell-race that I don't feel secure. I'm sure this is because of prison; being alone is your natural state, and contact is unnatural, and you've got to figure, realistically, that the other prisoners are always looking to get at you in some way. So you operate like that, with your back against a wall and your flanks covered, trusting only that against which you have a secure defense. But now I need to get away from that protective wall and take risks —I need that, and a lot of other things, if I'm going to make it. But mostly I need someone I can trust. To discuss things with, to confide in, but, primarily, to trust—and I feel that way about you. You're part of Arnoldo, and Arnoldo was the last person in my life whom I loved and trusted—and who trusted me. That's why it was important that I convince you that I did not foul his trust. And that's what I'm trying to tell you. Because of who you are, you're hooked to the life I had when life ended for me twenty-four years ago. So, what I'm trying to say, awkwardly I know, is that I need you. Just your participation. Because I know I can trust you—as I trusted your father. Just for now, just till I get my legs settled and my step adjusted. I didn't realize it until last night, after we had met, and now today it's very strong and certain—this need. So if you could bring yourself to get a little involved, just a *little* involved, it would be a great thing for me. I'm sorry if I embarrass you. I'm embarrassed myself. But if you could come up to Dongo . . . could you? It's not far, as you know, and if you spoke to Bis and Ted and Giorgio maybe you'd be truly convinced that I've told you the truth about your father and me, and if you really could accept that as truth, then perhaps you could trust me and help me."

I had not dared look at her; out of self-consciousness, I suppose, for I had certainly not intended to say all that but the words had started running out of me, unstoppable. Now I glanced at her. She had her hands under her chin and her eyes directly on me, the sadness of her face pronounced.

"I don't know what prompted all that," I said. I wrote down my Zonico address on a slip of paper and handed it to her. "Maybe you'll come. Now, if I promise not to say another word on the subject, would you have dinner with me?"

"No, I'm sorry I can't." She took the slip, and without looking at it, put it in her bag.

"I promise—no personal talk at all. I'll just be a stranger come to town."

"I wish I could, but I have an engagement."

"Shall I take you there?"

"I'm being picked up at my office."

I paid the bill and walked her across the street to the Nuvola entrance. "I'm glad we had our talk," she said. "I'm sorry it didn't turn out better." She didn't offer her hand. She didn't smile. She just turned and went into the building. I watched her legs climb the short flight of marble stairs and disappear through the ornate wooden door at the top. I stood on the sidewalk for a little while, adrift; then I slowly walked back to my hotel.

chapter fifteen

Bis had good news. The tentative mission to St. Zachary had paid off spectacularly. Ted and Bis had received a report via Father Piccionastro that one of the Zachary friars recalled information received in 1945 from a certain German officer, Otto Kisnat, who had been with the Nazi convoy that accompanied Mussolini. That information was that on the night of April 27, 1945, when the convoy was passing Tremezzo on Lake Como, Captain Kisnat, in an attempt to secrete some of the treasure and reclaim it after the war, had dropped two bags containing gold bars, jewels, gold coins and various folders of Mussolini's personal documents into the lake at a point directly opposite the entrance to the Villa Carlotta, an historic monument and one of the lake's tourist attractions.

"How did you manage to pierce the veil of ecclesiastical silence?"

"By sneaking around it. Ostensibly we had gone up to see the monastery, but then I began to reminisce about our mission here during the war and that way got onto the subject of the treasure. Ted said how strange it was that none of it ever showed up. That prompted old Piccionastro to say, yes, but there were rumors about it all the time. He mentioned the farm near Rachele Mussolini, and a few other things, and then he said that just recently he had taken a long deathbed confessional from one of his priests, in the course of which the dying priest divulged that he had taken Kisnat's confession about treasure bags in the lake."

"Has he told the authorities about it?"

"He said not yet."

"Why?"

"Given in confession. Privileged."

"Then why tell you?"

"Well, that's complicated. You see, we had just presented our part of the Roman artifacts to the monastery as a gift. Piccionastro is impressed by my allegiance, as Papal Knight, to the church, and although nothing was *specifically* discussed, Piccionastro had remarked, in accepting the artifacts, how poor and needy the monastery was, and it would be presumed, I think, that if we *did* pursue this lead and if we *did* locate the two bags, we would share our find with our benefactor."

Bis further reported that Ted had flown back to London to handle a business crisis and on his return would bring with him diving equipment that would enable them to explore the bottom of Lake Como for the missing bags. While he was there, Bis said, Ted also planned to put in motion a discreet inquiry into the life and good times of Judge Fernando Rambellini, formerly of Padua.

Giorgio also had good news. I had assigned to him the Squassoni puzzle—surely if one asked enough people someone would recall who the mysterious Squassoni was—and Giorgio had stumbled on the answer while diminishing a bottle of Strega one evening with the ambulance driver, Paulo Benfatto and his daughter, Lia, a lusty, full-breasted, laughing girl who worked in the Zonico ore and cement complex.

"This Squassoni, the whole thing we got wrong is—he's not a man."

"A woman?"

"No. A street."

"A street!"

"Before you think I'm Sherlock Holmes . . ."

"Giorgio, for Christ's sake, cut the comedy!"

"You are plenty cranky, baby, since you was to Como . . . okay, all right, everything serious: well, to be honest, I am in the Benfatto kitchen, barbecuing my guts with the Strega not just to pump the old man but because this Lia—man, have you ever seen such boobs? . . . She is too floody buckin' much!"

"Jesus, between you and Dan you'd think we were running . . ."

"Dan! I am not in the boat with Dan! I am talk about love! I am not hop this bed. That bed. You know me. When I say about this Lia, I am serious. About women I am always very serious. They are like land mines—you get a little careless and *whoom!* they blow up in the face."

"That isn't where a land mine gets you."

"I mean, it's quite possible I am in love with this Lia *and* with her beautiful boobs."

"All right, Giorgio, all *right!*"

"I may marry this Lia, who know?"

"All *right!* I wish all four of you great happiness. Now can we get on with it?"

"Hokay. So there I am, with all this Strega and falling in love with this Lia but above all comes duty so I ask the old man who's about to go under from the Strega if he knows this Squassoni and he mumble something I can't unnerstand, so quick I give him a little potch this cheek 'n that, and out it come, something about Via Squassoni. More potch and what he says is the little Via now call Sindaco Calli, which is Mayor Calli, who was the Dongo

mayor who disappear, this street before was called Squassoni. So, Paulo, we take a little walk along Via Sindaco
Calli, right?"

"You know, I once asked old Benfatto about Squassoni
and he just gave me a blank look."

"Oh, listen, baby, I don't think he meant to tell—he was
pissed on the Strega, you see, and I don't think he will have
memory of telling me because he slid off his chair about ten
seconds later. He was still there on the floor, asleep very
sound, when I leave a coupla hours after. Oh, that Lia, she
is like you get overrun by a hungry harem. Listen, Paulo, I
have woman experiences, you know I have experiences,
like there are flowers on the Spanish steps, but this one—oh,
Lord, baby—she is the Sistine Chapel."

The former Via Squassoni was a very short street. There
were two or three shops of little consequence: a tinsmith, an
herb merchant, a stationer-tobacconist; one shop of considerable consequence—the town's only butcher; and the
lesser of Dongo's two cinemas, Il Reggia, folding chairs on
the cement floor of what had once been a Fiat garage.
Only one of these establishments went as far back as 1945
—the butcher's—so we began (and as it turned out, ended)
our inquiry there.

Generations of Guistis had passed the butcher shop along,
and it was currently presided over by Rico Guisti, whose
father, now deceased, had been its proprietor in 1945. I got
him to talking about Dongo and then about how things
were there as the war ended. Rico, a talkative, sympatico
man, was not the least bit curious as to our interest in that
period and seemed to relish our queries about this shop
and how things were. He told us that he had been eleven
years old in 1945 and that he was already apprenticing in
the shop.

Rico's memory of people and events of that period was

very sharp; he recalled that by the close of the war meat was very scarce in the store but that suddenly, around the very time we were asking about, carcasses began to arrive, brought by men who were not the regular suppliers. Some of these carcasses were butchered for sale in the shop, but a few of them, Rico revealed, were loaded into his father's cart and taken away by his father the day after their delivery. There were several such deliveries, Rico said, and in each instance a few carcasses were carted away by his father the day after delivery. When Rico asked his father where he was taking them, the reply was that he had sold them to a butcher friend of his in Menaggio.

"The men who brought these carcasses to your father, do you recall what they looked like?"

"There were two of them. One I remember very well: he was extremely tall and extremely thin and quite a gentleman. Certainly not the kind of man I used to see delivering meat. I thought he might be a count or something. Looking back on it now, I suppose he was a little fancy, if you know what I mean, but as a boy I didn't know about those things."

"And the other man?"

"Oh, he was the tough kind I was used to seeing. He carried the carcasses; the elegant man just discussed things with my father. I'm sure he never carried anything."

"Anything special about the tough man you can recall? Any little thing?"

"Well, let's see . . . yes, one thing—he had a cheek scar—the way Germans get those saber scars on their cheeks. But a lot of Germans had that—it wasn't very unusual. I really don't remember anything else about him—that's a hell of a long time back."

"Was this man German?"

"I don't know. He spoke perfect Italian, and to me, as a kid, anyone who spoke good Italian was an Italian."

"They only came on three occasions, you say?"

"I think so. I can't be sure. They could have also come when I wasn't there. Sometimes I'd be out of the store making deliveries."

"Do you recall the name of either man, especially the tall, thin gentleman?"

"No. I don't think I heard their names."

I could have told him one name: Luigi Hoffmann. And I think I could have taken a pretty good guess at the other. But figuring out the game of movable carcasses was something else again.

"So that's how come Signora Gattamelatta wound up with a Claretta Petacci locket in her veal stew," Giorgio said as we walked back to the Villa di Cielo.

"Yes. Now we know how some of the treasure was hidden while it journeyed around. But where did Butcher Guisti take those carcasses which, let's presume, were the ones filled with treasure? Obviously Hoffmann was under surveillance so he needed someone to cover for him. It may very well have been that Butcher Guisti did not actually know that anything special was inside the carcasses he delivered. But certainly there was secrecy about it. But they were black-market carcasses so on that count Guisti may have participated in exchange for the other carcasses given to him. You can bet, though, that wherever he took them, it was not to a butcher friend in Menaggio."

"What about Signora Gattamelatta's veal stew?"

"I think that was probably a freak—one of the carcasses, after being stripped of its treasure, may have been put on the market, and that one jewel had dropped from its container and lodged somewhere in the meat. Otherwise, why hadn't many more of the jewels shown up that way?"

"You know, the more we dig around, the more everyone in this whole fucking scene seemsa been in on it."

"Well, just pieces of it. They've been in on little pieces of it. But I don't think anyone here got anything much out of it."

"Someone somewhere sure asa hell did."

"Oh, yes, someone did."

"You think that that someone who got it is the same son of a bitch who hung it on you?"

"Maybe." I thought about that as we walked in silence the rest of the way back to the villa. I thought about it intensely. I was surprised to find my fists clenched so tightly there were nail-arcs on my palms. That brought to mind my pledge to Gibio and I rubbed my palms together to relax them and tried to put my thoughts back where they belonged.

I was in my room before dinner that evening when Rosanna, the housekeeper, came up to say there was a Signorina Angelo to see me. Unknown name.

She was standing at the window with her back toward me but there was no mistaking her. We smiled at each other and she said she hoped she wasn't disturbing me. It was that hour of the early evening before cocktails when no one was downstairs. Ted was still in London, Dan was in Rome, so only Bis and Giorgio were in residence.

I took her for a twilight walk along the garden's white gravel walkways that wound through geometric privet.

"There is something that I have thought of that might help you. That's why I have come. But first I had to decide if I *wanted* to help you. If I believed you. I didn't at first. That first meeting. But you are identified in my mind with my father and that is something so terribly important to me that I forced myself to see you again. That second meeting, the way you told me about what had happened, and about yourself, and how you felt—well, you know how it is when you see a movie or a play and the next day, if it has rung true, it has a remembered impact even greater than when you saw it; you keep thinking about certain dialogue and scenes and the people. That is how I have thought about what you told me since you left. So I have decided to help you. I think you deserve whatever you feel is compensation for what you have gone through—although this does seem like a desperate, impossible gamble you are taking."

I stopped in the narrow path and turned to look at her. The sadness in her face was accentuated by the half-light. What she had said, this moment, was the first thing that had happened to me since I left prison that made me feel that I was really out of there and into the "free" world. Someone had finally accepted me for myself. Made me feel—all right, admit it!—like a man. I wanted to tell her that, but it was too awkward; perhaps she saw it on my face. I moved on. After these days and nights, especially nights, of constantly thinking about her and fantasizing seeing her again, and re-living our meetings in Como and what I might have said that I didn't say, and what I might have done that I didn't do, now I was finding it difficult to believe that she was actually compatibly walking beside me in this fragrant garden.

"I'm not at all sure that what I have to tell you will be of any real help to you. I rather doubt it. But there is a possibility . . . well, the fact is my mother kept a diary. Every evening, for as long as I can remember, she would sit down after dinner and write about the events of the day, her thoughts, things she had heard or read that she wanted to remember. She was a self-educated, literate woman, my mother. Sometimes she would read to me from the diaries. I remember one birthday, she got out her old diaries and went back and read to me what she had written on each of my birthdays. She kept her diary virtually till the day she died. They are all stored, those years of notebooks, in our house in Bellagio. The house has been closed for several years, but I'm sure they could be located. I just wonder what she might have written around the time my father was killed. When he was living in the villa with you, he phoned her every day, sometimes twice a day. I remember how we waited for his calls. Sometimes, when he was not pressed, he would talk to me. I had forgotten all about those diaries, but now I wonder if they might not just possibly have something in them that might prove helpful to you."

"I'd like very much to see them."

"Bellagio is only an hour from here. We don't have to go all the way around; we can leave the car at Cadenabbia and take the ferry across."

"Why do you keep your Bellagio house if it is boarded up?"

"Because it is family. Do you understand? It's all that is left. I used to think—*used* to think— that someday I might live there."

"You mean, someday, but not alone."

"Yes, that's what I meant. Now, there's something else I should mention—about why I am here. Your arrival in Como released a flood of feelings that I thought had left me long ago. But to my surprise they had not—and there they were, bothering me, tormenting me again. It is the kind of emotional stupidity that I despise, but it is in me, rekindled now—I have a deep desire to know who killed my father. After all these years, you'd think . . ."

"I know. The years I spent in jail before my trial, I was consumed with thoughts of vengeance . . ."

"I'm not sure it's vengeance. Perhaps it's just curiosity— perhaps it's just not knowing about my father. So long as I was able to make myself believe that you were the one who killed him—but now I can't any more. And as the price of helping you find the treasure, which you say is all *you* want, you must help me try to find out who the man, or men were who killed him."

My covenant with Gibio; my promise to myself. And yet I must keep her, for her help and for her presence. I simply must. "But honestly now—don't you think that what you want is vengeance? That that is really what you're after?"

"Perhaps. Yes—why not? And if it should develop that way, why shouldn't they get what's due them? I don't deny that I hate whoever killed him. What I want to know is who he is."

"So would I," I admitted.

The walkways had led us back to the villa. "I think it's time for negronis." I held the door for her. "Signorina Angelo . . . why Angelo?"

"I thought perhaps . . . things being what they are . . . that it might be best if it were not known in Dongo that Arnoldo Disio's daughter had arrived."

"Yes, I think you're right. And perhaps . . . for now . . . you should be Signorina Angelo here in this house too."

"Who am I?"

"A friend from Rome."

"We met when you were there?"

"Yes. Did you drive here?"

"Yes."

"Rosanna will get your things. There's a spare room across the hall from me."

"Perhaps I should stay in town."

"In Dongo? Where? You don't know Dongo. Besides, what kind of a Roman friend would they think you are if you don't stay across the hall from me."

Another thing about Giorgio, which I failed to mention, were his connections. They were not extraordinary by the accepted concept of the well-connected, i.e., those who could open the right doors or whisper in the right ears or grease the right palms, but although Giorgio's aim was oblique his results were right on target. Thus, given the truly challenging problem of how to pierce the impenetrable defenses of a Swiss bank against revealing the names on numbered accounts, his connection was not that he knew an officer of the bank or the mayor of Lugano or the chairman of the Swiss banking commission, but that the barman at the Bar l'Orange, in Lugano, had been his cell-mate for two years and owed him a gargantuan favor for having "arranged" certain events which had sprung the barman from his cell a year early.

The connection between the bartender and the bank's most guarded secrets, Giorgio explained, was that barmen were primary information centers and that he, Giorgio, operated on the theory that everyone, and that means *everyone,* has the same foibles. Bank presidents, to repeat Giorgio's simplistic explanation, screw like everyone else, and with the same results; sometimes not expected—and not wanted. To cope with these undesirable results, under sensitive conditions where the slightest stir of publicity would wreak havoc and ruin, has its high price—and, if need be, a small matter like whose name is on a particular numbered account could be included as a kind of price aftermath. (Giorgio disliked the word "blackmail.") So it was most rewarding to discover that the president of the Bank Nationale, and the president's son, ran afoul of the same unfortunate results with the same unfortunate lady.

"You mean your barman buddy runs an abortion service?"

"*Esattamente.*"

"And both the president of the bank and his son, unknown to each other, got involved with the same lady with the same pregnant results?"

"*Ecco.*"

"There's a run on the bank for you. There used to be a

bartender in a tavern close to where I went to university, who also operated such a convenience. He was heavily patronized by the students until several of my friends discovered that they had all knocked up the same girl whose abortions had been arranged by this bartender. When they also discovered that four of these alleged pregnancies and abortions had occurred over the same ten-day period, they began to suspect that something a wee bit irregular was taking place. So they cornered the girl and she confessed that she always used a diaphragm and that the bartender had no abortion facilities and that she was his shill. That night my friends went to see the bartender who said the girl was just a hysterical liar and a whore, and he refused to refund the hundred dollars each of my friends had paid, so they knocked him around with his own whiskey bottles and put a match to his place."

"That is not my friend," Giorgio said indignantly. "He is completely ethical about his abortions."

Before setting off for Lugano, Giorgio brought Lia to our villa for what he called an "occasion dinner." The soufflé of his love for her had risen in twenty-four hours and he had garnished it with a proposition of marriage which she had alacritously accepted with Papa Benfatto's approval.

Giorgio felt that the dinner was further made an occasion by the fact that just when he had begun to worry and wonder about me, I had finally produced a woman— and a beautiful one at that. Julietta had been friendly and interested in all aspects of our operation, but she was distant toward me and made no concessions to the charade of being my woman. That first night, with her across the hall, I had felt a kind of nervous excitement, fantasizing that she might come to my door on some pretext or other, or that I might invent an excuse to go to see her, but, of course, neither occurred.

You're lucky nothing happened, I finally told myself, just before I slept. Just what would you do if she did come? Overwhelm her with the same animal passion that victimized Iris and Keva? The only dream I remembered that night was getting on a bus and discovering when I tried to put my hand in my pocket, that I couldn't pay the fare because I had forgotten to wear my pants. The people in the bus got a good jeering laugh out of it and the bus driver put his shoe on my bare ass and gave me a shove as I got off the bus, causing me to fall into the street. The people in the bus laughed like jackals.

I was a bit concerned that Julietta's attitude—obviously not that of a woman involved with a man—would be noted, but Bis was busy preparing for the underwater exploration at Tremezzo, and Giorgio's eyes only saw Lia.

It was a good party. There was plenty to eat and drink, and Giorgio was an absolute addict at proposing toasts. He was imaginative and amusing and the toasts were often rhymed wittily, but I finally pushed lusty Lia at him to get his arm down and finish off the speeches.

I looked around for Julietta but she had gone upstairs to her room. Her door was partly open and she was sitting in a chair by the window, reading. I knocked.

"Wouldn't you like some dinner?"

She smiled. "I snuck out to the kitchen and had some— I was famished. Fresh gnocchi. Ummmm."

"I'm sorry to have delayed going to Bellagio, but it was very important to Giorgio that I stay."

"I understand. He's your friend. You told me."

"We'll leave first thing in the morning."

"Where do they think you're going? Not to Bellagio, I hope—that would give me away."

"No. One of our leads, which we got through Scotland Yard, involves a farm near Milan where Rachele Mussolini lives. They think we're going there, and I will go on there after Bellagio. Did you get a chance to talk to Bis? I mean, just to get him to talking about how things were back in 1945? I'm sure you could lead him into it without tipping him off about who you are."

"You don't seem to understand—I've settled all that. I told you I believed you. That's why I'm here. To help you if I can, but also to see if, in the process, we can find out who might have killed my father."

"Then you no longer have doubts about me?"

"No, not about you. Once I've made a decision, I don't keep nibbling away at it."

"How does it look to you, our cover here? The way we're set up?"

"Oh, I don't know. It's done very well, I guess—you certainly look like a full-scale archaeological enterprise. But whether it will achieve the results you want—it does seem far-fetched."

"I know. But one or two breaks could turn it all around."

"By the way, I was walking around Dongo this afternoon and went into the church, and to my surprise I saw a priest there whom I recognized."

"But have you ever been here before?"

"I didn't recognize him from here. For several years after my father's death, Uncle Pietro lived with us in Bellagio—right up to the time he left for Germany. On a few occasions . . . I told you that he had been a novitiate in Zonico in the early part of the war, didn't I?"

"Yes."

"Well, on a few occasions Uncle Pietro was visited by a very tall, very fat priest who had not a hair on his head but a full scraggly beard to atone for it. A very unique priest. Not one you would be likely to forget or to confuse with any other priest."

"And he's the one you saw in the Dongo church?"

"I'm sure of it. But I don't think he was *of* the Dongo church, since he was wearing the vestments of St. Zachary."

"Do you remember his name?"

"No, just the breadth, baldness and beard."

She came downstairs later to say good-bye to Giorgio and wish him well with Lia. Afterward she unobtrusively withdrew and returned to her room.

Later, when the celebrants had thinned, Giorgio and I talked privately.

"She's a rare bird you got there. Beautiful like that, and a lady. Is she sexy?"

"Oh . . . oh, sure. I mean, well—sure."

"Those kind always are. Very deceiving. I once had this royal bird in London—Lady Something-or-Other. Very snooty. But let me tell you, it was like getting laid on a roller coaster."

"You mean very uncomfortable?"

He laughed. "A mink-lined inner-spring roller coaster! Listen, before I forget, I'va got this contact in London who's look into these race horses of this Judge Rambellini. My contact is a very big bookmaker, knows about the horses. I thought maybe we could find out something about this judge through his horses. Anyway, my contact will send me the words on him. It may take time—but patience and saliva, we get to this Rambellini."

"Maybe we should have Ted talk to your bookie."

"No, no, my bookie musta be keep secret. That'sa how it is with contacts. And, *senta,* while I think on it, you don't tell no one about my contact in Lugano, do you? We musta always protect the contact."

I wished him good luck on his mission and happiness in his Lia alliance and he embraced me and pounded my back and said he hoped my girl worked out for me too.

"*Senta,* Paulo, we get this treasury, okay, we are the fat cats and we live it up like a coupla friggin' Pashas— but ifa we don't, fuck it, we got our women and a little place to live somewhere and every night warm in the bed— so who care? Either way we got it made."

Lia came over and put her arms around him from behind and kissed the back of his neck.

"Oh," he moaned, "oh, have we got it made!"

Julietta and I did not leave the following morning. When I went downstairs to arrange for an early breakfast, Rosanna told me that Dan Reeder had arrived and was in his room. This was a surprise because Dan was supposed to be on an assignment in Israel and had not been expected for at least another week.

The shutters in Dan's room were closed and at first I didn't see him sitting in the far corner. The room smelled of licorice.

"Dan?"

"Hello, Paul."

"What the hell you doing in the dark?"

"It is not dark. I can see you perfectly. It is only dark when you can't see. I can see you perfectly."

He was sitting in an ornate high-backed arm chair with no clothes on. On the end table next to the chair was a bottle of Pernod and a pitcher of water. He carefully poured some Pernod into his glass, carelessly added a splash of water with a flourish, and holding the glass too close to his eyes, swirled its contents around until the colorless Pernod had turned chalk white.

"Observe, I am naked and ready for my return to the womb," he said. "It's the 'in' place to be." He began to laugh at his joke, the laughter intensifying until it turned into a choking cough.

"What is it, Dan?"

He proffered the glass. "Will you join me?"

"No, thanks."

"Lest you think I have come back only to drink, you will observe on the mantel a little acid, a little grass, and a great big beautiful bottle of goofs."

I went over to look. He wasn't kidding. There wasn't much LSD or marijuana, but there must have been five hundred amphetamine tablets. I took the jar of them and put it in my pocket. "Why don't you concentrate on the Pernod, for now?"

"I gotta get back to the womb. You think Pernod will get me back to the womb?"

I turned on the lamp beside the chair. Dan's face was the putty color it had been when he had stood in the docket at his trial. He reached up and knocked the lamp down, the bulbs smashing as they hit the floor. Then he leaned his face forward into his hands and began to sob. Dry sobs without tears.

After a while he got up and went into the bathroom. The tap water ran for several minutes, then he emerged wearing his bathrobe. He sat down on the edge of the bed. He kept his head bowed. I had trouble hearing him.

"She's gone. Every trace of her. Really gone."

"Who?"

"Natalie."

"Natalie left you?"

"Natalie has gone on to something grand, see? Something really grand."

"What? Why, that can't be. When she was here—just a few days ago—she spent an hour telling me about how you got in heat for each other in Siena and how much she is in love with you."

"Siena? How *we* got in heat in Siena? Well, *she* got in heat, all right; Natalie always does all right in bed, you can count on that, but not with me, oh, not with me."

"She said you were watching the race from your hotel room and you wound up in bed making love while the race was on and you both had a great bang just as the winning horse crossed the finishing line."

"There's no limit to her perversion. You want to know

the truth? It was the jockey on that horse who was into her, not me. The night before the race we had gone to a party given by that *contrade* and Natalie had gone for the jockey. It's a wild thing, watching her work. Always the same. Like a pointer working the field, looking for quail, that's the way she circles and crosses and smells around till she sets up her point—and then, look out! She moves right in on it, right for the balls, and I've never seen her bird get away. The male bird is called the cock, you know."

"Dan, you're insane, *you're* the one who chases around and pursues until he makes a score."

"Sure, sure, that's how it looks, but the truth is that's all window dressing, all that smokey action, all that cunt talk, just propaganda, that's all. Oh, I tried leaving her. I *did* leave her. It didn't work. I've got this thing about her, a rotten sick hang-up, I admit, but it always brought me back. I'd try to discuss it with her. She was always very honest, I'll say that for her. She said that in bed I was like a toaster that gets plugged in and two minutes later pops up, all done. Natalie cut balls and hung them on her chastity belt like hunters hang their game. But she always wanted me waiting back at the ranch. She always needed that base. And I guess, these last couple of years, I was able to pretend that what was awful didn't exist, and what was good was total. Now she's gone. What was awful is all there is."

"Who has she gone off with, do you know?"

Dan looked up. He smiled at me in a crazy way. "You won't believe it. But I *did* tell you that he once was hot after her. Well, he was *always* hot for her, but she had moved off him."

"Who?"

Again the crazy smile. "Gibio. Aging billionaires are in the ascendancy."

"You mean Gibio—you mean she's gone off with *Gibio?*"

"That's what he gave me to understand. Marriage."

"You've seen him?"

"He came to Tel Aviv. Oh, you've got to hand it to Constantin; he's got class."

"Did Natalie come with him?"

"Who said Natalie had class? Of course not. Natalie was already on his island in the Benggai Archipelago."

"Will all this . . . well, affect our project?"

"Not a bit. Gibio is a man of honor. He even offered to settle a large sum on my head for having taken my wife."

"Probably to buy your good will toward a speedy divorce."

"No, I had already told him that I'd give them that."

"Did you let him settle the large sum?"

"No."

"Why not? At least that."

"What would it buy me? Anything of what I'm losing?"

"Do you *really* think you're losing anything?"

"Yes. By my cock-eyed lights, everything." He got up, stiffly, and went over to reclaim his Pernod glass. He added some Pernod and the contents of the glass got whiter. He sat down in his chair again. "Everything," he repeated.

"Tell me what I can do, Dan? How can we lift you up a little."

"I have to be by myself for now."

"That will just make you more black-ass."

"I'm all right, Paul. You go ahead with your trip."

"I'll stick around today, just in case."

"In case what?"

"Just in case . . . oh, if you want to talk . . . or anything."

"Suit yourself. I'm just going to stay here for now. You may as well go."

"Maybe she'll be back. Maybe it's just another of her tears and she'll get tired of it and come back."

"Not this one. No, it's different. She hasn't got a bed

thing for Gibio any more. I have reason to believe, from Natalie's reaction to the brief thing they did have, that he's not much of an improvement, in that respect, over me. No, this is for the billion marbles and the private islands and the castles in Scotland and game preserves in India and the ocean-going yacht and the international power. That's what she's really after—the power. If you're Natalie, you want to make it slow down and speed up at your command. As for the rest, she can get her men as she got them with me."

"Unless Gibio chains her to the mast and nails her to the deck. It seemed to me that if you scratched under Gibio's polite, urbane exterior you'd find a granite epidermis covered with porcupine quills. I doubt that Natalie will fool much with that."

"Well, just let's see. Natalie likes the tough ones. She likes to pick them apart—quill by quill. She did it once with Gibio. She'll do it again."

"I'll look in on you later."

"You should go on your trip."

"Not today."

"Paul . . ."

"Yes?"

"It's Marseilles, all over again."

"I know. And you recovered from that beating."

"But I'm a lot older. I don't heal nearly as quick. And . . . listen, Paul, I'm shit sick of getting hit. Maybe I just want to toss in the towel and call it quits. I've got open sores that have been running for years. Enough is enough."

"I'll look in on you later."

I went up to see Dan several times that day, twice bringing him something to eat, but he just sat at the window staring out, sipping Pernod, not wanting to talk, not eating.

That night, before going to bed, I thought I'd give it a last try, but this time the door was locked.

chapter sixteen

It was not easy to find Signora Disio's diaries. The house had been closed for a long time and Julietta had forgotten where things had been stored. But finally, in the back of the attic behind some surplus kitchen utensils, we found a cardboard box that was full to the top with thick, lined notebooks. It took time to find the right notebook, since the dates were not always explicitly marked, and Signora Disio's handwriting was tiny and choppy and, for me, not easy to read.

It was Julietta who found the notebook we were looking for; we carried our prize down to the living room. It had been a gray, blustery day and now slants of rain peppered the windows from off the lake. Great rolling black thunder clouds had invaded the northern sky and the lake water was churning froth at the edges. The electricity and other utilities in the house were disconnected; I built a fire in the large stone fireplace that almost filled one wall of the living room, and Julietta found thick squat candles which she placed on tables near the hearth. She also found a cache of first-rate Bardolino to counteract the musty dampness of the house.

Sitting on the rug in front of the fire, we set our wine glasses between us. The driving rain made a metallic-sounding din as it smacked the windows. Julietta worked her way slowly along the pages. I tried to watch the fire, fed quickly to full life by the well-aged birch, but mostly I looked at her. Twice I refilled our glasses.

"I think this may be it," she said. She read on for a bit. "Yes . . . yes, I have found it. Yes, here we are." She ran her eyes ahead a little, then she retreated and started to read: " 'Tonight Arnoldo telephoned from Como. We were cut off but he called again. He was waiting for someone but he said he did not know who. I did not like the sound of it. Oh, why can it not all be ended? Why must he go on? It is the same now as it was all those years with the mystery and danger of the underground, but now that the war is over must it go on? I don't understand about tonight. I asked him where he was, and he said a bar next to Leonardo's restaurant where he was to meet some person—that this person had valuable information they were seeking. I don't know what that information is—Arnoldo never tells me these things—not that he doesn't trust me but only because then I might be sought out and involved. But I did ask him why, if he was to meet in Leonardo's, he was in the bar. "Because I'm alone," he said. "Paul is guarding the Villa. I would prefer to watch the Leonardo entrance and see who my informant is before he sees me. As I am talking to you I'm watching the door." I would have felt better if Paul had been there with him. Suddenly Arnoldo said, "Ah, there is a friend of mine arriving at Leonardo's. I hadn't expected to see him. That's fine. I'll have an ally there if things get rough. I must catch him before he goes into the restaurant." He said he had to hang up. I begged him to phone later. He said he would if he could and hung up. I feel disturbed. I feel something that makes me nervous. I don't know why I have this feeling, but I am definitely agitated. Maybe because there is a storm blowing in over the lake. There are flashes of lightning. I am always terribly afraid when I am here without Arnoldo and there is a storm. The lake amplifies the thunder and the lightning cracks around this house like a whip on fire. It will be a bad night for me and for little Julietta, I know."

Julietta shut the notebook and picked up her glass. She was illuminated by the orange of the fire and the yellow of the candles, and a touch of rose ricocheted off the wine to her face. "Would it have made a difference, do you think," she asked, "if my mother had given that testimony at your trial?"

"I was just thinking that. I don't know. The evidence against me was so strong. Why do you think she didn't testify?"

"I guess because of what happened to her after father was killed. Her mind became . . . well, not sharp. She began to have less and less recall of events that preceded his death. It became so bad she even got to the point of having to ask me his birthday and even the date of their wedding. So you can see . . . how long was it until your trial—three years?"

"But why not right away, when I was first arrested?"

"That period was even worse—for six months she was under doctor's care and never left her bed or saw anyone." A white knife of lightning cut the black sky and the night's first thunder roared into the room. Julietta shivered and pulled her glass against her chest. "God, how I hate electrical storms here. That's one of the reasons I stopped coming."

"You and your mother."

"Yes, when there was a storm I always slept in my mother's room and we comforted each other." The lightning and thunder hit again. "We had best start for the ferry dock. It's a little early but it's the last one and we mustn't miss it. I saw some old rain things on the kitchen porch. Here, you take the notebook. Does it make any sense to you, what my father is quoted as saying? What friend would that be?"

"I'll have to think about it. We will have to read it again and think about it."

It was much worse outside than I had thought. The wind was furious, cross-whipping the rain at an angle that blinded. Julietta held my arm tightly as we struggled toward the dock; every time the lightning struck, her grip dug into my arm and she gasped. A constant tremor ran through her body.

By the time we reached the ferry slip we were soaked to the skin, the rain disdainfully penetrating our raincoats and boots. There was no one at the dock. On the door of the little ticket shack, a notice read, "Ferry canceled due to weather." The turbulent lake water had inundated the dock.

The rain was now so heavy and coming so nearly horizontal that as we turned into the wind to retrace our steps, it was as I would imagine swallowing water while trying to swim in heavy seas. The rain suffocated my nostrils and mouth and as I struggled to breathe I was aware that Julietta was beginning to sag under this impact. I took off the rubber seaman's hat I was wearing and put it across her face, then I placed myself in front of her and she held onto me, her head bowed forward in the lee of my back. By keeping my chin tucked against my chest, I was able to breathe but it was hard to keep an eye on the road and we made slow, staggered progress against the force of the wind.

I was thankful that there was still a layer of hot coals in the fireplace. Julietta quickly revived. She foraged about,

using one of the fat candles for light, and found some
blankets which enabled us to hang our wet clothes on the
screen in front of the fire, which we nourished quickly with
the aged birch logs. And the wine warmed our insides.
Although the storm did not abate, the lightning became
less frequent and more distant.

"Are you hungry?" Julietta asked. "I'm positively famished."

"So am I. But I guess there's not much we can do about
it."

"Let's see."

I followed her into the kitchen, the two of us clasping
the front of our blankets with one hand and a candle in the
other. I felt like I was being initiated into some secret order.
Julietta found some sealed packages of pasta, cans of to-
matoes and tomato paste, an unopened can of olive oil, tins
of anchovies, a big jar of pimientoes, several tins of tuna,
plenty of dried herbs and a variety of other preserved
commodities.

"I wish we had some dry clothes," she said. "You have
to be an Indian to cook in this costume."

"I thought I saw some clothes in one of the boxes in
the attic. I'll get them."

The box contained men's clothes which Julietta identified as having belonged to her Uncle Pietro. They were a
size too big for me, and of course mountainous on Julietta,
but by rolling and tucking we managed to size them down.

An empty plant tub outside the kitchen door was brim
full of rain water; I filled two pots from it and hung them
from hooks in the fireplace. Julietta cooked the pasta in
the boiling water and concocted a splendid sauce from the
haphazard ingredients she had found. We both ate raven-
ously, drank a great deal of wine, and talked very little.
The unabated noise of the surrounding storm was oppressive.

"Would you believe, from this performance, that I am one of those Italians who dislikes pasta?" She laughed at herself as she displayed her empty plate.

"You have elevated the lowly spaghetti to the heights of the Châteaubriand."

"Would you also believe that I am not a cook?"

"Here's to the glory of the non-cook." We drank.

"Have you thought any more about my mother's diary?"

"Yes. Who could that 'friend' have been who arrived at the restaurant? That's what I've been pondering. Friend. What friend? He wouldn't have referred to your Uncle Pietro as a friend. Or in fact anyone your mother might have known. Whoever she had known he would have referred to by name. So this was a friend of his but a stranger to your mother. He must have been a member of the partisan underground with whom Arnoldo had worked. And of course, one must strongly suspect that this alleged friend was the one who had contrived the rendezvous for the purpose of eliminating him."

"Why would he want to do that? My father had been a staunch partisan, loyal to the organization . . ."

"Yes, *had* been. But these were Communist partisans and Arnoldo was not cooperating with them in their attempt to get hold of the treasure for the Communist party. Not only wasn't he cooperating, but he was working *against* them as a member of our Allied investigative team which was trying to locate the treasure for its own purposes. We don't know what happened that night. Maybe the unknown friend tried to make a deal with him. Certainly he knew about the stuff we had hidden in the organ machinery at our villa and he was eager to get his hands on that. Obviously, he—and I presume he had allies—had set their elaborate plans to implicate me in advance of seeing your father. But whether his murder was contingent on conditions that he had to meet . . . no way to know. But I think the time has come to try to run down some of the former partisans who may still be around the Dongo area. A friend. That's what I must find out—who were his friends, the men he trusted the most?"

Julietta put me in a bedroom which faced the water. We couldn't find sheets but there were enough blankets to use one to cover the mattress of the large, four-posted brass bed. We made up my bed, then we made up the bed in a room at the opposite end of the hall for Julietta. It was a small room with one window that Julietta covered tightly with its shade.

I was very tired, over-fed and quite drunk from the wine; I immediately fell asleep with all my borrowed clothes on. I had turbulent dreams which abruptly ended with a detonation of thunder that literally rattled my room. I sat up, momentarily terrorized; it had seemed, in my sleep, that the house had exploded. The thunder vibrated the room again, and I realized that the electrical storm had circled back and was attacking even more viciously. I had never seen lightning bolts strike with such rapidity, fresh thunder rolling in on the waning growl of its predecessor, the house lighted as if with arc lamps. My door was flung open and Julietta burst in, a blanket wrapped around her. She was panic-stricken. "Please, just till it passes!" A luminous streak, very near, broke the sky and snapped at something quite near, roaring triumphantly. Julietta flung herself across the foot of the bed and buried her face in the covers. She was emitting little whimpers of apprehension. I put my arm across her back to comfort her.

"I'm sorry to disturb you," she said. "I'm so terrible about lightning. This was my mother's room. I ran here when the bad storms struck."

"So I'm a mother-substitute, am I? Can't I at least be a father-substitute?" This time the lightning actually struck

a nearby object, the sharp *clak* of the thunderbolt topped
by the eerie *cre-e-e-ack* of the strike itself. Julietta gasped
and pulled herself against me, trembling. I could feel the
full softness of her breasts through the thick fold of the
blanket. Her face was pushed against my throat, buried
there, a frightened ostrich. My body felt warmed and ex-
cited by hers, but there was no panic rise or rise of sweat.
This was nothing more than a lovely frightened girl who
needed sanctuary. There would be nothing more. No challenge. No cause for alarm. I held her tightly, knowing there
would be no consequence. The undulating thunder did not
abate, but I could feel some of the tenseness go out of her.

We fell asleep like that, mummy-wrapped in our individual blankets, her forehead buried in my chest, my face
in her hair.

When we awoke the next morning, a brilliant day belied
the night storm. Our clothes were dry, the ferry was back
in service, and by noon we were on our way to Carpignano.

chapter seventeen

It was late in the afternoon by the time we reached Carpignano, a small town about sixty kilometers northeast of Milan. We had stopped in Cernobbio on the way down to have lunch, and had stopped again in Como so that Julietta could attend to some matters at the Nuvola offices. It was really too late in the day to do little more than to size up the Carpignano area.

Rachele Mussolini's house was readily identified for us by an obliging Carpignanian, and following the needle on my compass, we drove two kilometers due southeast. What there was at that point was a section of farmland which ran right up to the highway. On the highway itself was a Supercortemaggiore gasoline station, and a small, old stone church which looked abandoned. Another kilometer down the road was a large farmhouse which probably housed the farmer who tended this field, but if two kilometers was an exact reading, the farmhouse would have to be ruled out.

We got out of the car and walked onto the field, keeping our feet carefully between the orderly rows of egg plants whose lavender blossoms decorated the field. It was apparent that, above ground, that was all there was for the eye to see. But perhaps a meticulous inspection might reveal some marker, some sign indicating a burial spot; that would have to be on the next day's agenda.

We returned to the car and drove the short distance to Milan. Bis had suggested the Cavour Hotel on Via Fatebenefratelli; when I asked for two rooms the young desk clerk, after glancing at Julietta, smiled softly and, it seemed to me, approvingly, and said yes, of course, he had two very nice adjoining rooms on the fourth floor. We gave him our passports, told the *bagagliere* which suitcase went into which room, and followed the young receptionist to the elevator.

The rooms had a connecting door which he unlocked but discreetly did not open. Julietta had gone over to look out the windows. The receptionist supervised the arrival of the luggage; I did not know whether to tip him or not, so elegant was he in his striped pants, black jacket and starched white collar, but I long ago learned that in Italy, when in doubt—tip, and from the subtle, practiced way he palmed the folded lire, I could tell I had done the right thing.

"Is the room all right?" I asked Julietta after the young receptionist had left.

"Oh, yes. Slightly better accommodations than last night." It was the first reference either of us had made to the previous night. The day's talk had mostly been about fabric design, prison life, Italian food, automobiles (about which she knew a surprising amount), skiing, French food, American tourists, Italian aristocracy, movies and lake fishing.

"Oh, I don't know. I personally enjoyed the accommodations," I said. "Although the hot tub here does have its allure. Would you like to take a nap and eat late?"

"No . . . but if you'd like to?"

"No, I'm not a napper."

"No siestas at Santo Stefano?"

"Only in solitary. See you later." I started toward the corridor door.

"You can go through there," she said. I smiled at her and used our mutual door, carefully closing it behind me.

I felt a knot tie in my stomach as the door shut. I am in love with her—and she feels something, I do not know what, but *something* for me; we have a night alone in this splendid city and we share these rooms but this time, without lightning as your ally, you will not be able to evade the "moment." This time, if you love her, you will have to love her as any man loves any woman but all you will do is dissolve into gelatin and sweat. What about that? What about that ordeal? How many times have you heard Iris' anguished outcry ringing in your ears? How many times must it be repeated before you realize? . . .

All *right*, I realize! Do you think this is something I sought? Didn't I try to steer clear of involvement? Didn't I resign myself to the reality of how I was, of what had happened to me? Of all women—this one—who is surely not my ally. I couldn't help loving her. It was as inevitable and natural as succumbing to sleep when I have gone too long without sleep. I am not to blame, God damn it! Don't berate me. What shall I do? Pack up and leave her a note and run? Why not? That's what you did to Keva, isn't it? I didn't love Keva. All the better: you should make sacrifices for someone you love. Oh, Christ, you are lethal, Selwyn. You are an ambulatory plague. Talk about the kiss of death—you are the kiss of half-death. Step up, folks, see the man-freak—he talks like a man, he comes on like a man, but does he come like a man? Watch him turn from man to goat before your eyes. And watch his victims as they writhe upon their beds of frustrated pain.

Cut it out! Stop chopping yourself up. Maybe this will be different. You do love her and *there's* the difference and maybe, just maybe if she responds to you, it will level out for you and you will be the way you were before they wrecked you.

We walked from the hotel to the Galleria Vittorio Emanuele, where we had drinks under the wondrous high-vaulted glass arcade. From there we walked across the Piazza del Duomo to Giannino's, a restaurant I had heard about for as long as I had been in Italy. To begin with, it *looked* like a great vintage Italian restaurant should look: its waiters were obviously born to their cloths and its food was beyond expectation. I also supplied a large measure of comic relief by ordering their specialty, *risotto certosina,* as *risotto certosino;* Julietta explained, when she could stop laughing, that *certosino* was a Carthusian monk.

"Now just a minute—you've never had shishka monk? Delicious. Of course, it's only served on Fridays."

On the way back to the hotel, Julietta asked if I would mind if she went into the Duomo. When she entered, she did not take holy water or cross herself, nor did she cross herself when she knelt at one of the side altars to pray with her forehead resting on her hands.

"You're very religious, aren't you?"

"No. Not at all; what I am is *not* religious, but I like to pray. You didn't see me make obeisance to the Christus, did you?"

"But kneeling and praying is religious."

"Oh, no. I do not pray to anyone, or anything—like Jesus or Jehovah—I just like to create an inner church and meditate. Churches are fine. It's just religions I don't like."

When we got to our rooms, I unlocked her door for her and for an awkward moment we stood in the corridor indecisively. I felt very close to her; she was someone I had known a long time. I put my hand on her bare arm, touching her lightly. She smiled at me. I wanted to kiss her desperately, but my rising desire brought fear with it.

"May I talk to you, Julietta? I really must talk to you."

"You mean *talk*?" Her smile was mocking me.

I laughed. "Yes, *talk*."

She took off her shoes and sat on the bed pillows, her back against the headboard. "You take the Father chair," she said. I loosened my tie and took off my jacket and sat down facing her in the room's one armchair.

"I want to tell you something," I said. "After last night . . ." This wouldn't work, sitting there, looking at her, beautiful on her pillow perch, her hair softly against her cheeks, one leg tucked under her, the other clasped at the knee, looking small and pale in the bed lamp's brightness. I got up and turned to the windows and watched the traffic below on the Via Fatebenefratelli. I can't do this, I thought. I'll never be able to do this. Why should I?

"Is it that difficult?" she asked.

"Yes," I answered, keeping my face at the windows, "it's that difficult."

"Well, then, why . . ."

"Because I've got to! There are some things you've got to do!" Too strong, calm it down. Handle it, evenly now, handle it. I was facing her, half-sitting on the window ledge. There was air conditioning coming up through the vents and it made my ass cold. "I am very attracted to you—let's start with that. That first time—when you walked into the café . . . it was crazy of me, there was every reason to believe you would run off the minute I told you who I was—of *course* it was irrational—but you had a beauty . . . I don't want to go into that. You know what I'm saying. Every man has his dream, who *the* woman will be, and my dream was deeper and longer than most. But that's not what I want to tell you. What I want you to know is about me. I'm . . . I'm not normal. I mean, as a man—with a woman. I used to be. But something happened. Those years in prison . . . it's very difficult to talk about this, but I have to, it will help me, I don't want to fool myself, or you. It isn't that I had homosexual relations in prison or that I am turned off women—it's just that I'm . . . not *able*. They took that with everything else, but I still desire and want you. Last night, the feel of you against me, sleeping in my arms . . . Can you imagine what last night meant to a man who has not slept with a woman in his arms for all those years? But since I was released, I have tried with two women, attractive women whom I desired and who wanted me, and it was terrible. I mustn't put myself or a woman through that again. That's why I'm telling you this. *Making* myself tell you this. To keep myself—and you—from that agony. I hope this doesn't have any self-pity in it. I'm trying to avoid that. Of course, I have anger about it. But self-pity is such a worthless thing. I hate it. I hate it all. I want to love, so damn much, and all I have is this hate. Of myself, I guess. Sure, of myself. But you're part of the dream. I want you to know that."

I had not been able to look at her. I felt exposed and humiliated. I picked up my coat and went to my room, not using the connecting door. There was enough light coming through the windows to find the bed without turning on the lights. I took off my shoes and flopped down. I felt a tight band around my forehead, and I was cold. I pulled up the blanket at the foot of the bed but it didn't help. I tried to think of other things: of the farm we had seen that afternoon, of the lake vista while crossing on the ferry, of the choreography of the waiters who served us at Giannino's; but they were brief diversions and where my mind returned relentlessly was to her. The cold I felt turned to a chill. I turned on my stomach and buried my head under the pillow. Oh, Christ, how will I get through this night? I should have kept my mouth shut. Yes, and then what? Then—nothing. Why couldn't we just keep on as is. Which is what? Like it is—friendly, just as friends. Why do I have to presume we must wind up in bed? Who says she wants that? Because that's where it was headed. You can't keep your eyes off her. You can't restrain yourself from touching her. Where does that lead—to an exchange of friendship rings? So don't kid yourself. All right. In six hours there will be daylight. You've got six rough hours, that's all. What's another few hours on top of all the other black ones?

I didn't hear her at all. The give of the bed startled me. She was wearing a silk robe and she smelled freshly of soap. She took me in her arms and pressed my face against the soft hollow at the base of her throat.

"Oh, God!" came out of me in a whisper.

She held me like that, motionless. A tear dropped on my forehead and rolled slowly down to the bridge of my nose. I could feel her underthings beneath the silk robe. My head rested on her arm, just as hers had been on mine the night before. I guess she understood that I was as fear-struck by my storm as she had been by hers. But my storm would not abate with the morning sun although there was a moment's respite here in the silk-sheathed warmth of her body. And in the fact that someone cared. It had been a long time since anyone cared.

It turned out that the people in the farmhouse did not own the field but simply worked it for the owner who was also the proprietor of the Supercortemaggiore gasoline station. I explained to him that I was an American journalist come to do a piece on the buried treasure.

"You're about a year too late. They already dug it all up and found nothing. Pretty exciting here for a couple of days, though."

"Would you mind if we looked around? We'll be careful of the crops."

"Sure, go right ahead. Anything you find we split fifty-fifty." He laughed loudly at his joke and went to service a car that had just pulled up.

We made a very careful, thorough search, slowly going down one furrow and then back up the next, furrow after furrow, every inch inspected. The sun was hot and the plants were infested by flies that clung to our moist skin.

"Paul, I just realized that we measured two kilometers only on the southeast road. But what if the measurement was not taken along the road? What if someone walked off the measurement on a due course? It might come out somewhat differently."

"It just might. Let's give it a try."

We went back to the Mussolini house, took a reading, and followed a straight course over backyards and fields. I didn't have the automobile's speedometer for measurement, but I maintained an even stride. Exactly two kilometers, by my stride count, put us at the entrance to the deserted church. It was cool and dark inside, and vegetation grew through cracks in the walls. From the condition of the ground it was evident that the searchers' shovels had worked it over. Where there had once been an altar, there was now a heap of stones. An old wooden crucifix was still in place and some of the wall nooks contained stone urns. Against the rear wall, flanking the entrance, there were two sarcophagi: the one on the right, possibly of limestone, was eroded and deteriorated; the sarcophagus on the left, however, was of a harder stone and of more recent vintage, and its elaborate frieze-work was intact. Atop it was a stone image of the worthy within, probably the nobleman who once was lord of this domain. There was nothing else in the church.

I poked around at the base of the altar rubble with no results. By lifting Julietta at her ankles, she was able to see into the wall urns; they were all empty. We carefully inspected the heavy stones in all the walls but none gave evidence of ever having been dislodged. Nor did any of the stones in the newer sarcophagus. I then squeezed behind the older, deteriorated one, which stood away from the wall, and scraped off a layer of green mold which covered the rear surface. It seemed to me that the two center stones were not flush with the rest of the surface. Julietta squeezed in from the opposite side. She agreed.

Working slowly and carefully with the leather punch on my pocket knife (my invaluable Swiss Officer's Escape knife which was the only possession they returned to me when I left prison), I worked loose one of the stones which, with Julietta's help, came away from the coffin. The stone next to it easily came free, then the edges of the surrounding stone crumbled a bit. I tried to push up the lid, but it was no go. Putting my hand through the opening, I probed about the shallow interior. The first object I came upon was a large thick section of bone, and further up there were a number of smaller bones, and then, the skull. Working my hand down in the opposite direction I found nothing but more bones. The excitement of possible discovery died off.

"But those two stones had obviously been removed," Julietta insisted.

"Maybe someone scavenged jewelry that had been on the dead person. Could have been something like that."

"Are you sure you covered the whole area?"

Something was bothering me. Did I imagine it or was the skull elevated? I put my hand in again and, palm down, pushed upward toward the skull. No doubt about it, an abrupt rise just before I touched the skull. I rolled the skull aside and probed around beneath where it had been. Under a thin layer of silt, there was a flat metal box that had once been covered with canvas, but the canvas had mostly rotted away. It just barely fitted through the opening. The metal was lead-colored and unrusted, but the padlock that secured it was badly rusted. We quickly refitted the two stones and tried as best we could to smooth things out.

I put the box, which was not more than two inches or so in thickness, under my shirt and we walked unhurriedly back to the car and drove away.

We stopped in Como and took the box up to Julietta's apartment. There was no assurance, of course, that what was inside the box was Mussolini treasure, but as I studied the lock my fingers trembled with expectancy. The loop of the lock was so rusted that it broke away under the first sharp hammer blow. Inside, sealed in a thick fold of oil-skin, were papers and documents. I took out a blue card-board folder tied with a blue ribbon. The paper was excellently preserved. Blue ribbon, blue folder. Across the face of which was written: "Entrusted to Benito Mussolini. Secret." I untied the ribbon and handed the contents to Julietta, who carefully spread them out on a table. Across the top of each document the words "Secret. To Benito Mussolini" were written in large red letters. The documents themselves covered a wide variety of state matters: the war, the Trieste situation, arrangements for Mussolini's entrance into Switzerland and his stay there, reports on partisan activities in the north, various military reports; all of this exactly as it had been described in the deposition given by the partisan Urbano Lazzaro, who in Mussolini's presence in Dongo searched his leather briefcase and found these items and others which he inventoried.

A second folder was filled with letters and documents exchanged between Mussolini and Hitler; Hitler's letters all had typewritten Italian translations pinned to them, the Mussolini letters were carbons. The letters themselves were typed but many of them had postscripts and marginal notations written in longhand by the two dictators.

Also in this folder was a sheaf of prewar correspondence between Mussolini and Winston Churchill. This puzzled me, because as I recalled the Lazzaro deposition, he stated that the Churchill correspondence was in a thick file of its own.

The last item in the oilskin bag was a diary, on the cover of which was written, "That the Italians May Know IV," obviously the fourth volume of the Duce's long-sought and highly valued diaries. I identified these items for Julietta, and explained that in my estimation the Churchill letters and the diary did not rightfully belong in this assemblage but had somehow become detached from their original folders.

"What does it mean, Paul? Who would it be—the one who knew about these papers being buried there and would confess it to a priest in London? And how did they happen to be buried so close to the home of Rachele Mussolini? Do you think without her knowledge? Surely without her knowledge, or wouldn't she have dug them out?"

"All unanswerable. But we do know that the confessor was a religious man who must have been fearful of confessing to a priest in Italy and perhaps the trip to London was his first chance out of Italy to ease his conscience. But his nervous behavior at the confessional box certainly illustrates his fear. He knew something—the hiding place—that others who might have recognized him wanted to know."

"Did he give the London priest permission to tell Scotland Yard?"

"Yes, or else, as a privileged communication, the priest would not have had the right to divulge the information received during the confession."

"So the informer wanted the papers discovered?"

"Yes, and wanted them to be discovered by Italian police so that they would be returned to the Italian government. Obviously an altruistic informer."

"So what it comes down to is an Italian, fearful of making a move in Italy, goes to London and *fearfully* tries to pass the information there."

"You know, Julietta, I think you've just described someone we know about. Not know, but know about."

"Who?"

"Judge Rambellini of Padua."

"The one who stopped the trial? But why in the world would he want to give up these papers for nothing?"

"That's hard to say. But a man's conscience sometimes howls him down."

chapter eighteen

The Carpignano church discovery had a profound effect on my fellow members of the Spedizione Internazionale. I was no longer skeptically indulged; the reality of the Hitler letters and Churchill letters in their very hands made Bis and Ted, who had just returned from London, true believers. Even Dan, who had not left his room since our departure, came downstairs to congratulate me. I wished that Giorgio had returned from Lugano so that he could have been in on this.

That afternoon a boy bicycled up from the village with an envelope for me. He was a utility boy who worked at the Dongo café, serving drinks to the bocce players in the open yard in the back, helping on the espresso machine, clearing tables, fetching newspapers. The envelope, which had no markings on it other than my name, contained a white index card on which was printed:

"I have information related to your non-archaeological interests. Come alone tonight 10 o'clock to Dongo cathedral. Confess at box for French-speaking. Use words,

'E Pluribus Unum' to identify yourself. Be sure you are not
followed."

The utility boy said that he did not know who had given
him the envelope. He said that when he had gone to choir
practice at the cathedral that afternoon, the envelope was in
his cubbyhole, above his choir robe, and pinned to it was
one hundred lire and a note saying, "Please deliver to Paul
Selwyn, Villa di Cielo."

As I stood there watching the boy ride away, holding the
note in my hand so similar to the note of long ago, I felt,
eerily, that Arnoldo was coming down the stairs.

I looked up to see Ted descending the staircase. "No need
whacking about the bushes with you, Paulsky, so here it is,
right out: Bis and I are a bit stirred up over your having
installed a lady friend in the villa. Not that she isn't first-
rate, charming, beautiful, no aspersion intended, but, after
all, dear fellow, we must have some semblance of security,
n'est-ce pas? I mean, have you checked out this girl? Background and all that? She could put us out of business one-
two-three, don't you know?"

"It's okay, Ted. She's Julietta Disio."

"She is? Not Angelo? Why Angelo?"

"She wanted it that way."

"What is she afraid of? I mean, not even to trust her fellow archaeologists?"

"She does now. At first she was tentative about mas-
querading like this."

"Will you tell her we know?"

"Yes, I'll tell her. But you'd better keep on with the
Angelo—she doesn't want the town to know who she is.
She's not sure how certain people might react to the Disio
name."

"What does that mean?"

"It means whoever killed Arnoldo may have come from

around here; *probably* came from around here. You can imagine what cause and effect the sudden presence of Arnoldo Disio's daughter might have. Right?"

"Jolly right."

I started to show him the note but the housekeeper announced the arrival of Father Piccionastro, who had come to propose some new dig procedures.

The sound of a siren usually blends with the noise of a city, but in Zonico, where emergency was rare, its wail was the wail of stark calamity. Our housekeeper telephoned the barman at the Dongo café, who had an eye for her; he said there had been a serious accident and the ambulance had been summoned. I looked at the hall clock: it was seven o'clock.

By the time we arrived at the scene, virtually all of Dongo and Zonico was there. The ambulance, on its first official mission in two months, stood at the mouth of one of the little streets that feed into the Piazza Dongo. A verbal bulletin was circulating through the crowd: a priest was dead in the street, probably hit by an automobile, but no one had actually seen what had happened. You could hear, "a priest left dead" . . . "a priest has been killed" . . . "a priest" . . . "a priest" . . . simultaneously buzzing through various parts of the crowd. A car arrived in the square, bearing the doctor, and the crowd made a respectful path for him. I followed in his wake. He was old and he heavily listed toward the weight of his medic bag.

The body of the priest lay about twenty yards down the little street, well-illuminated by the lights of the ambulance. The priest's hat and one of his sandals were in the gutter further down the street. The priest was fat, bald and heavily bearded. I twisted around to look for Julietta; she was standing a few feet away and from the look on her face I knew that this was the priest she had seen in the Dongo church.

Paulo Benfatto was importantly standing in front of his ambulance, waching the doctor examine the corpse.

"What happened, Paulo?"

"Nobody knows. Nobody saw or heard anything."

"Do you recognize him?"

"Yes, it is Father Laekla. He *was* Father Laekla when he was in the Dongo church, but then he went off and when he came back he entered Santo Zacharia so now he is Brother Laekla. He was of the administration, with Father Piccionastro, so he circulated outside the monastery. There was a meeting scheduled tonight at the cathedral for eight o'clock and he was on his way there."

"You say he left Dongo—where did he go?"

"On a long sabbatical—various places."

"Where? Do you know?"

"Where? Ummm, let's see, what did he tell me? Oh, I don't know, all around Italy, and then Lourdes, and then, oh, yes, he went to see relatives in London."

"When was this?"

"This was last year, or the year before—I can't recall which."

"Did he tell you much about London?"

"How do you mean?"

"Well, who he saw there, what he did?"

"Not that I remember."

The doctor was finished examining the body and Benfatto enlisted several young men to hoist it and carry it to the ambulance. Benfatto went over to talk to the doctor; I stayed close enough to listen.

"Doctor, what do I enter on the report?"

"Death from multiple interior injuries resulting from a massive impact delivered from the back of the body."

"An automobile?"

"Most likely."

"But from the back?"

"Definitely from the back."

"He must have been walking with his back to the car."

"I wouldn't know."

Or, I thought, trying to run from the automobile. I took Julietta's arm and guided her through the crowd, which started to disburse as the ambulance doors clanged shut.

I felt a tug on my coat jacket; it was the little old helmet lady. She seemed terribly agitated; her lips trembled and her breath was gaspy.

"You kept my secret so well about the helmet. I know I can trust you. Promise never to tell on me."

"I promise."

"I saw it. I was . . . I was . . . there's a little alley that goes to my house and I had just passed Father Laekla, when there was a commotion, I don't hear very well, but there was this autocar with no lights and it had run down Father Lackla, and a man from the autocar got out, there were two men, one man driving and this man, and he took his foot and pushed Father Laekla onto—to his back and then he went through his vestments looking for something, then back to the autocar and I was hugging the shadow of the wall and they did not see me and very fast they were, they were gone and I was too scared to go to look but you must promise not to . . . to say who told you. You must promise, or that man, that man would come after me . . ."

"I promise. It's all right. I do promise. Did the man get what he wanted from Father Laekla's vestments?"

"I can't be sure. The street light is dim and my eyes are old but I think he took something." She had stopped trembling.

"What kind of a car? Could you tell?"

"Oh, sir, I do not know cars."

"Well, little, big?"

"Medium. A medium autocar, like you see so many."

"Did you see the man's face—anything you can tell me about him?"

"No. He was all in black. I did not see his face at all."

"Was he tall, short, fat . . . ?"

"I don't know. It was all so fast. I was so scared. He seemed very large to me, but my fear probably made him so."

"You say large, do you mean fat?"

"No, just, just large. Perhaps tall. Yes, tall; he was very tall. I must go. I must not be noticed. Oh, poor Father Laekla. Poor man. He confessed me many times when he was in Dongo. But he was now at Santo Zacharia, you know. I must go pray for him. Poor man."

It was, of course, pointless but nevertheless we went through the motions of going to the church. Obviously Father Laekla had planned our rendezvous at the confessional box after his church meeting and he was murdered to prevent it. It was already well past the appointed time. Not able to find us, Ted and Bis had driven back to the villa in the Volkswagen. It was a full-mooned night, a nice night to walk, and Julietta and I took the back road, which was downhill and, at this time of night, deserted.

"Don't you think it rather odd that Father Laekla and Judge Rambellini both were in London?" Julietta asked.

"I was certainly wrong in my guess that the London confessor was the judge, wasn't I?"

"But both in London, Paul . . ."

"Yes. Suspicious coincidence. Let's see what it could mean: if the story about visiting relatives was just cover, then perhaps Laekla went to see the judge . . ."

"Or was sent for."

"Yes—*ordered* to see the judge, and as a result of that meeting, decided to make some kind of disclosure about the hidden papers."

"I've been thinking about that old church. So close to Signora Mussolini's farmhouse. Why would Father Laekla hide those papers there?"

"You think he had visited Signora Mussolini?"

"Yes. Either to offer her the papers—or get them from her."

"Why would she give them to him?"

"Well, this was twenty years ago—maybe there was some kind of blackmail, some kind of threat to Rachele Mussolini's security."

"Perhaps a threat to her children. Perhaps Vittorio. Don't forget that Vittorio had actively helped his father to escape. He had been sent by Benito to Switzerland to contact the government, to make all arrangements for Mussolini's internment. There was a partisan price on his head."

"He escaped to South America, didn't he?"

"Yes. But what if he were *allowed* to escape as part of the deal?"

"But if Father Laekla was simply a courier and did not deliver the papers to whomever had sent him . . ."

"Yes, but what if he delivered *part* of the papers and kept part—the part he hid. You said that some of those things had been detached from larger files—like the Churchill letters. The diaries."

"So what you suggest is that Laekla went to Carpignano to effect a deal—something Rachele Mussolini wanted in exchange for certain letters and papers in her possession. That's unlikely because these papers had been captured in Dongo. How would they have reached Rachele?"

"Then what about the other postulate—that Father Laekla brought those papers to exchange for something that Rachele had?"

"I doubt she had anything of more value than those papers. But there's one other possible speculation—Father Laekla could have had those papers without anyone else's knowledge. After all, he was one of the priests in the Dongo church at the time of Mussolini's capture. Now if he were a man of conscience, he could have wanted to give those papers to Signora Mussolini—and perhaps that's why the trip to see her."

"Then why would he leave her house with them?"

"Because, as you suggest, those years were perilous ones, and Rachele Mussolini undoubtedly had already been threatened by the men who were after this treasure—threatened to cough up everything of value in her possession. I should think that with her children threatened, her own safety in peril, the last thing she would have wanted in her possession were old letters and papers of no immediate value. Certainly the treasure-seekers had grilled her about such possessions, and you can bet they had been to Carpignano on more than one occasion. No, not old papers. If Father Laekla had brought money or gold that Benito had had with him, she might have risked taking that. But there was Laekla with these hot documents, not wanting to turn them over to the ruthless killers who were after the treasure, but also not wanting to keep them in his own possession. So what did he do? After his visit with Signora Mussolini, he walked a short distance away and cleverly concealed them in the first likely place he came to—a deserted church."

"But why, after all those years, did Father Laekla suddenly and very nervously decide to disclose the whereabouts of the papers? And why so mysteriously—two kilometers southeast but no specific details?"

"Well, I think he intended to give a full description of the hiding place but the Scotland Yard report said that he broke off in mid-sentence, which makes me think that he probably saw someone enter the church who was known to him."

"Someone who had followed him?"

"Very likely."

"And Rambellini—why would his outfit become suspicious of Laekla twenty years later?"

"We can't really figure Rambellini into this until we get

more information about him. Obviously something boiled up that turned attention to Laekla—maybe Giorgio's bookie will be of some help. Or Ted. Ted was going to run a recce on him."

The road descended steeply at the point where it passed the vicinity of our villa and we were by now almost to the bottom of this stretch. Julietta, walking toward the outside of the road, had her left arm linked with my right, and occasionally she would reach out to pluck little blossoms from moonlighted bushes. She stopped now at a bower of honeysuckle and broke off a twig which she put under my nose. Perhaps I glimpsed something as I turned my head to the honeysuckle, or perhaps I only sensed it—however it happened, I grabbed Julietta and dived off the road, hurtling in a sprawl among the bushes as the car, no lights, no motor, sped from the long noiseless descent, shushed past. The right fender of the car nicked my right foot, but my foot was in the air and gave with the impact. It hurt from the blow but it did not seem serious.

Julietta was all right except for a bleeding scratch across her forehead. Just beyond us the sound of the car's brakes, then the churn of its starter as the engine came to life with a whoom-whoom magnified by the silence. The car was backing up. I grabbed Julietta's arm, got her to her feet, and holding her firmly, started running along the field, using the bushes for cover as much as possible. The moonlight was both ally and enemy, exposing us if they came onto the field, but lighting the way to where I knew a round-pipe culvert, now summer dry, cut under the road so that we could get to the other side and make it to the villa.

The car stopped, doors opened, bushes rustled, Julietta and I hugged as close to cover as we could, bent low, running, the moonlight merciless, but suddenly sliding into the unseen culvert, sliding down its dirt-smooth pebbled side, dustily to its bottom, then through the large round metal

road tunnel, corrugated bottom, the sound of men's voices
in the field, the moonless tunnel suddenly black, a round of
light to target us through, then out in the culvert again,
running along its pebbly bottom, slipping, Julietta carrying
her shoes, now up the side, a hand down to Julietta, her
shoes tossed up, both her hands grasping mine as up she
came, and grabbing her shoes, moving swiftly now through
a brambly field, then the villa's back fence to the high iron
gate squealing rustily on its hinges, and along the privet
path and into safety. Gasping, scratched, clothing ripped,
Julietta's leg cut, her forehead still bleeding, my foot so
painfully swollen I could not remove my shoe.

Julietta helped me up the stairs and into her room. I did
not want Ted and Bis to know what had happened.

"But why—why shouldn't they know?"

"Because they may pack up and go. They had their
doubts to begin with—and their fears about the dangers
involved. This would be all the proof they need."

"They're right, Paul. You know now what you're up
against; no one's imagining it."

"You want your father's murderer. I want the treasure
he took. There's risk in that—but not enough to stop me.
No amount of risk could stop me, but I think it's different
for you. You don't have the fire in you that burns in me.
I *can't* back off. I've *got* to go on. If I hadn't shown up you
would never have involved yourself in all this. I think you
should go back to Como. I will do my best to identify the
killer or killers, but there's no sense in your sharing this
risk. You must go back."

She had taken the lace out of my shoe and pulled out
the tongue and now with great care she freed my foot.
There was a sharp pain as my foot emerged from the shoe,
but then, with the pressure gone, the foot felt measurably
less painful.

Julietta went into the bathroom and washed the blood from her forehead. She returned with a scissors and gingerly cut the sock from my foot, which was puffed and blue at the ankle. She put her arm around me and helped me hobble into the bathroom. She ran hot water into the tub, then helped me sit on the edge and soak my foot in the steaming water.

"Do you really want me to go?"

"For myself? You know the answer to that. But for you . . ."

She had taken off her torn stockings and now she joined me on the edge of the tub and put her scratched feet into the water besides mine.

"For you—what do *you* have here?" I asked. "The peril of someone who either wants to frighten you off by feigning a murder attempt or who really wants to kill you. It seems more likely that tonight's attack was aimed solely at me, and at you only because you were with me, but that may happen again. And for what—a man who wants you but can't make love to you, who can only sleep with you like a sexless blanket."

"Has it occurred to you that that is maybe all I want?"

"What are you talking about?"

She reached down and gently circulated water around my bruised ankle.

"I'm twenty-nine years old. I live alone—I can assure you, by choice. I don't deny that I liked the way you held me these two nights, and the way we slept. But I don't want anything beyond that. Not any more." She lifted my foot from the water, examined it, and carefully set it down. "What I mean is—I can't *feel* any more than that. *Feel.* Beyond just holding, sleeping, it's all quite dead. I think I should tell you . . . I've never told anyone, but you have been so honest with me. . . ."

"I wish you would."

"Well, not everything, but . . . When I left home, I studied fabric design in Florence and apprenticed in Milan. It was hard work, long hours; by then my mother was in a nursing home and we were quite poor. I had a boyfriend in Florence and another in Milan although neither was important to me. They wanted to marry but they were nothing serious for me. Then, when I was twenty-four I came to Como to work for Nuvola. I met a man there—he was married and much older, semi-separated from his wife. Perhaps his being older . . ."

"How much older?"

"Forty-two—so eighteen years older. We were two magnets. Right from the start. I would see him during the week, then weekends he would go to his wife and children, two children; they had lived in Milan before he was transferred to Como, recently transferred to Como, and his family continued to live in Milan. The thing with this man was that for the first time in my life I was able to react. The two men I told you about, and a few others, I was never truly attracted to. I had resigned myself never to have fully realized love, to feel deeply, but with this man—he released me, he made me feel all the things I wanted to feel as a woman. I had never felt that before. I had never liked myself as a woman, never felt I was attractive, never felt my body was sensual or sexual, but he changed all that and lifted me up and made me alive, not just in bed, but totally alive. Naturally I fell deeply in love with him. And he loved me.

"Well, after a year he finally left his wife and lived with me all the time. We had a small place, five flights up—most of my salary went to the nursing home to support my mother, and his salary went to his family—so we were very poor but very happy in our high-rise nest. I really didn't think much about marriage or care about it as long as we were together, but he wanted to marry me. He was Italian but his wife was Swiss and they had had a non-Catholic marriage in Geneva so divorce was possible for him. Complicated but possible.

"For more than a year lawyers worked on the divorce. But as I say, I wasn't too concerned. I thought about marrying him, and I wanted to, but I was in no hurry. I didn't want to have a child just yet and it did bother me that he was eighteen years older. Sometimes I would think about how old he would be when our children were ten or fifteen. But I wanted to live with him forever. I know it sounds crazy, that kind of thinking, but marriage was real commitment, and since my father's death and the terrible grief I had over his loss, I guess I had made a practice of not committing myself to anything, of standing back at a safe point, or rather what I *thought* was safety. So that's probably why I wasn't pressuring about marriage, but in terms of our relation I was certainly totally committed. We were compatible in so many ways, but especially in bed. I don't suppose you can understand what it means to a woman when a part of her is born with a particular man. That man is both father and child of this birth, for he conceives it and is conceived by it.

"Well, three years passed. The divorce papers were finally drawn. This was in the autumn, two years ago. I had received a letter from a cousin of mine who lived in Milan and who, besides being a first cousin, was my closest and dearest friend. In fact, the only close friend I had. When I apprenticed in Milan we had lived together, and as kids she used to spend summers with me in Bellagio. Flora wrote that she was coming to Como for two weeks and could she stay with me. Of course, she didn't know I was living with a man. Despite our closeness, she was, after all, family, and I just couldn't bring myself to tell her; we didn't have that kind of openness with each other.

"So for the two weeks, Pietro took a room in a *pensione*.

I think, as I look back on it, that he resented my pretense about living alone, resented being moved out. Also, as he explained later, he had subconsciously been gathering a deeper resentment—that my enthusiasm for marrying him had not kept pace with the movement of the divorce proceedings toward finality.

"At any rate, Flora came—Flora is pretty and vivacious and two years younger—and we were together, the three of us, every night that she was in Como. We got along fine, but after she left (although I didn't associate it with her leaving), my relation with Pietro was not quite the same, not quite as sharp, as intense. Twice he had to make weekend business trips to Verona, and once to Venice, although before that he had not traveled at all.

"Then one day I went by his office to give him something. He wasn't in, but on his desk was a letter—the letter was open—he had read it and left it in a corner of his desk pad. I read it. It was a love letter, the letter of a woman who was deeply bedded with a man. It had references to specific joys they had shared during a weekend in the Albergo di Due Torre in Verona, along with other references about me, guilt about me, what should we do about poor Julietta, all that.

"It was Christmas by then. I always spent Christmas with my relations in Milan. So I felt I had to go. Flora or no Flora. I shared Flora's room, as I always did, and as I was unpacking, *literally* I was unpacking when I opened a drawer to put in my things and there at the back was a large manila envelope that contained a stack of letters to Flora from Pietro. That he had been able to sleep with me and write letters like that! I confronted Flora and she admitted everything quite honestly. She said, though, that Pietro had given her the impression that there was nothing serious between us. I don't know if he had, or not—it really wasn't important. What was obvious was that, in leaving the letters in that drawer, as she did, either consciously or subconsciously Flora wanted me to read them.

"What followed were six months of hell and torture for me. Pietro trying to keep contact, trying to atone, trying to hold on to what he had renounced—and lost. But all those lovely, strong, passionate feelings I had had, dried up and died. It wasn't that I hated Pietro for what he had done—it would have been better if I could have hated him —but I didn't, I just went dead. Not just on him, but on everyone. After a while, I went out occasionally. I tried to make love once or twice, with attractive, virile men who liked me, but not only did I not care, but it was, in a strange way, demeaning—an irritant.

"I saw Pietro a few times after he got his divorce. I even went to bed with him—but it was dead and hopeless. Then my feelings seemed to congeal—almost two years ago—and I stopped seeing men altogether. There is nothing I want from a man, nor that I feel for a man. That's why I can hold you in my arms, or be held, and feel comfort but nothing beyond that. Nothing woman to man. You say your prison experience wrecked you as a man. Well, this experience of mine wrecked me as a woman. I'd say we are a couple of wrecks well met."

She had taken her feet from the water and dried them, and now she helped me swing my legs from the tub; while I sat on the edge, she carefully patted my ankle with a towel.

"I suppose it's an old story, losing your man to your best friend, but why did he keep on living with me and making love to me and making me feel such a part of his body, that there was me and only me? I could understand if they had just had a fling while Flora was in Como—she is terribly attractive and sexy in a lusty way, which I'm not—

but why did he pursue it? The letters and trysts. Why didn't he leave me? After all, I wasn't his wife. He had no ties to me. Yet—he kept on loving me. And you know . . ."

She helped me up, and using her shoulders for support, I limped into her room and stretched out on the bed. A ledge of tears stood precariously on her lower lids. She sat on the edge of the bed, her back to me, her shoulders sagged.

". . . you know, after I stopped seeing him, and it was all over, he never saw Flora again. He finally left Como—it was hell on both of us for him to stay on—and although, after that, he was in Milan several times, he never got in touch with Flora. Or wrote to her. Or phoned her. He used to write to me. Lovely, poetic letters, full of his heart. I've never answered any; there is nothing in me that reacts. I don't even know where he is now. I don't want to know. It's been a long time. And now . . . now I am almost thirty. I gave—no, gave is not the word—I *used up* so many good years—years to have a child—and make a home—in Italy, thirty is old for a woman. Thirty is a spinster. Thirty means you're passed over. Does your foot feel better? I think the swelling is . . . down."

The tear ledge had lost its balance and a thin tributary flowed to each of her cheeks. She lowered her head to the pillow, beside mine, her legs still over the bed edge, at a right angle. "It doesn't mean I don't like you, Paul. I do. You have a sweet warmth, and there hasn't been much of that for me." She pulled her legs onto the bed and turned her eyes to the ceiling. She floated far off. The scratch on her forehead was bright red and deeper than I had thought. It ran unevenly from the outer edge of one eyebrow to the inner edge of the other, resembling the graph of an erratic stock. She reached one hand toward me, vaguely, and it came to rest on my cheek. She moved her finger tips back and forth across my cheekbone.

"It must be terrible for you, Paul, to be impotent," she said, softly. "But, then . . . so many of us are."

The underwater expedition to Tremezzo to probe for the two bags of treasure allegedly jettisoned there by Nazi Captain Otto Kisnat, was scheduled to depart early the following morning. But since my ankle was still swollen and tender, Bis and Ted set off without us. (They had readily accepted our explanation that on returning from Dongo we had fallen into the unseen culvert, thereby incurring the ankle and the scratches.) Their plan was to drive down to the little lake town of Acquaseria, where they had arranged to charter a thirty-foot sloop that slept six. Ted had brought all the required underwater gear from London, but it would be necessary to take on fishing equipment and galley supplies in Acquaseria.

The scheme was to cruise south, anchor off Tremezzo, directly opposite the Villa Carlotta, and under the cover of fishermen-tourists, probe the depths for the Kisnat treasure bags. It would take at least a day to outfit the boat and get down to Tremezzo, and I planned to join them there the following day. But before they left, I hobbled down the hall to Dan's room to see if I could convince him to go along—it would be better to have three men on the boat.

The shutters in Dan's room were closed and so were the windows. The room was oppressively hot and it fetidly smelled of liquor, dead cigarettes and uneaten food. I opened the windows.

"Jesus, what a stinking oven! Can't you drink with the windows open?"

"And who invited you and your senstive nose in here?"

"The Zonico chapter of Alcoholics Anonymous."

"I wish to make it clear," Dan said, speaking formally, "that although I am drinking I am decidedly not drunk." He was very drunk.

"Good. Then what do you say to a nice boat ride on the lake? Bis and Ted are ready to take off for the Tremezzo project and they could use you aboard. Be good for you."

"No—I can't leave the think tank."

"You mean the stink tank. What the hell you trying to prove, Dan? That you can drown in your own seepage? Now, come on, shave off that grimy bristle and take a belt of mouthwash and I'll tell Ted to wait, you'll be right down."

"No way. No fucking way. I am spending the summer in this room, and now, if you don't mind, put my windows and shutters back where you found them and get your ass out of here."

"Dan, you jerk, don't you realize your whole performance is out of date? Man with busted heart withdraws to darkened room and drinks himself stupid, thereby invoking the world's pity and commiseration. Do you think Natalie will get wind of your plight—you know, she just *might,* the smell being what it is—and come rushing back to you, snatching you from the jaws of the monster Booze? Or are you simply enjoying one more marvelous masochistic kick, the role of the staunch mariner wrecked on the nefarious shoals of Underhanded Natalie."

"Go fuck yourself, Paul. Please withdraw from my inner sanctum and go fuck yourself. What you don't understand is that I am no ordinary man. You are looking at one of the last of an almost extinct animal that has stopped propagating because he can suck his own cock."

"Dan, she's gone. For good. She's given Gibio the key to her chastity belt, and he's given her the key to his counting house, and at this moment she's sitting at a solid gold desk counting her millions. But, actually, she's been gone for a long time—and you know it. You have tolerated the intolerable but now even the intolerable has been taken away from you. So you've set up this substitute flagellation

—drinking yourself stupid in this stinking room. But it's ersatz. Nothing can replace the exquisite shit you wallowed in with Natalie. Accept no substitutes. Maybe you'll just have to enjoy other things. Maybe even dial your enjoyment adjuster all the way around to the other side and take on a woman who likes you and doesn't cuckold and demean you every chance she gets."

Dan picked up the bottle he had been drinking from and flung it at me. The bottle was drunkenly off target and it hit high up on the wall in the back of me and fell to the floor, miraculously unbroken.

He was right. Every man should lick his wounds in his own way without the interference of other wound-lickers.

I shut the windows and the shutters and left.

That night, Julietta and I took a long time to decide where to hide the Mussolini papers, but Julietta finally solved it by producing a gaily colored Moroccan vest which, she said, had matching bell-bottoms. The vest was padded and stiff, like a matador's tunic, and by opening the seams and removing some of the stiffening, Julietta was able to fit the papers and letters into the vest to replace the removed material. She did it expertly, and afterward she wore the vest to dinner and it was impossible to tell that it had valuable stuffing.

We ate dinner alone. We had given the help the night off, and Julietta cooked chicken breasts and made fresh asparagus hollandaise. We ate dinner by candlelight at a small table on the veranda and it was as if we were married and this was our home and the children were asleep upstairs.

We had slept together, now, for three consecutive nights, under the strangest circumstances: the lightning of Bellagio, my confessional collapse in Milan, and the previous night in the villa when, bruised and battered, we slept through the night on top of the coverlet with our clothes on—but three consecutive nights they were, however they were contrived; going up to bed this night, no crisis or trauma involved, I wondered, in light of Julietta's self-conscious revelations of the previous night, whether there would be a fourth. I desperately wanted her in my arms. She had said it didn't matter to her, and for me it mattered enormously: I wanted to further my illusion about who we were, one illusion further. But she had seemed distant, perhaps distracted, during dinner, and when we went upstairs she helped me to my door and abruptly left me there and went to her room.

I undressed and washed and brushed my teeth. It was very hot and airless. I opened my door to get the air moving —hers was closed. I vacillated over whether to go to her but I couldn't. Perhaps later. I took off my robe and peeled down the bed and got in it. At first I covered with the sheet but it was too hot even for that. I thought about how it would be if I went across the hall and opened her door without knocking and just slipped into bed with her. No, leave her alone. If she wants you—what word did she use? —comfort—if she wants to be comforted, she'll let you know. That's your function—comforter.

I got up and put on my robe and limped down to Dan's room. I had been a sanctimonious horse's ass and I wanted to apologize.

The door of his room was open. I turned on the light. He was not there. Stuck to the mirror was a note for me: "Dear Paul: What schmucks we mortals be. Ciao, Dan."

How had he departed without my hearing him?

I went back to my room, using the wall for support. I stopped outside Julietta's door and listened for sounds but there weren't any. I had my hand on the door knob and I wanted to turn it but I couldn't.

I left my door open, took off my robe and went back to bed. Julietta was there.

"Where have you been?"

"To see Dan. He's gone." During dinner, I had told her about my visit with him.

"Good. Or is it?"

"Yes, I think so."

She was wearing a short silk nightshirt embroidered with blue flowers at the throat. I put my arms around her; she was not wearing any undergarments. The feel of her against me shortened my breath.

"You turn, I'll hold you," she said. I turned my back to her and she put her arms around me and fitted her body against mine. One hand nestled in my hair.

"I like to hold your hair," she said.

The crickets in the garden were boisterous. A night bird called rhythmically. Julietta's hands relaxed and I knew she had fallen asleep. I could feel her slow sleep-breaths on the back of my neck. I had a sense of belonging. My whole body seemed to rise up. For the first time since I had left prison I felt alive; I felt an erection grow strong and insistent. It was for her—from her and for her—as she had said—when sex is born with someone that someone is parent and child, conceiver and conceived.

Slowly, not wanting to wake her, I turned around, to hold her that way, so I could feel her body against my erection. But as I pressed against her she stirred and mumbled something out of her sleep and I was afraid—afraid, I suppose, that at this moment, at least, she would discover that I was an imposter—it must have been that, for my erection fell and I felt disorganized and on my forehead I felt the familiar, dreaded outbreak of sweat.

chapter nineteen

It was late afternoon by the time we arrived at the boat. We had stopped in Cadenabbia, just short of Tremezzo, and rented a skiff with an outboard motor. That way our arrival would attract less attention, and the Spedizione Internazionale van would not be parked at the dock, advertising our presence.

Bis and Ted were on the afterdeck fishing. There was no sign of underwater gear or activity.

"Too many boats buzzing about," Ted explained, "and boat people are notoriously nosey. There's been a surfboard sex-pot skiing by here, flashing her tail at us, for the past . . . here she comes now . . . note the praiseworthy boobs . . ."

A speedboat cut across our bow with a bikini blonde, long hair flying, in tow. Two boats were following her, presumably with binoculars.

"It's like this from dawn to dusk," Bis said, "fishing boats, water skiers, lake cruisers—so we've decided to operate only at night."

"We have undersea lights and it should work out all right," Ted said.

* * *

We started as soon as it was totally dark. Ted, expert at this, had drawn up a search-grid which, when followed, gave us a pattern that would methodically cover the area without repetition. We had two skin suits and two tanks, so that we could have two down, two resting on deck throughout the night. Despite my swimming deficiency, I was determined to participate, and convinced Ted to let me try since there would always be someone with me. He gave me tank and breathing instructions on deck; with considerable misgivings (not allayed by the rope line tied around my waist), he descended with me.

It was easy and natural and exhilarating; the weighted suit carried me down, the breathing apparatus was no problem, and maneuvering on the bottom, the fish flashing through the lights, it was all easy. In fact, after my second tour I had no doubts that I would now be able to swim without benefit of face mask and flippers.

We had covered a considerable area by dawn—an area that had to be inspected carefully because years of floor silt would certainly obscure the bags—but there was no sign of Kisnat's contribution to Como's deep.

We anchored a small buoy to mark our position, then moved a short distance up the coast so that our continued presence in one spot would not attract attention. Once anchored, we hauled up mattresses from below, where it was too warm for comfort, spread them out on the deck and in the well, and flopped asleep. Julietta and I slept on separate mattresses, but close together, in the well. Neither sun nor buzzing boats roused any of us until noon.

During the afternoon, while Ted and I fished from the stern and Bis read and Julietta alternately swam and sunned, I asked Ted what he had found out about Rambellini when he was in London.

"Not much, I can tell you! The judge has a security screen that beats Central Intelligence. Oh, little stuff, but not anything we're after. Triplex flat near the Connaught; very attractive mistress, young Swedish dish, two heads taller than His Honor; Jaguar with chauffeur; much partying; much race-track activity, has a stable but not entirely his, a syndicate involved but he's front man and members of the syndicate are shy fellows who are absolutely anonymous. Last year the judge's big score was the Lord Derby handicap at Epsom, which he took with a new 19–1 outsider, Leading Light. A couple of last-minute bets went down on her, the size of which just about capsized the totes. Great wad of money won there. Huge."

"It would be interesting, I should think, to find out who's in that syndicate."

"Which was exactly my thinking. Put a very good man on it, first-rate sleuth, experienced, tough, nose like a starved bloodhound, and we found him one morning in the back of a Chinese restaurant in Soho beat to a pulp."

"Dead?"

"No, but really chewed up."

"What was the story?"

"That's the sad part—no story. He tailed the judge and his blonde smorgasbord to a party being given in the upstairs room at the Six Friends restaurant in Soho, but somehow, after arriving in front of the restaurant and before making a move, he was wiped out."

"What did the restaurant say about his battered body being found there?"

"You ever try to interrogate Chinese cooks? I mean even getting the recipe for boiled rice out of them is hopeless. No, just blank stares and streams of Chinese and smiles, all the time smiles—let me tell you, the third degree was not invented for Chinese."

"So I guess the judge is now aware that there's interest in him?"

"Aware but seemingly not worried."

Later on, Bis and Julietta took over the fishing rods, which had yielded nothing but undersized chubs, and within an hour they had hooked, between them, two fat pike, several yellow perch, an eel the size of the Loch Ness monster, a half-dozen trout, two king-sized chubs and a pair of *agone,* which is a species of shad and the great delicacy of the Como deep.

Bis, a *chef accompli,* undertook a rather original bouillabaisse and I volunteered to assist him.

"Bis, tell me about that monastery."

"St. Zachary? Not much to tell. You know Italian monasteries—cold stones and hard beds."

"But what about Father Laekla? What if I told you that he wasn't a hit-run victim but had been run down intentionally?"

"You mean murdered? Oh, that's preposterous!"

"What if someone saw it?" I told him about the old lady.

"I don't understand—why didn't you tell us about that? How could you keep that from us?"

"Well, we were distracted by that accident we had—falling into the culvert—and then you left first thing the next morning. Besides, it didn't seem important except as gossip. Whether a priest is hit accidentally or on purpose —what does that have to do with us?" I had no intention of telling him about the note; if I did, considering Bis's jittery concern for his own hide, I ran the distinct possibility of a swift departure for Stockholm.

"It just *may* have something to do with us," Bis said, testily. "Who knows? When many pots boil on the same fire, they all contribute to the steam—Swedish proverb."

"Well, you see why I asked about the monastery—why would two men murder a monastery priest in the street? What does it mean, Bis?"

"It means the murdered priest—what did you call him, Laekla?—obviously had sinned against the tenets of the

order, which commands total noninvolvement with the outside world."

"Oh, now, Bis, what theological bullshit! 'Sinned against'
—good God!"

"All right, it means the corpse was probably trying to put
the nab on some wordly goods—how's that?"

"Better. But where did you pick up 'put the nab on'? We
may have to recall your Humphrey Bogart rosette."

"Trying to glom onto?"

"Attaboy! But what about Laekla—he worked with
Father Piccionastro, didn't he? Now what about *that* pious
phony?"

"I don't think he is—phony, I mean. He is a pushy church
type one finds everywhere, the huffer and heaver who makes
up for all his docile brethren who keep their eyes to the
heavens. After all, the Catholic church is one of the most
pugnacious organizations in the world—and it needs its
own canonical Mafia to keep it that way."

"Still and all, I would like to talk to Piccionastro about
Laekla."

"All right—do it first thing when we get back."

"Just ask him some questions."

"By all means. We'll invite him for dinner."

The aromatic harbingers of the bouillabaisse began to fill
the air.

"Praise be, what messengers of the gods seek my nostrils,
mischievously entice my stomach, and cause a river of
saliva to gush from my quivering mouth?" Ted had been
sitting on the bowsprit, reading, but now, for his declama-
tion, he had risen and balanced himself full stride on the
bowsprit shrouds, his arms akimbo.

"If this be promise of delights to come, then subscribe
me to your rolls, for I am fallen to your wafted spell and
verily will follow thee, sweet messengers, wherever you will
lead, to highest sky or darkest deep . . ."

Bis picked up a chub by the tail, and rising up from the galley, flung it at the rhapsodizing figurehead, catching him smack under the neck and somersaulting him backward into the deep, where he disappeared, the chub and his book remaining on the surface as buoys to mark where he had sounded.

Julietta had something to show me. She had been doodling on a pad throughout the afternoon, working on C, S, + : on her pad opposite C, she had "Communisti"; opposite S, she had "Stranieri" with a question mark.

"Foreigners," she said. "Why not? Luigi Hoffmann would be one of them. Perhaps there were others."

"Yes, yes, that seems right!" I asked Bis and Ted. They agreed it was possible but they did not share my enthusiasm.

"What's wrong with you guys? Now if we can decipher the plus sign, we'll know the entire disposition of the inventory."

"And then what?" Bis asked. "So we will know that Communists, foreigners and plus men got the treasure. What Communists? What foreigners?"

"I don't know but I have a feeling that when we crack the plus, we'll know something. And if Giorgio comes back from Lugano with the Bank Nationale bacon . . ."

"Don't count on it," Ted said. "There are only three sure things in life—taxes, death and the sanctity of the numbered account."

"Shouldn't he be back by now?" Bis asked. "Will he come straight away here?"

"He'll check to see if we're at the villa first—but he's not due back until tomorrow."

"How did he expect to go about it in Lugano? Does he have contacts?"

"Oh, you know Giorgio—he can make life-long friendships on a ten-minute bus ride."

"I thought he did have a con—" Julietta started to say, but caught my look. The promise to protect Giorgio's barman was absolute.

"What were you going to say, Julietta?"

"I was thinking of Carpignano, Giorgio's contacts there. I don't know anything about Lugano."

Julietta took the skiff and went into Tremezzo to get a few ingredients vital for Bis's bouillabaisse. I had wanted to go along but she had refused my offer because my ankle was still bothering me and I was needed at my post as second cook. Watching her move away from the sloop toward shore, I had a clutch of unreasonable panic: that she was not coming back. I realized how deeply I was involved with her; all right, say it—in love with her. Around her all the time, I was nonetheless filled with longing for her; for to be with her this much, to sleep with her at night and not make love to her—not *able* to make love to her—was as if we were being kept from each other by some heartless chaperone. But, then, my very inability was what attracted her to me; that is the irony: to have a woman attracted to me because I can't have a woman.

Bis read me, as my eyes followed her to shore. "So, agreed, she is a thing of beauty—do you intend to make her your joy forever?"

Ted groaned. "Good God, Bis, I hope that's not original."

"Well, original to a point—what you probably do not realize is that the poet John Keats . . ."

"Are you kidding? I went to school with Johnny Keats."

"All right, why *not* a joy forever, Paul? I'll give you a Swedish wedding with all trimmings—there is nothing like a formal Swedish wedding."

"And I'll give you a year's supply of the pill as a wedding gift," Ted added.

"Look, Paul," Bis said, "I know when you first left

prison you were terribly alone and without hope, but now it seems to me you might re-think what you're doing. It's true you've turned up some papers and letters, and we do have a few leads like these bags, but we also have a bit of ominous stirring. If Father Laekla was murdered, as you say, it is, in my opinion, cause for some alarm. It may very well be that Piccionastro got his information about these bags from Father Laekla and just said they were from a deathbed priest."

"But that's what we're after, Bis. Get the pot boiling and see what happens. Okay, it has finally come to a boil, and if we're patient . . ."

"But the more it boils, the greater the danger of its boiling over."

"You once said, in describing yourself," Ted said, "that when a man puts no value on his life, then he has nothing to lose, and with nothing to lose, that man has no fear. But now you do have some sense of value—I can tell—young Julietta, there's a value, for one. So *now* what about fear? We are in a dangerous area—we've always known that. But I can sense a change in you. I think you have developed a sense of value and with it, you have developed fear, just like ours, because now you have something to lose."

"Let me tell you how I feel about fear, Ted. When I was with the anti-submarine outfit, our base in North Africa was attacked and I was wounded and hospitalized. Had never been hospitalized or operated on before. Operation was scheduled for eight A.M. I was wheeled into the operating room and prepared, strapped onto the table, needles taped into my arms, all that sort of thing. Well, this was the time of the morning for my bowels; they operate like clockwork, and just then happened to be the moment on my movement clock. But it had taken forty-five minutes to get me ready, all those needles set with adhesive tape and all the rest, and I just didn't have the nerve to say undo everything while I take a shit—but at the same time I was scared to death that when I went under the anesthetic, I might, during the operation, let loose on the operating table. Well, all this consternation and fear showed up on whatever gauges they read, blood pressure or whatever, and the surgeon came over and began giving me a little lecture about how there was nothing to be afraid of, it was not a dangerous operation, blah blah blah, when all the time my fear was just shitting out of turn. That's how it is with fear, Bis. You read a situation and make a judgment but what reads for you doesn't necessarily scan the same for me."

Toward dusk it started to rain, not a storm, but the water got a bit choppy. Promptly at dark we moved the boat back to its search position and, sustained by the bouillabaisse and a lusty Valpolicella Julietta had found in town, we resumed our descents; two hours into the night, the search was over.

Bis and Ted surfaced ten minutes after their second descent had started, and Ted had the bags. They were much smaller than I had imagined—I had been expecting something the size of mail bags—and they were in infinitely better condition than we had anticipated. Bis thought that was attributable to the vast quantity of waterproof material stuffed into the bags and to the protective silt that had buried all but the very top of one of them.

We opened them on the cabin table and there it all was— gold bars, jewels, coins, and a variety of documents—but moisture had ruined the documents, which had been reduced to clumps of sodden washed-out paper fiber. It seemed incredible to me, having dreamed of it for so long, that here it was—heavy in my hand as only gold can be— some of the treasure I had promised myself I would find, not very much in comparison to the total, but surely a healthy six figures' worth; we all sat there around the cabin table and picked up the gold pieces and put them down, and held the unset jewels in front of the kerosene light. No one said anything because none of us had really in his practical heart expected to find this eyeless needle in this deep-sea haystack and, having found it, we were speechless.

"I must confess, Paul," Ted finally said, "that Bis and I had never expected . . . well, we had thought to humor you for a time, although honestly trying to locate the treasure—but then, having done our part, to ease you out of this. But now . . . can you really believe this, Bis?"

Bis simply shook his head.

"If indeed it was Laekla who knew about this," I said, "*and,* let us presume, about other things which he had also been keeping secret—no wonder they killed him."

"And tried to kill you," Julietta said.

Bis's head jerked up. "Killed who? Paul? What was that?"

Julietta looked stricken over having unbagged that cat. "Oh, I'm . . . oh, Paul!"

"It's okay, Julietta."

"*Now* what are you keeping from us?" Bis demanded.

I told them.

"I've had it! God damn but I have had it!" Bis was in a fury. He slammed both hands on the table as he pushed himself to his feet. "God knows what other little secrets you have! All these lies about how you got your ankle and Julietta's cuts and bruises—and supposedly we are your partners! Don't you realize an attempt on your life is a warning signal to us to keep a sharper eye on ours?"

"I'm truly sorry, Bis. You're right. I was just being selfish—trying not to scare you off."

"Well, you have lost me! But good! I didn't want into this crazy business to begin with and you have just now convinced me I was right. You can have my part of what has been found—divide it up any way you like. But leave me out of it! I do not want any of this deadly stuff! I am going

to get out of here and out of Zonico just as fast as I can."
He started to throw his belongings into a duffel. "I am going
back to the villa—I will take the van—and pack up and get
out of there pronto. And you, Ted, what about you? You
intend to wait around for your funeral?"

Not waiting for an answer, Bis turned toward me, his face
contorted and very close to mine. "You are crazy! Crazy!
That you got your hands on anything before they killed
you, as they have killed all the others who gave them
trouble, is a miracle. A bloody miracle! And with your
record, if you are found dead—or half-dead—do you think
anyone will care? And do you not think they know it?"

Now to Julietta, screaming at her: "Can you not talk
sense to him? You like him, do you not? Well, do you want
to walk behind his hearse to the cemetery? You were there
in the road when they tried to run him down—and still you
let him go on. Crazy! Both of you!"

He was finished packing. "What do you do, Ted?"

"I'll help return the boat tomorrow."

"And then?"

"I'll help wind up Zonico, if Paul agrees. Otherwise . . .
I'm sorry, Paul, but Bis is right. He's too emotional, but he's
right. This is no place for sane people who care about
living."

Bis said, "I am too emotional—but I know what I'm
saying." He slung his bag over his shoulder and climbed up
the stairs to the deck. A few moments later we heard the
outboard motor start, and Bis was gone.

Ted put the valuables back into their sacks, tied them
up, handed them to me, and with a barely audible "Good
night," went to the aft cabin.

Julietta and I sat at the table for a while, and then I went
up on deck. The rain had turned to mist. I stood at the
starboard rail with the lights of Tremezzo panoplied around
me and tried to evaluate what this defection would mean, or,

rather, whether I could continue without them. And perhaps without Julietta. Most assuredly without Julietta because certainly Bis was right in his assessment of the foolhardiness of continuing in the face of obvious and certain peril, and I must not let Julietta stay any longer.

Julietta came up beside me. She put her arm consolingly around my shoulders. I tried to think. My mind went back to the litany of years in that nightmare cell, the promises to myself, constant as drips from a washerless faucet, promises and promises of reparations: for the rats, for the sadistic guards, for the revulsive inmates, for the wretched food, for the loss of life, liberty and the pursuit of love . . . love, this arm around me and her face looking up at me in the thickening mist and oh, Christ, won't any of it work, not any of it? Why not? Why *not?* Why does it have to go on and on and on from prison to prison to prison.

I felt her arm tighten as she eased me away from the rail toward the hatch and then down the stairs out of the mist. We went to the forward cabin and I sat down on one of the bunks and put my head in my hands and again tried to force myself to think about what had happened and what my position was and whether it all had ended, as it seemed, or was there a way to go on?

Julietta took off my sandals and unbuttoned my shirt and eased my head down to the pillow. "Don't think about it, Paul. Not now. Tomorrow." It was warm in the cabin but a slight breeze made it bearable. The breeze carried some mist with it through the porthole and it felt good on my face. I slipped off my dungarees and rolled over on my stomach, crooking my arm into a cradle for my face, which felt hot.

Julietta came in from the head and turned off the cabin light and got into my bunk. She lay there quietly, only touching me with an inadvertent strand of her hair which had fallen across my shoulder. The boat rolled gently in the rain-teased water. The cabin was pitch dark but the running light on the spar outside the porthole threw a back-wash of light on the bunk.

Now that she lay next to me, there was only Julietta and nothing else. Whatever it was I had with her, it was all I had, and it transcended everything. For the first time I felt released; we *did* have something, and it generated its own power and, inexplicably, at this moment I felt no re-straint, no fear, of what was clearly ours. I turned toward her and she put her head on my shoulder and as the port-hole light caught her turning face, illuminating her beauty, I put my lips to hers and kissed her tenderly and then tenderly again and then unrestrainedly, holding back nothing, releasing my lips and tongue which were finally able to speak for me. I felt my body grow with that kiss and my whole groin come alive, breaking from its prison, run-ning free, and her body responded, at first reluctantly, straining against itself, but then released from *its* prison, flooding over its dammed restraint onto my body, our bodies fitting as dowled wood, my over-body now shutting out the light from her face, and she cried out with joy and so did I as I entered her and filled her and attached her to my body, creating the oneness I had felt but had not been able to express, now expressed, unfettered, intense, airborne, diving freefall, her lips pulling away from mine to breathe, I wanting desperately to tell her how it was, a whirr of passing moments to catch and hold but elusive sun moats bursting in my eyes, "Oh, God!" she whispered, "Oh God! Oh God! Oh God!" She rolled her lips onto mine, fully onto mine to mute in each other's mouths our simultaneous cries; then, just as we were, joined, arms around, deep in each other, we floated off somewhere.

And in this way we slept.

In the morning it was as it had been in the night but now I could see her face in the early light, see it as it responded

to me, and I was making love to her, making love, such unexpected joy after all the long years followed by the impotent hopelessness and despair, and then, miraculously,
making love, with her, making it all come to life, to con-
ceive and be conceived by it, yes, yes, exactly right; my head
and my heart so full to bursting I couldn't hold back when
the tears came, so I let them come. I, who never cried, let
them roll down my face, drip onto her, unashamedly, for I
knew she knew why I cried and, as if to tell me, she cried
too, holding me as tight as she could, sharing my tears, as
we had shared this night, everything else.

4

POINT OF RETURN

What of my dross thou findest there, be bold
To throw away; but yet preserve the gold.
What if my gold be wrapped up in ore?—
None throws away the apple for the core.

The Pilgrim's Progress

chapter twenty

Julietta and I returned to the villa in the early afternoon.
The van was in the garage, but there was no sign of the
maids and neither Bis nor Giorgio was in his room.
Giorgio's suitcase was there, so it was clear he had returned,
and Bis's was in his room, indicating that he had not yet
departed.

Calling out to them as we opened all the doors, I finally
found them in Dan's room. Giorgio was sprawled across
a small rug at the foot of the bed, dead, his head at a crazy,
broken angle. Bis, lying in the corner, his face battered,
was badly beaten but still alive. The place was a shambles—
whoever they were, they had not killed Giorgio easily. We
carried Bis into his room and put him on the bed. Julietta
tended him while I went back to examine Giorgio.

His neck was broken and there were contusions on his
face and throat. His hands were swollen and bloody—the
assailant or assailants would bear noticeable evidence of his
struggle. I picked him up and put him on the bed. He was
light in my arms and seemed smaller in death. I fixed his
head on the pillow in such a way that you could not tell his
neck was broken. One of his eyes was slightly open, but I
could not close it.

I straightened his shirt and his coat; he looked like he would wake up any minute. I went through his pockets but found nothing related to his Lugano trip. Nor had there been anything in his luggage about the bank account or any communication from the bartender in London.

You were my good friend, Giorgio, and I loved you and who will take your place? I thought we would get rich and enjoy life and what a fine time you would have had playing your wicked games with all that money. And what about Lia, your almost wife? What shall I do about her? What a shit-end of the stick you got. Well, I hope you have a good trip. I'm a son of a bitch for having put you in this. I'll miss you, Giorgio. You *will* be mourned—by me. I took his lucky piece out of my pocket—the Russian tobacco disc from the Palermo whore who had loved him—and put it in his shirt pocket. He had given me his good luck which he would need now, wherever he was headed. Julietta called to me. One last time I tried to close Giorgio's eye; then I went down the hall to her.

Bis had regained consciousness. He had a terrible headache and could barely talk. Giorgio, he said, had returned to the villa around noon; Bis had gone to his room to greet him. They had only exchanged a few words when they heard a noise down the hall. They went to investigate, and that took them into Dan's room. Bis entered first, and as he went through the door he was hit and stunned but able to fight. There seemed to be two men but that first blow had muddied his head and everything after that was hazy.

Could he describe the attacker?

Not really. So muddy. Just a blur of being slugged about the face and in the stomach . . . everything so fast . . . and so quickly all over . . . no real recall . . . struggle . . . landing a few punches . . . swinging wild . . . then brilliant explosions in both eyes and out.

What about Giorgio?

Don't know. Think he was also fighting but too over-whelmed with self-defense to pay attention to Giorgio.

I told Bis that Giorgio was dead and it hit him hard.

What about the maids? Were they in the house?

Yes, as far as Bis knew.

Had Giorgio told him anything about Lugano or given him anything?

No, no opportunity. Had barely said hello when they heard the noises down the hall.

Julietta located the maids. They were locked in the base-ment. They had been busy at the washtubs from ten o'clock on; when they tried to go back upstairs they had found, to their surprise, and then fear, that the door was locked. They had pounded and called for a long time but no one had responded. They had heard nothing, which was to be expected since Dan's room was on the third floor. They had not heard or seen any vehicle arrive or depart. No, they were not aware that Giorgio had returned. We did not tell the maids what had happened, and kept them busy in the kitchen, out of the way.

The problem was: Should we inform the authorities of Giorgio's death? A crime like this would undoubtedly bring police and detectives from the regional headquarters in Como, just as they had come when Arnoldo was murdered; with the regional police would come the kind of thorough investigation that certainly would unmask our whole opera-tion and, if it also revealed my true identity, would send me right back to Santo Stefano. My sentence was twenty years to life; I had been released at the end of twenty years on the condition that I would leave Italian soil. If I were identified, as I surely would be, I would be remanded immediately and forced to serve out the remainder of my life.

* * *

Bis stayed in his room until nightfall; one look at him, in his condition, would have elicited a thousand questions. He was in pain, especially the left side of his swollen face, and when Ted returned and looked at him he thought his cheekbone might have been fractured.

"I want you to know, Bis," I said, "that I am now convinced. I may be stubborn but I'm not *this* stubborn. Just as soon as we can close up shop, it's good-bye to Dongo. I blame myself for Giorgio's death. I was the one who insisted on fanning the fire, but Giorgio, poor Giorgio's the one who got burned."

"I don't mind the beating so much if it induces you to leave. I meant what I said—my share of the bags is yours."

"And so is mine," Ted added. "You can give the papers and letters you found to Gibio and that will be his payoff. Then you and Julietta can arrange about the contents of those bags as you see fit."

"If you want to go to work for me," Bis said, "my offer still stands."

"Thanks, but now I want to get back to the States."

Julietta came to the door. "Could I please talk to you, Paul?"

I walked downstairs with her. "I want to speak to your schoolteacher. I have something to ask her that might explain that inventory—if you would like to know about that before we leave."

"Yes, I certainly would. And on the way in, I want to stop at the boat supply store to get a spinnaker bag."

Elenora Campisi was in her classroom grading papers. Julietta put the inventory sheet in front of her.

"Signorina Campisi, what puzzles us is this plus mark. On the original inventory which you typed, these symbols were marked by hand, weren't they?"

"Yes."

"Then when you typed up the inventory, you typed the symbols as they appeared."

"That's right."

"Well, this plus—can you show me how it was written?"

"Like this—a plus." Elenora Campisi took her pencil and made a plus sign on the paper.

"Could it have been more like this?" Julietta asked. She made a plus, but raised the arm a trifle, so that it looked like this:

†

"Why, you're right! That's exactly how it was! How did you know?"

Julietta thanked the schoolteacher and we left. We went to the café and had a coffee. Julietta got out the inventory. "It breaks down very neatly: all entries indicating lire or Italian assets are marked C, Communists. All items of foreign currency went to S, foreigners. And all items that were less negotiable—jewels, manuscripts and documents, gold bullion—went to †, the church. But as Bis or somebody said, breaking the key really doesn't lead anywhere . . ."

"It may lead further than you know. It may explain Laekla and other pieces of the puzzle that didn't fit. It was obvious that since none of the jewels and the like had ever appeared on the market, they were being held by someone who was in no hurry to sell them—the church. Why didn't I think of the church? Now to find out . . ."

"Paul, you're not going to keep after this—you're not, are you?"

"I just want to *know* something, that's all. I've *got* to know something. I'll just need a day. Not even that. Maybe just a few hours tonight." Her eyes were troubled and she was holding her thumbs in her fists. "But, darling," I said, "if it worries you, I won't."

"It troubles me because you sound like the skiier at the end of a long day who says just one time more down the course and that's the run he breaks his leg. Oh, Paul, can't we just stop? We have found this lovely thing together, can't we just have that, won't you settle for that? You have the Kisnat treasure all to yourself, and the gold which Elenora Campisi gave you, why not settle for that?"

"And you?" I put my hand on hers and her thumb emerged from her fist like the head of a turtle.

"You mean what do I have?"

"No, I mean, do I have *that* gold?"

She looked down at my hand. "The way you touch me I have never been touched. It is as if I am connected to something more direct than your fingers."

"I love you, Julietta. What could be more direct than that?" Her hand sensuously folded around mine and I marveled at the easy, strong response I felt to it. "Let's go back and have a siesta," I said.

"Let's."

"Would you do something silly for me?" I asked Julietta.

"I just have."

"Even sillier. Would you play dead? Just roll over and play dead."

"Oh, you think of the nicest games. Ka-ploom! I'm dead!" She flopped onto her back and let her arms dangle.

"Now, Julietta, be serious. I want you to be seriously dead. Dead all over. You have just died—the blood has stopped running, your heart has stopped beating, you are limp and lifeless. That's it. A vegetable, ready for the soil. Okay, now stay that way. Absolutely dead. I'm going to pick you up but you stay dead. No tensing up. That's it. Fine. What a talented corpse you are!"

I put her back on the bed. Immediately she sprang at me and demonstrated her reincarnation by twining herself around me, pulling my hair and covering my face with resounding kisses. "Now," she said, finally subsided and looking down at me with her elbows on my chest, her hands under her chin, "what was that all about?"

"An experiment in criminology."

"Ah, Perry Mason, and what have you deduced?"

"Now, Della, you know I never discuss details until I'm sure of my man. How would you like to take a little drive tonight?"

"Where?"

"Switzerland. I have a sudden hankering for a cup of hot chocolate."

We fell asleep and I dreamed we were lost, looking for each other in the stacks of my law school library, but endless cascades of Corpus Juris kept falling from the shelves, blocking my way. I woke abruptly and put my arms around her and rolled us over.

"Would you please spend the rest of your life being my wife?"

She rubbed her feet along the back of my calves and batted her sleepy eyes at me. "It's not fair to propose while making love to me. A girl is supposed to be clear-headed and realistic when entertaining marriage."

"Are you stalling?"

"Do you think this is proper? I thought it was supposed to be on one knee with a bouquet of flowers in your hand."

"All right. It sounds a little awkward, but let's try it that way." I withdrew.

"No—oh, come back in me!"

"But we must observe the proprieties . . ."

She reached down and put me back and fitted her body into mine and buried her face against my neck and wet my skin with her lips.

"Yes, marry me, Paul, marry me, oh, yes, marry me, marry me." She said it over and over.

At twilight Bis said good-bye and got into the Volkswagen; Ted was to drive him to Milan where he would board the night plane for Stockholm. In the back of the Volks, in addition to Bis's luggage, there was the large canvas sail bag I had purchased in Dongo, with Giorgio in it.

I waited twenty minutes, then backed the van out of the garage, and Julietta and I drove to Lugano, Switzerland, which is less than an hour south of Zonico.

This was the last inquiry we would make before leaving Zonico. I had promised her that.

"But why Lugano, Paul?"

"Because Giorgio returned here with certain information which caused his death. I would like to know what that was."

"And what will you do if you find out what Giorgio knew?"

"I don't know. Knowledge precedes action. First to know, then to do, or not to do—that is the question."

"But this is the end of it, Paul. You have promised, haven't you? But what if you find out some things that make you want to do? Will you then be a man of your word? *That,* darling, is the real question."

The Bar l'Orange was staid traditional—none of that chrome and neon and beer signs bubbling—but quiet and dim with English club-room tables and chairs, hunting prints on the wall and a padded leather arm rest along the edge of the bar.

When I told the barman, after the drinks had been served and we had broken the conversational ice, that I was a friend of Giorgio's, his face washed out and there was an overt shift in how he looked at me.

"I'm Paul Selwyn. Giorgio and I attended the same college together—Santo Stefano." There were three other people at the bar, but at the other end, and I was speaking softly.

"I told Giorgio that whatever was between us was between *us*," the barman said.

"I know. He told me—but I was in on it."

"Well, that's how it is." He left to check on the needs of his other clients.

I pushed my empty glass forward, forcing him to return. As he put the fresh drink in front of me, I said, "Giorgio was murdered this afternoon. I want to find out what he learned from you." He gave me a hard, shut-off look. "You'll get the same protection from me that you got from Giorgio," I said.

"I'll bet—he told *you*, didn't he?"

"Look, you gave him a piece of paper—correct?"

"Yes."

"That's all I want—give me a duplicate."

"No way. I should have never given him that one. Who's got it? You know?"

"Whoever killed him."

"But you don't know?"

"No."

"That's great—and it's in my handwriting."

He started to walk away—I put my hand on his arm. "Would you answer a question?" He hesitated. "Did you give him the names of the depositors who opened numbered accounts in 1945 right after the one opened in my name?"

"Yes. You were MLZ-674. Giorgio wanted 675 and 676. But I told you . . ."

"I know—you refuse to write down the names for me.

But would you do this?" I took a piece of paper from my pocket and wrote a name on it. "If I write the names, will you just check them out?" I showed him the name I had written on the paper.

He hesitated, undoubtedly debating the advisability of even this much cooperation. "Yes, that was 675."

"And this?"

"No."

My hand felt unsteady as I wrote down the third name. "And this?"

A newly arrived customer called to the barman; after serving him, he slowly returned. He picked up my piece of paper and looked at the third name, then put it back down on its face. "Yes, that was 676—you sure you didn't see Giorgio's list?"

I picked up the paper and put it in my pocket.

"If Giorgio's been tagged, there will be police . . ."

"There won't be police."

"If there are, they better not show up here . . ."

"I told you there won't be police." I paid the bill, adding a sizable amount as a tip. "I appreciate your help. You have nothing to worry about."

The barman put his hand on the money, but did not pick it up. I helped Julietta off her stool and we left.

In the car, on our way back to Zonico, I handed her the slip of paper. The three names on my list were:

Luigi Hoffmann
Ted Middlekey
Bis de Jong.

The barman had answered "yes" to one and three.

chapter twenty-one

It was not so much a process of deductive reasoning as it was deductive disturbances. My insight into the black interior of what had really happened was myopic; but truth, I found, comes not in big vessels but in little slips.

To start with the latest deductive disturbance: that afternoon I had lifted two bodies—I had picked up the unconscious Bis by his shoulders, Julietta had his feet, and we had carried him to his room. Shortly afterward I had put Giorgio on his bed. I didn't realize what it was that disturbed me at that moment, but later, when I was talking to Bis about what had happened, it struck me how different the two men had felt when I had lifted them. That's why I had conducted the experiment with Julietta. Despite his apparent flaccidity, Bis's body had a tenseness—as we carried him through the door, his shoulder had brushed the door jamb and his instinctive tensing belied his unconsciousness. Lifting Julietta substantiated that.

Another disturbance was that the alleged assailants, who had, according to Bis, used their fists, apparently had come on their mission without guns, knives or other weapons. Highly unlikely. Also, why would they be in *Dan's* room, of all places? If they were seeking the Lugano bank information which Giorgio had—and that's what they must have been after because I found nothing on his person or in his luggage—wasn't Dan's room a strange place to look for it?

Why *were* they in Dan's room? Giorgio knew that I was in Tremezzo with Ted and Bis, so Dan was the only person at the villa whom Giorgio could confide in about the startling discovery he had made in Lugano that Bis de Jong opened a numbered account at the same time that mine had been opened. Giorgio did not know Bis was in the villa—and it occurred to me that Bis had put on his leave-in-a-huff act on the boat so that he could intercept Giorgio at the villa and determine if he had indeed been able to get the numbered accounts identified. When he heard Giorgio coming into the house, Bis must have stayed out of sight, locked the maids in the basement, and then stalked Giorgio to Dan's room.

But some of my suspicions considerably predated the Giorgio incidents. The Mera River box was the beginning— I could never bring myself fully to believe that the box, which Bis had failed to mention and which Dan and I had discovered by accident, had been empty when Bis stumbled on it.

I had also been disturbed by the manner in which that car had managed just barely to miss me in the road. Anyone behind the wheel who had really *wanted* to kill me, could have done so easily. No—that car had swerved just enough. Whoever it was wanted to get rid of me, but not as a corpse.

I had been telling all this to Julietta on our way back from Lugano. When we arrived in Dongo I drove to the post office, hoping that a letter from Giorgio's bookmaker would be in our box. As I fitted my key into the lock, I could see a packet of letters through the glass. There were bills, a letter from the manager of Gibio's office, and an air-mail from London:

Dear Giorgio,

   I would rather get you a sure-shot in the Irish than crack a mother-humper like this. The Jock Club guards syndicates like you guard your pecker in a fag sauna. But pussiverence, me lad, is my middle name, so here are the lucky gents who own the secret pieces of Rambellini's Leading Light . . .

Four names were listed, three of whom were unknown to me; the fourth was Ted Middlekey.

"Oh, God, Paul—not both of them! Did you suspect Ted?"

"Not really. But when things began to heat up—when we brought back the manuscripts and what all from Carpignano —if Ted were really broke and in on this he would have come alive."

"But they did assemble the Kisnat lake mission, and they did find the treasure bags, didn't they?"

"I wonder."

"What do you mean? What a silly thing to say. You wonder what?"

"If they did find that treasure."

"Oh, Paul, love—you are losing your mind."

"You saw the size of those bags—that was another thing that bothered me. Are we really to believe that after twenty years, with that enormous area to search, and the bottom as soft as it is—they could ferret out those two little bags?"

"But, Paul, how else?" Her brow creased and she squinted her eyes and tilted her head. "You think they were planted? Is that it? Oh, Paul, you saw how they looked."

"It's easy to age metal."

"But where did they get that stuff? You think it wasn't part of the treasure?"

"Oh, it was part of the treasure, all right."

"Then where—?"

"That's what we're going to find out. When you remarked that once you decoded the plus symbol on the inventory you might unlock a great deal more, you were certainly right. I think the cross of the church will indeed unlock most of this; how often the church has come up: Father Laekla's confession in London and his murder in Dongo; the papers secreted in the deserted church; the curious Father Piccionastro; the tip on the Kisnat treasure coming from St. Zachary via Piccionastro; the fact that Bis and Ted are both staunch Catholics and Bis a Papal Knight; that your Uncle Pietro was once a St. Zachary novitiate; and, as we have said, who is in better position than the church to hold valuables for a long period of time without exposing them to the market?"

"You say we're going to find out . . ."

"Yes, from Ted."

"What makes you think he will come back?"

"It doesn't matter too much. Zonico or London—what he has to say will sound the same."

Ted came back the following evening.

"Did Bis get away all right?"

"Yes. We had a few drinks at the airport and that eased him a bit."

"And Giorgio?"

"I arranged for him nicely—a cemetery just outside Milan."

We made ourselves drinks in the library and Julietta came down to join us.

"I have a suggestion," Ted said. "I think we should pack up and leave tonight. Wake up the maids and go."

"And the digs?"

"Leave them—just as they are. Who would ever trace us?

Why would they? They'd have all our tools and supplies. In the light of the attempt to kill you and Julietta, and now this attack on Giorgio and Bis, who knows what they'll try next—or when."

"I think you're right," I said. "Who do you think they are, the killers?"

"No idea. Not a clue. Have you?"

"Not who the killers are. But I have a pretty good line on the men who could tell us."

"You do? Who are they?"

"Two men, to be exact. These two." First I handed him a slip with the names of the numbered accounts, and then, after he had looked at it, I placed on top of that slip the letter from Giorgio's bookmaker.

"I would like to hear the story, Ted. The whole story. Don't leave out anything, and don't invent anything." He looked up at me, his face bewildered, and he started to say something, but I cut him off. "And don't go through a dumb act. You can skip that. Just level with me, Ted. I want to hear it, and I want to hear it all."

He again inspected the two slips of paper, started to hand them back to me but put them on a table in front of me instead. He looked at Julietta, not at me, as if she could rescue him. He sucked in some breath, let it out, and with his hands clasped tightly, began to talk:

For you to understand everything that happened—and why— you have to know about Luigi Hoffmann.

Luigi Hoffmann—Luigi, an Italian mother, Hoffmann, a German father. He was born in Munich but raised in Geneva, where he became a very sharp financier, banker and investment genius. In 1936, he was thirty-two years old and was in Rome when Mussolini made his famous speech from the balcony of the Palazzo Venezia, extolling his victory in Abyssinia. Hoffmann was among the four hundred thousand thronged in the piazza, and he became caught up in their wild adulatory reaction, the ceaseless and hypnotic "Duce! Duce! Duce!," the mass hysteria that gripped that crowd gripped Hoffmann.

Hoffmann had always been a mystic, an intellectual mystic, one who was a Catholic and a Theosophist and somehow found a way to blend the two beliefs into a fervid religiosity. And arising out of it, not superimposed on it, was his candent adoration of Mussolini. Partly attributable to the fact that he was homosexual, no doubt, the way homosexuals, both declared and undeclared, become identified with matadors; during the days of Dominguín and Ordóñez, when I used to follow the bulls and got to know those two brothers-in-law and sometimes went to their rooms before or after a fight, I was always amazed at the number of men of class and position who simply sat around the matadors' rooms while they dressed or undressed, or clustered around them in the hotel lobbies and sent them expensive gifts and secretly or openly admired them. Well, that was undoubtedly a part of Hoffmann's Mussolini obsession. Mussolini's strutting, black-shirted, superman braggadocio would certainly have been a keen object of a homosexual's affections. In Hoffmann's case it was fantasy affection. Whatever the osmotic process, that was compensation enough.

Through his banking connections, Hoffmann became acquainted with the Duce and in many ways had more access to him, and more effect on him, than Mussolini's own ministers. It was Hoffmann who first planted in Mussolini's mind the concept of an entente with Hitler, stirring Mussolini's bombastic imagination with the word "axis." It took a lot of doing, for Mussolini disliked and distrusted Hitler and referred to Mein Kampf *as "that boring book that I have never been able to read."*

Hoffmann became a regular member of Mussolini's ex officio court, but had the good sense to keep well in the official background so as not to arouse the animosities of Mussolini's ministers and other functionaries.

But in 1943, when Mussolini's regime collapsed and he was

arrested and imprisoned on the island of Maddalena, it was Hoffmann who went to Munich and worked tirelessly on Mussolini's behalf, trying, through his German connections, to induce Hitler to liberate his axis partner. Hoffmann finally succeeded, and when Mussolini was restored to power as president of the newly formed Saló Republic, Hoffmann's influence and position with the Duce became even greater.

But the Saló Republic didn't last very long. The Allies drove on Milan; General Wolff, the German commander of Nazi forces in Italy, surrendered; and Mussolini was put in a state of panic and flight. There was only one reasonable place to go—Switzerland, and there were two possible cities: Lugano, which was very near, and Lausanne, which was much further north. Mussolini sent his son, Vittorio, to Lugano, and Hoffmann to Lausanne, each to try to determine what kind of reception the Duce would get on entry, and how he would be dealt with. Besides funds for arrangements, Hoffmann bore a letter that Mussolini had received from Hitler that verified the fact that Mussolini had successfully urged Hitler not to invade Switzerland—in this role, as Swiss saviour, Mussolini hoped that Hoffmann could convince the Swiss government to protect him.

This mission to Switzerland explains why Hoffmann was not present during the flight along Lake Como, why he was not in Dongo at the capture and execution, and why he did not have a hand in the assembling of the treasure loot.

By the time Hoffmann received word in Lausanne of the Dongo debacle, and arrived on the Dongo scene, Mussolini was dead and the treasure had disappeared. But Hoffmann was not to be denied. He had resources and a small but loyal and fiercely dedicated group of men who had been around him for years, sustained by his affluence and by the bond of homosexuality. They were a cruel, unscrupulous pack, blindly obedient to Hoffmann; in fact, their attitude toward him was not too unlike his attitude toward Mussolini—really a chain of worshipful command.

Hoffmann's men returned to Dongo to ascertain the whereabouts of the treasure which had not yet been disbursed, and there were two groups for Hoffmann to play off against each other—both the groups were partisans who had fought all through the war as one unit, but had now split asunder, one group Communist, the other group anti-Communist and loyal to the postwar government. Hoffmann assessed their relative strengths, found the Communist partisans stronger, and made a deal with them to join forces in collecting the diffused treasure from the various banks, officials and individuals who were holding it. The partisans would get all negotiable treasure. Hoffmann would get foreign and non-negotiable treasure. In exchange for this split, his group would guarantee safe passage of the Communists' share to their headquarters in Rome—that meant liquidating the anti-Communist partisans who stood in the way.

To effectuate his operation, Hoffmann needed a Dongo base and St. Zachary was made to order. Hoffmann knew that Piccionastro was a man who aspired to a better life for himself and his monastery, and when he suggested that in exchange for sanctuary he would donate his share of the treasure, Piccionastro eagerly consented. Hoffmann and his followers were given accommodations inside the monastery's walls and it proved a totally effective cover against the loyal anti-Communist partisans who incessantly hunted Hoffmann and his henchmen.

Hoffmann also obtained Pietro Disio from Piccionastro. He needed a plant inside the loyal partisan ranks and Piccionastro brought Hoffmann and Pietro together. Pietro, as you know, had been a novitiate at Zachary before joining the partisan underground. He was in no way homosexually oriented but he was bitter and disillusioned over the solidarity of the partisans being shattered by their cupidity, and he became even more embittered, later on, when his brother-in-law, Arnoldo, appeared as a member of an Allied team that was, as far as Pietro knew, hell-bent on grabbing this Italian treasure for their own foreign governments. So when Hoffmann suggested that Pietro was as entitled to a cut of the treasure pie as anyone else, and adroitly fanned Pietro's smoldering bitterness, Pietro threw in with him.

Through Pietro, then, Hoffmann discovered which loyal partisan leaders were hostile to the Communists' treasure grab and were trying to transport the collected treasure back to the government treasury in Milan. Hoffmann's men quickly disposed of these loyalists. Captain Neri "disappeared." His mistress, Gianna, who had been in charge of the inventory, was anonymously warned not to look for her missing lover; but she did, and her body was later found washed up on the Como shore. Gianna's girl friend, seeking Gianna's whereabouts, was beaten to death by the Hoffmann pack and her body was similarly pitched into Lake Como. Gianna's brother, Cesare, also went to look for her but he was luckier than Anna—a machine gun ambush missed him and he escaped with his life, but he fearfully gave up his search for his sister. When the loyal partisan Lino divulged certain facts about Mussolini's execution and the treasure inventory, Lino was found dead a few days later in what police called mysterious circumstances. His friend Sandrino also disappeared, as did the loyalists Pedro and Moretti, who were involved in transporting some of the treasure lode.

The net effect that Hoffmann achieved with these murders and disappearances was to impose a silence of fear on the people of Zonico and Dongo, and on many anti-Communist partisans who had exhausted their appetites for heroism.

The treasure was methodically collected from its various dispersal points and some of it—the jewels—very cleverly transported back to Dongo in the carcasses of black-market meat. The butcher Guisti received all the carcasses and then put those earmarked for St. Zachary in his cart and trundled them up the mountain to the monastery, going along with the secrecy and subterfuge because he thought St. Zachary was fearful that it would be revealed that they were using black-market meat, and not at all suspecting that the carcasses contained treasure. From Hoffmann's point of view, the carcass maneuver was necessary because anti-Communist partisans were on sharp lookout for Hoffmann and for any sign of the vast quantities of treasure that had disappeared.

The inventory sheets, as finally marked by Hoffmann and the Communist leaders, apportioned the treasure: C went to the communists, the cross indicated what went to St. Zachary (Piccionastro's price for his aid and abet), and S, the stranieri, the foreigners, indicated the take for Hoffmann and his group. Hoffmann was sure he was free and clear but our Allied investigative group suddenly appeared on the scene, and there was an entire new set of threats to combat.

Your discovery of his well-hidden cache in his Como villa enraged him, and Bis and I were making him very apprehensive with our activities in Dongo. He had to deal with us in some way other than the murders that had eliminated previous threats.

What he did was to make contact with Bis, in the course of which he probed for Bis's soft spots and found them. Bis had lost everything in the war—his family, his home, the family business, his money and his possessions. That he was a stripped and penniless man is what Hoffmann went to work on. Before the war had officially ended, Bis was disillusioned and embittered to see the same Fascist power men being restored in Holland. The same big industrialists, and so many of the evil political leaders who had collaborated were finding their way back to postwar power. Hoffmann recognized this truculent strain in Bis, and very cleverly exploited it, convincing Bis that the very treasure he was seeking, risking his life in the process, would undoubtedly wind up sustaining the power grabs of old-line Fascists who would resume command with new paint on their faces. Eventually Hoffmann's reasoning that Bis deserved to be repaid for the loss of all his loved ones, and all the things he loved, prevailed. Hoffmann gave Bis certain negotiable assets and arranged for the funds to be deposited in a numbered account in Switzerland.

As for me, my cupidity has never needed much teasing. As a Scotland Yard worthy I confess that I had many times fallen from grace—short, noiseless falls. When Hoffmann appeared, I was filled with the long privations of the war, apprehensive about the future—I had no intention of returning to Scotland Yard, but had no resources to pursue anything else. So it didn't take much for Bis and Hoffmann to convince me to take part in their "arrangement," which seemed pretty foolproof and which, Hoffmann convinced me, could harm no one.

But complications arose when Lefevre sensed that something irregular was going on and confronted Bis, who of course denied Lefevre's accusations, but not convincingly. Fortunately for Bis, Lefevre had also had a long war and he did not want to pursue his suspicions. But he was vituperative toward us and effectively sprung himself from us by feigning an attack of jaundice, which was already on his medical record, and getting himself returned to France. But you can see now why he was so belligerent toward you when you went to see him in Paris.

Another complication was that Hoffmann wanted to recover the treasure which you had found in his villa, and which now was hidden in your Como house. To that end, Hoffmann sent that note asking for the rendezvous at Leonardo's. While you were out of the villa, his men were to remove the treasure and plant the implicatory bank number in your book. Bis and I knew nothing about that part of the operation—implicating you —we thought Hoffmann simply was going to remove the treasure from the villa. Of course, if we had known how he planned to frame you, we would have opposed it. It was necessary to implicate you, Hoffmann later explained, because Allied headquarters in Milan already knew about this recovered treasure and this would connect you with its disappearance and simultaneously achieve Hoffmann's other goal, which was to create a disturbance that would cause our investigation to be terminated, and our team to be disbanded. In the event that both of

you did not go to Leonardo's, Hoffmann had arranged for who-
ever stayed to be drugged. But in his scheme of things, Hoff-
mann had not intended that any killing occur. I'm sure of that.

But Enrico, who was just an assistant to us in Dongo but a
very shrewd one, got wind of what was happening, was out-
raged by it, and tried to get to Leonardo's to warn Arnoldo
before Hoffmann and Bis arrived. He was able to tell Arnoldo
just enough before Hoffmann and Bis got there to make him
aware of Bis's complicity. Hoffmann now had to deal with
Arnoldo straight on, something he had not wanted to do. He
took Arnoldo to a rather remote meeting place and tried to
induce him to make a deal similar to the one he had made with
Bis and me; not only would Arnoldo have none of it, but he
also attacked Hoffmann and in the fight that ensued, Arnoldo
was killed by one of Hoffmann's men. Enrico was cold-bloodedly
executed, and his body buried in Hoffmann's favorite cemetery,
Lake Como.

Arnoldo's body created more of a problem, for his disap-
pearance or the discovery of his murdered body would bring a
military investigation into the area—just what Hoffmann didn't
want. So he decided to broaden your crime, Paul, from em-
bezzlement to murder. Bis, who had been forced to stand by
horrified and helpless during the killings, tried to argue Hoff-
mann out of it but Bis's involvement had left him powerless.

I didn't want to hear more, the son of a bitch, but there
were still questions to be answered.

"How did Hoffmann steal the treasure from the organ-
machinery hiding place in our villa and in the course of the
theft, plant evidence of a numbered account in my address
book—how could he possibly have had the number of an
account at the very time he was stealing the money for
that account?"

"Another example of Hoffmann's cunning—he knew that
thirty-three million lire was the amount you had in your
hiding place. So several days before he cleaned you out—at

the same time he opened accounts for himself and for Bis— he used his own thirty-three million to open a numbered account for you."

"Why did you and Bis let him incriminate me for the murder? Didn't it matter to you that I would be put away for life?"

"Yes, of course—it mattered terribly. And we did try to turn it around, but Hoffmann had us by the short hair and knew it—what could we do? One peep out of us and we'd either be wiped out by Hoffmann's barracudas for getting out of line or jugged by our own people for our crimes. What could we do? Hoffmann had let us know that we were to cut off the investigation and get the hell out—and that the first step we made toward interfering with the frame he had on you, would be our last step."

"I suppose everyone got some kind of payoff—is that how Julietta's Uncle Pietro wound up a pre-fab tycoon?"

"Yes. Hoffmann had important connections in Dusseldorf —Nazi pals who had successfully sung Germany's postwar hit tunes: 'I Only Took Orders,' and 'I Didn't Know That Anything Wrong Was Going On.' By sending Pietro to Germany, Hoffmann paid him off and got him out of the area."

"What about Father Laekla? Where did he fit in?"

"Well, how he first became involved was when he was with the Dongo church; the man who was then mayor came to confess and told Laekla, who happened to be receiving confession that day, that he was disturbed over information he had received that St. Zachary was being used as a shield for certain nefarious operations that were surely at variance with the religious nature of the monastery. Alarmed at what such a public revelation would do to the area's churchdom, Laekla went to see Father Piccionastro and revealed what the mayor had told him. Naturally, Piccionastro told Hoffmann, and shortly after that the mayor mysteriously disappeared—it was for him that the name of Via Squassoni was changed. Father Laekla was transferred to St. Zachary to become Piccionastro's administrative assistant."

"It was Laekla who went to see Rachele Mussolini with the documents, wasn't it?"

"Yes—I suppose Laekla was deeply troubled by the complicity he had been forced into. The silence of fear worked only to a point with him, and every once in a while his conscience rebelled with no regard for the consequences. You guessed right about Signora Mussolini having refused the documents, and that Laekla had secreted them in the deserted church."

"Where did he get them?"

"From some parishioner who had confiscated them but then became fearful about keeping them. No one knew that Laekla had them until his confession to the priest in London."

"Why was he sent to London—to see you and Rambellini?"

"Yes. He was Hoffmann's courier. He traveled extensively in that capacity. Hoffmann depended on Piccionastro and Laekla—they were his eyes, ears and nose."

"Why did Hoffmann need eyes, ears and nose—with his super-capabilities?"

"Because once he established himself behind the walls of St. Zachary, he never left there. Not to this day."

"Hoffmann is still there? Now?"

"Very much so."

"What!"

"Yes, he has been as committed to the walls of St. Zachary as you were to Santo Stefano. Only the style of commitment was different."

"Is he a member of the Order?" Julietta asked.

Ted smiled indulgently. "I'm afraid I haven't properly conveyed the pomp and grandeur that is Hoffmann. No— he hasn't joined the Order. To go back: once he got his hands on the treasure, Hoffmann divided it into two parts; that which he wanted to keep—jewels, documents, medals and the like—and that which he wanted to convert—gold, silver currencies, and so forth. That's where Benno Barbelli and his little business came into it. You were correct in your supposition that the Barbelli ore and cement complex was financed by treasure proceeds. But Barbelli was just a mild little man who asked no questions, did as he was told. The Barbelli industry with its thirteen hundred employees is totally Hoffmann's operation; he runs it by remote control —but make no mistake—he runs it."

"Where do the profits go? He must earn a prodigious amount . . ."

"Oh, he does, he does. Once he was set up and had murdered off the 'interferers,' over the years Hoffmann had only two threatening situations to contend with. The first was the Padua trial, and he solved that, as was obvious, by buying off Judge Rambellini with a little Barbelli profits and exiling His Honor into my care in London. Once I discovered that the judge had been deprived of the carnal pleasures of life and had an insatiable appetite for same, my job was easy."

"What about that story you told me—hiring a detective to track the judge and how the poor detective got his brains beat out in that Chinese restaurant? You made the details so damn convincing . . ."

"That's because it really happened—but not quite as I told it. The dective whom I described was really a secret service man who had been dispatched to London by the Italian government a few years back in order to investigate the judge whose abrupt resignation, departure and reputed high-style of living had reached the attention of officials in Rome."

"And it was the Italian detective who got the Chinese treatment you described?"

"Precisely."

"Under your direction?"

"Hoffmann had ordered me to discourage him."

"And after that the Italian government just gave up? With the sacrifice of only one detective?"

"The condition of the fellow when he returned to Italy made it difficult to find any more volunteers. Besides, Hoffmann's purse bought a few additional favors in the interim."

"What was the other threat? You said there were two."

"You. Bis and I had not told Hoffmann that we were working on your release, but his radar network of informers is so sensitive it picked you up the minute your *vaporetto* came into the Naples harbor. Hoffmann's immediate order was to kill you—but Bis and I let him know, no matter what the price, that if you were found murdered, or disappeared mysteriously, we would blow the whistle on him and his entire operation. He knew we meant it. And he knew it was no good to kill us because in the event of our deaths, we had set up machinery that would go into motion and reveal him just as surely as if we were alive. So he was forced to go along with our plan, which was to dissuade you from your treasure project—by noncooperation, by scaring you off, by delaying you, by setting you up in business in America— by any means we could think of. When it became apparent that nothing would dissuade you and you were determined to go it alone if we didn't cooperate, then we had to switch horses and ride with you because we had promised Hoffmann to keep you under close surveillance. We thought that if we could create an atmosphere of peril, and if you came to realize how real the dangers were, and if we could provide you with some treasure, then you might be induced to leave."

"That's why you set up the fakery at Tremezzo and gave me your share of the planted 'find'?"

"Yes."

"If part of your scheme was to let me collect enough

treasure to induce me to leave, then what about that box you found on the banks of the Mera? It certainly wasn't empty, was it?"

"No—but that was not a planted box. That was the one real surprise we got—stumbling on that crate. If it had contained gold or currencies we would have revealed it and given you its contents but it contained something that Hoffmann wanted very badly, and had searched for for a long time—the gold eagle which had once hung above the Duce's desk in the Sala del Mappamondo at Palazzo Venezia, and later in the prefecture in Milan."

"Why did Hoffmann want that?"

"The eagle was the symbol of Mussolini's regime. Hoffmann needed to add it to his collection. Look, I don't know too much about Hoffmann at St. Zachary—I haven't seen him since 1945—but I know that behind the monastery, he has scalloped out of the mountain a cavernous interior where he and his Black Shirts exist. One of the functions of the Black Shirts is to keep constant surveillance on the friars."

"You mean the St. Zacharians are prisoners?"

"Virtually. As far as I can tell, they have only one function that relates to Hoffmann's world. Every midnight—for twenty years every midnight—they participate in an elaborate mass. I had a late meeting with Piccionastro one evening, and at midnight, before I left, I saw the monks assembling for the mass. At that time Piccionastro told me it was a nightly event that took place in the Hoffmann compound. He also told me that Hoffmann had collected the bodies of Mussolini and Claretta Petacci and all the Fascist ministers, and that the mass related to them. But that's all he would tell me."

"But there must be some purpose to Hoffmann's operation. Is it that when he feels the country is ready, Hoffmann will emerge as Duce II?"

"No, I don't think that's it. I told you Hoffmann was a fanatic—a brilliant one. But my guess is that a fanatic like Hoffmann doesn't have any clear purpose beyond indulging his own fanaticism. It's true that he and his men wear the uniforms of the Black Shirt elite, but only as protectors of whatever it is Hoffmann has created inside that mountain— and not with any thought of projecting themselves into the outside world."

"But how was Hoffmann able to collect all those bodies?" Julietta asked.

"It wasn't too difficult. After the Dongo executions, the fifteen bodies of the men who had been shot in the piazza, were loaded in a lorry, which stopped in Azzano to pick up the corpses of Mussolini and Claretta. All these bodies were taken to Milan and dumped in front of a gasoline station in the Piazzale Loreto. Eventually they were strung up by the heels so that everyone in the vast crowd which gathered could see them. Proof to all that they were indeed dead. Bodies of other executed Fascist leaders were brought to the Piazzale Loreto and added to the collection.

"Eventually these corpses—twenty-three in all—were carted to the Musocco cemetery, but in plain coffins and buried in one long grave. Mussolini's coffin was buried beside Claretta Petacci's. The ground was leveled off and unmarked except for a stake with the number sixteen on it, driven into the soil above Mussolini's coffin. After the burial, for months there was a steady stream of visitors to the grave —partisans, anti-Fascists, former political prisoners, all of whom came to the grave to express their contempt for Mussolini by covering the gravesite with urine and shit.

"Hoffmann had kept tabs on the whereabouts of these bodies but before he was able to get set up and send for them, a group of young people, sympathetic to Mussolini, went to the graveyard in the dead of night and surreptitiously dug up the body, wrapped it in a blanket, and took it to Milan where arrangements had been made to turn it over to two monks of the Ambrosian Order; these monks had agreed to care for the body and to pray for the peace of the Duce's soul. Curiously, during the war these same two monks had provided cover for partisans of the resistance movement who were being sought by German and Italian secret service.

"Word of the Mussolini body-snatch got out, and there was considerable public furor—and, incidentally, great consternation on Hoffmann's part—until the body was finally traced to the Ambrosian monastery. At that point the Italian cabinet was convened in Rome to decide what to do with Mussolini's body. There was much controversy because the cabinet was presided over by a Catholic Party leader who blocked any attempt to provide Mussolini with a Christian burial. It was finally decided to take the body from the monks and cart it off to a secret, unmarked place that would never be revealed to the public.

"Somewhere along the line, perhaps while the cabinet debated, Hoffmann got to the corpse. Another body, of identical dimensions, was substituted for Mussolini's, and that is how Mussolini now happens to be at St. Zachary. Subsequently, Hoffmann had all the other bodies clandestinely removed from the Musocco grave and transported to Zonico. Substitute corpses were put into the Musocco gravesite to replace these pilfered bodies."

Ted had been standing in front of the fireplace, occasionally leaning on it for support. Now he went over and poured himself another whiskey. There was nothing more to tell. That was everything. He sat down beside Julietta.

I said, "So—the man who killed Arnoldo and took twenty-three years of my life . . . and the treasure I want as payment . . . all in one place. Right up there on the mountain."

"Don't forget *me*," Ted said. "I'm as much to blame for

what happened, for what you have endured, as anyone else. The crime of nonfeasance—standing by and not doing that which I was obligated to do. In order to save my own hide."

"I'm not interested in you, Ted," I said. "Or Bis. In a funny way I feel sorry for you. I don't want your money or your help. I feel a certain violence toward Bis for Giorgio's death, but so much of my time is gone, I don't want to use up any more in pursuit of hatreds. But about the treasure—have you seen any of it, or do you know what Hoffmann has done with it?"

"No—nothing about the treasure. But what about Hoffmann? Will you go after him? After the treasure?"

"I don't know." I looked at Julietta. Her eyes were dark and worried.

"How much of the treasure do you think is there?"

"At least half."

"Eighty or ninety million?"

"At least. If you want to go after Hoffmann, you can count on my testimony."

"No, I'm not interested in him. But perhaps Julietta wants to . . ."

"No!"

"The treasure will be very hard to get to, Paul. I'd say impossible, but considering what you accomplished since you left prison . . ."

"I have to think about it. Do you think I could make a deal with Hoffmann?"

"No—and make no mistake about it, Paul—the very second you reveal your knowledge to Hoffmann, you will be dead."

"But you said that you and Bis . . ."

"We guaranteed that we would get rid of you—keep you away from St. Zachary. We have lost our position."

"What you mean is—I have lost mine. I thought you

were all choked up about making amends for what you did
to poor old Paul . . ."

"Believe me, Paul, I have suffered enormously about you.
So has Bis. All these years. The tortures of the damned.
And now Giorgio to add to my . . ."

Maybe it was hearing Giorgio's name in the unctuousness
of Ted's voice; whatever, it came up fast, a sudden rumbling
from somewhere deep in me, and then up like hot lava and
the whole volcano erupted and with extraordinary calm
and quiet I came at him with all the compressed fury, fury
for Arnoldo and myself and Julietta and Giorgio, my hands
locked on his throat; and as I pressed him to the floor he
was clawing my hands desperately. My eyes filled with
venom, my head gone, feeling the muscles in his neck start
to give, feeling the vibrations of his strangled sounds
through my fingers I began to yell at him, screaming everything, all the frustrated vengeance, oppression, jails, judges,
prosecutors, prison guards, inmates, charity people, getting
back, for my taking it, taking it, taking it—now, you son of
a bitch, you get it, I am going to kill you for all those bas-
tards who shit on me and still do. You die for all of them,
you *are* all of them. My fingers dug into his neck, my arms
straight out, leaning into him, yelling, screaming at him for
what seemed an eternity over his dying sounds, when she
came at me, straight at my chest, hurling her body at me,
knocking me backward, freeing Ted as she grabbed me
around the body, locking onto me, legs around, arms in
back of my neck, intertwined, and I fought her, pulled at
her arms, all my might, fingers dug in, trying to peel her
off, but she stuck, her head jammed under my chin, her
arms interlocked, binding me with her body and legs and
arms as securely as rope, squeezing with all her strength,
pulling herself tighter and tighter, her pelvic bones dug
into my bones, her heels locked behind my calves, her head

pushing up hard under my chin as I thrashed all over the
floor with her, not hearing what she was pleading, then
finally the beginning of the drain, feeling it start to move
out of me and burst and run out as fast as it had filled, an
angry boil lanced, empty now, laying there with her on top
of me, her hold gone, just laying there on top of me, breathing hard, her face wet with tears and perspiration, her
dress ripped at the shoulder, Ted moaning and trying to
suck breath and if he lived, I lived, and this saved life of
mine was hers.

chapter twenty-two

We were lying across the bed before the open window, our spent bodies moist and viscous; one of Julietta's legs was between mine, a patch inside her thigh cemented to me with the drops of after-love. I felt weightless and eternal. My eyes closed, I listened to the distance-muffled sounds of hawkers' voices and calliopes at a somewhere carnival, borne into the room on sirocco wings. It was a moment to hold and preserve, as in a store window in Milan I had seen a butterfly immortally imprisoned in a square of thick clear acrylic.

"What will you do, Paul?"

It was the first reference to Ted's revelations. We had gone to our room to think, but it was suddenly important to go to bed to affirm ourselves.

"What do you think I should do?"

"Keep your word."

"My word?"

"Your promise. That you just wanted to *know* and that would be the end of it. Now is it the end of it—or not?"

"How can it be the end, knowing all this?"

"Quite easily. By turning your back on it and getting away from here."

"And not facing something that has haunted me for twenty years. I'm too literal for that, Julietta. I can't end anything like that. It's like when my father died. The cancer had been at him for several years, a big, strong healthy man who had to endure the ignomy of having his strong body slowly humiliated by four surgeries, each removing a part of him. Until finally, hacked and withered and martyred with pain, he surrendered. At his funeral the coffin was kept shut, but after the service, when everyone had gone and the room was empty, I went back alone and before they took the coffin away to the crematorium I asked the fat undertaker with the pencil mustache if he would open the coffin so I could see my father.

"Why? Because I couldn't put an end to him that way. He would just go on living and I knew I'd have a hell of a time ever burying him.

"The fat undertaker said, 'I thought the deceased wasn't to be viewed.' Then he said, 'Well, let me see if we did his hair and prepared him for viewing.' I stood outside the door and he came out and got me and took me in and left me at the coffin. Dad looked the way he was before he got sick. His cheeks were full and he had color. But he was dead. I could now *see* he was dead. I touched my fingers to his forehead. I can still feel how it was when I touched him. He was really dead—I had convinced myself and it had registered inside me."

"And if you see and hear and smell what goes on at St. Zachary, if you can see that treasure—then what?"

"I don't know. But I *have* to see it. And the man who knifed me in the back."

"And what about the risk? You know that as far as Hoffmann is concerned, you're a cheap candle—one puff and you're out."

"I realize that, but my desire has always overcome my fear—if it hadn't, I wouldn't have you."

"Desire for what, Paul? What in God's name are your

values? All you seem to care about is getting paid in treasure and money for your lost time and your suffering. But what about all the important things you were deprived of? All the unheard music, the unread books, the unseen movies, the plays and art and dances and speeches, and watching children—maybe *your* children—playing in the park? You don't even *mention* the world around you—not once have I heard you discuss anything except your money-avengence for your wrong. How about getting paid back in love and caring, and building something that is really yours? You see what we have, you and I. We can put ourselves anywhere and live fine."

"Doing what?"

"I don't know just what—but you want guarantees, is that it? Can't you just *believe?* Can't you look for something of value in life beyond stacking up gold pieces in a counting house? You talk about writing. That's what you seem to care about—the only thing you have mentioned. To go back to writing. Then what about that? I would think that other writers would have used up so much of the materials of their lives by the time they're your age . . ."

"What materials? Do you think I have been living and storing up experiences? I have been dead for twenty years."

"But you must believe in *yourself!* Why can't you believe in Paul Selwyn? We can have everything—it's ours—but you want to go up that mountain slope to St. Zachary and commit suicide. Why? *Why?*"

"To open the coffin and touch the body and know that it's dead."

"You did promise me, Paul."

"I know."

"I relied on that promise."

"I know."

"Paul—it's not just the risk, or simply a matter of principles. It's a terrible rejection."

"Rejection of what?"

"Me. You could have me and my love and our good life but you're rejecting that."

"No—no, of course I'm not. I am saying, just indulge me, just for this one important thing, and then it will be over and we'll go off and be fine."

"Aren't you doing what Ted and Bis did? The treasure at any price. Was Hoffmann any different? Paul—you're still living in 1942. *Things* were all that mattered then, and that's all that matters to you now. But that isn't today—don't you want to *want* to live in *this* world?"

"Don't tell me that these times aren't just as materialistic as times were twenty years ago. More so. This is a world of *have*. That's one thing that has been impressed on me. I see it everywhere I look."

"You see what you want to see. Sure, money and power —there will always be that game. But that's not for you. That's not you, Paul. As it's not me. Why can't you just let me love you and see what happens? Can't you believe? Can't you start your life from here? Here on out?"

"Yes. I'm going to finish off tonight—then I'll be ready. I'll be quit of it. We'll be fine, Julietta."

"No, Paul, we won't."

"How do you mean?"

"I won't be here when you get back."

"Of course you will."

"You'll see."

"Where will you go?"

"I don't know—out of this."

"Back to Como?"

"No—and don't come looking for me."

"You'll be here."

"No—I honestly won't."

"Julietta . . ."

"Please don't. You made a promise. You gave me your word."

"All right, God damn it! I've got to go back on it! I've *got* to! Why can't you understand?"

"What I wanted for you was for both of us. I think of *us* —you think of *you*."

"You talk about values. Value is just another word. Value is something that matters; whatever matters has value."

"Oh, you know what I mean by values! Values and value are night and day. The difference between making love for pleasure, and making love to have a baby—those values! You couldn't *make* love until you *loved*—until you committed yourself. The potency of loving, the potency of believing. That's how you are, Paul. That's what I like most about you."

"I worship you—and believe in you—and I will prove it to you. I may not know who I am, but I know who we are."

"But you're going?"

"Will you promise to be here?"

"Why, of course I *promise*."

"Please . . ."

"Unless I have to go back on it."

She covered herself with the sheet. I looked at my watch. I would have to hurry. I got up and dressed quickly.

"I'll be careful. There's nothing to worry about. I take care of myself, don't I?"

She didn't answer. She had buried her head under the pillow to muffle her weeping.

chapter twenty-three

I stopped the station wagon about a hundred yards short of the entrance to St. Zachary and turned off the motor and the lights. "Getting into the monastery without being seen will be easy," Ted had said, "but the Hoffmann enclave is something else again."

The road to St. Zachary had been a steadily precipitating corkscrew climb and now I could feel the effect of the thin air as we stepped from the car and started toward the forbidding front wall of the stone monastery which was nestled right up against the mountain. Ted had done what he could to discourage me from coming here—it was his neck as well as mine—but now that he was in it, the possibility of instant extinction would certainly motivate cautious but inventive moves on his part.

He did not use the main entrance. Instead he took me around to a side wall where a small old iron gate led into a meditation garden. A huge dark crucifix loomed starkly against the night sky of rolling white clouds which partially hid the moon. Beyond the garden was a courtyard and beyond that, the monastery. There were no lights and no sign of life. I looked at my watch: eleven twenty-five. Thirty-five minutes to the midnight mass.

Ted led me across the garden and the courtyard and entered the monastery through the kitchen. He paused to check for noises, then continued through a series of large, bare, flagstoned rooms, which eventually led us to the main entrance hall. He cautioned me to wait there, and disappeared. It occurred to me that this could very well be a trap, with the lights suddenly flooding the hall and Hoffmann and his men arranged above me at the second-floor balustrade that overlooked the stairwell. I backed off to a position in the doorway leading from the hall, as if, illogically, that was, under the ominous circumstances, protective.

But at the end of those interminable minutes, with old house creaks stabbing their points into me, I heard Ted's single pair of footsteps returning. He was carrying two habits and accessories, and we got dressed quickly. He then led me to a pantry where he inspected me in the circle of his small flashlight. It was a blessing that the rough brown habit had a full conical hood that jutted forward of the face all around, thereby providing a mask of shadows. Ted adjusted my rosary and showed me how to walk in the processional, hands clasped inside the wide-mouthed sleeves, head bent, sandaled feet shuffling slowly forward.

Somewhere above, causing me to jump, a sonorous bell unloosed a cascade of terrifying peals through the monastery, terrifying because each toll brought me nearer to that which had been my preoccupation for so long; I knew very well (intellectually) that this object of my preoccupation should, under these circumstances, have been avoided at all costs. But just what would the costs be? Undeterminable.

Ted motioned and I followed him to an alcove in back of the stairwell. Looking up from our position, I could discern robed forms, my brothers, carrying torches, igniting the long-necked oil lamps along the stairs and foyer walls. After a pause, the bell intoned again, in a variant rhythm, and this time my brothers began to appear in large numbers, many of them coming into the hall from a doorway to our immediate left. Ted took my arm and adroitly infiltrated us into the file of assembling monks. Once I was part of the mass of silent, identical, bent-headed Zacharians, I felt less threatened.

We shuffled slowly forward in absolute silence, a heavy prison-familiar rancid smell suggesting that my brothers were as unwashed as they were silently devout. As we passed from the spacious foyer into the corridor, the unshaped group formed into twos, Ted carefully maneuvering us so that we stayed together. But now I felt exposed again and my breath shortened and caught in my chest. The shuffling leather on the flagstones made an eerie and ominously echoed sound. I kept my head bowed low and my eyes determinedly on the heels of the sandals in front of me.

What if they counted the friars as they entered the mountain? I had quizzed Ted on this, but he thought they had no such security check on the monks. But what if they did and Ted was wrong? The slow route to the Hoffmann entrance was unnerving—it seemed we would never get there. I began to think about Julietta. I could still hear her sobs. It was the first time I had heard her cry. A few emotional tears. But not cry. What if I *were* caught? What a foolish gamble when she was all that really mattered—and all of this, as she had tried to impress on me, had no true meaning, especially without her. But there had been a compulsion to go. I felt how much I loved her, felt it wind its way through my body, and felt it moisten my eyes and dry my mouth. She's got to be there. But, Christ, what if she isn't?

The sandals in front of me dropped out of sight, and I felt my body contract as Ted and I, in our turn, started down the steps. This was the connecting tunnel that joined the rear of the monastery to Hoffmann's mountain retreat. The descent was pitched steeply, turned twice, and abruptly we were in a large stone chamber with the entrance before us. Massive bronze doors, flanged to the stone. Giant silver oil lamps sending their black-plumed flames to the vaulted roof. Above the doors, set into the stone in gold: EGLI VIVRA PER SEMPRE NEL SUORE DEL SUO PO-POLO. (He will always live in the hearts of his people.)

At each side of the entrance, tall and starched, two Black Guard elite: black shirt, black tie, black fezlike tasseled cap emblazoned with the gold Fascist eagle, white leather sash, red-and-white belt, black jodhpur pants fitted into glistening black knee boots, ornate sword suspended from the belt.

My upturned eyes were on them but my head was down, the hood a perfect shield, and I shuffled perfectly to the gait of the preceding friars. But I could feel the hot pierce of the Black Shirt eyes as we passed through the doors into—I almost froze in the surprise of recognition—into what was an exact replica of the Sala del Mappamondo, Mussolini's Roman headquarters.

A sonorous recording of the Beethoven Violin Concerto poured down on us, the Duce's favorite piece of music. I had seen the original Sala del Mappamondo in the Palazzo Venezia in Rome (we had held a conference there in 1945 prior to leaving for Como) and this was a spectacular re-creation in all its minutest details: a huge room, dominated by Mussolini's massive, ornate desk at the far end; floors of exquisite inlaid marble; in back of the desk, an enormous fireplace with a triangular-shaped frieze above it, the center of the triangle filled with a laurel circle bisected by a fasces, Caesar's symbol of Roman power, which Mussolini adopted. Heavy marble columns ringed the walls from high, baroque bases.

And everywhere Mussolini's possessions: his books,

violin, uniforms, fencing swords, the flags and banners that flew from his palaces, villas and automobiles, and flags that were carried in his parades; his saddle, ornate silver tack and riding gear; his hunting equipment and shotguns; an endless array of gifts he had received from rulers of other countries, in particular some ivory splendors probably "contributed" by Emperor Haile Selassie; wall maps of marble mosaics depicting the geography of his triumphs. These mosaic maps were on the side walls; on the end wall, on each side of the fireplace, between the marble columns, were two mosaic scenes: the one at the left depicted Mussolini leading his followers on the march to Rome, which put him into power; the right mosaic, in elaborate uniform, black tunic and tiers of chest medals, the Duce in heroic pose with Adolf Hitler.

As we shuffled slowly across the room, headed toward a door at the far end, we passed a dozen or more tables on which were displayed most of the diaries and documents which had been part of the missing treasure.

It would have been difficult to think of a facet of Mussolini's life which was not preserved in some way in this room. Huge leather books, gold-embossed *"Fotografia"* on their covers, indicated that significant events in the Duce's existence were depicted therein.

We were now approaching the rear door. Perched above it was a large, profiled gold eagle which, I presumed, had been the occupant of the Mera River crate.

The door was small, another flight of sharply pitched stone stairs, narrow, dank, dimly lit, then we were in a crypt. Stunningly, in a crypt. Gaspingly, in a circular, low-domed, treasure-laden crypt. The treasure. There it was. Right there before my eyes—the gold bejeweled crown of this bizarre and frightening crypt.

My eyes did not know where to focus; so overpowering; so immediate; so involving. Now in place of the Beethoven symphony was Mussolini's voice, booming from some balcony over the heads of a once-assembled multitude.

As they entered the monks raised their heads, abandoned their slow, shuffling gait, and formed themselves in rows, shoulder to shoulder, in the open area before the altar. To right and left of the altar, faced toward the assembling Zacharians, Hoffmann's Black Shirts. Perhaps a hundred. Matched men. In rows, at attention. Eyes front. Two black rectangles.

Solidly around the walls, one contiguous to the other, were the marble biers of Mussolini's henchmen—his ministers and generals who had been executed in Dongo and Milan. Their bodies were entombed in ornate stone sarcophagi, but the men were not depicted lying atop the sarcophagi in traditional death poses, but in active stone postures on the walls above the funeral biers, some sitting, some standing gesturing toward each other, reaching across to shake hands, General Cadorna astride a rearing horse, Marshal Graziani with sword aloft, all their names clearly stone-cut beneath their likenesses:

MEZZASOMA	BOMBACCI	PAVOLINI
PETACCI	ZERBINO	ROMANO
LIVERANI	PORTA	GATTI
COPPOLO	DAQUANNO	NUDI
CASALINUOVO	SALUSTRI	HINTERMAYER
STARACE	FARINACCI	GRAZIANI
BARRACU	CADORNA	CALISTRI

Mussolini's voice was now at its fullest, the final crescendo, bombastically vital, the words as such not saying much, only their rhythmic thrust important, rising to a climax in a Beethoven pattern; this was the genius, shared with Hitler, this kettle drum and brass of thundering invective, pulling listeners up to imagined heights, the blood of the listeners rising as the leader's face grew red with his own upflowed blood, this hypnosis, spilling the mind, firing the emotions, injecting the followers, now bombarding us in this rotund mausoleum, none of its thrust diminished, the deep-throated tattoo of words, beating out the final soaring bars, then cymbals and a last sustained chord, a triumphal animal cry for the Fatherland, for Destined Greatness, for the Greatness of the Fatherland, Fatherland, and all around me, the friars in unison, *"Duce! Duce! Duce!"*

This was the only yield to the stricture of silence: the St. Zacharians could talk each midnight at this mass for Mussolini's soul, which was being kept alive here at this shrine by Luigi Hoffmann. Facing the altar, their heads up, the friars knelt as Father Piccionastro, in silken robes of the high mass, incense swinging in an ancient silver pot, began intoning the Latin words for the preservation of the soul; monks on their knees as he entered, hands clasped once to the brow, then in unison the cross etched in the air, not on the body, but in the air where circulated the soul of Mussolini.

The altar: solid gold (I could not even estimate the number of bullion bars that went into it!). And directly over it the ceiling domed, a parachute design, covered with Mussolini's gold: gold coins, the wedding rings of the women of Italy, religious medallions of gold, gold medals, a glittering canopy reflecting its powerful golden glow on the altar and on the glass-enclosed figure that was mounted there, the corners of the glass sarcophagus supported by rounds of onyx, and inside, mummified, preserved in vacuum, the face black, the skin cleaved to the bone, but the jutted jaw and massive forehead unmistakable: BENITO MUSSOLINI. Full military dress. Boots polished. Black hands, the nails opaque gray, the hands at the sides. A thin white stripe of teeth showing beneath the slightly parted lips. Eyes sunken. The glass coffined vacuum doing for the body what the nightly mass was attempting for the soul.

Three sides of the sarcophagus and its top were glass but the back panel was solid and mounted on it were the jewels. All the jewels. Backdrop for the Mussolini corpse, painting the body with their mobile luster, in dense array the great jewels of the Dongo treasure. Gold above, jewels within, their animate colors blending on the dead black skin.

Set in letters at the base of the altar, just below the coffin, these words in Italian: "Here lies one of the most intelligent animals that ever appeared on the face of the earth." The epitaph Mussolini had written for himself.

On a level below this inscription, a plain, stone sarcophagus with the name "Clara Petacci" on its side.

Two servers were at the right and left of Piccionastro, holding incense pots swung out from silver holders. Father Piccionastro knelt.

Piccionastro: "In the name of the Father, and of the Son and of the Holy Spirit, Amen."

Monks: "I will go to the altar of God."

Piccionastro: "To God who gives joy to my youth."

Monks: "Our help is in the name of the Lord."

Piccionastro: "Who made heaven and earth."

Ted knew the responses but I was faking them, apprehensively trying to move my lips just behind the words as I heard them, desperately hoping none of the Black Shirt eyes dead ahead would single me out. Piccionastro put a wafer and a goblet of wine atop the Mussolini coffin.

Piccionastro: "I await the resurrection of the dead. And the life of the world to come. Amen."

Monks: "Amen."

From behind the altar, up the stairs and now in view, two Black Guard officers and then, slowly, majestically, a man of tall leanness, flowing white silk robe, purple cross covering the chest, with the Fascist insignia in the transverse of the cross. White hair, white eyebrows, white mustache, face without color, whites on white, El Greco hands, luminous, frail, esthetic beauty, a Jesus face, the man flowing forward as if borne legless on an obedient breeze. Slowly to one knee, two fingers as long and tapered and white as the altar candles, putting the sign of the cross on his chest, then the fingers forward to etch a second cross for Mussolini.

Piccionastro: "I am the Resurrection and the Life; he who believes in Me, even if he die, shall live, and whoever lives and believes in Me, shall never die."

Hoffmann now prostrated himself beside the body of Mussolini, assuming the identical position, his long white hair flowing to the sides of his face.

Piccionastro: "Absolve, O Lord, the soul of the faithful departed, Benito Mussolini, from every bond of sin. And by the help of Your grace may he deserve to escape the judgment of vengeance. And to enjoy the blessedness of light eternal."

Monks: "May he deserve to escape the judgment of vengeance. And to enjoy the blessedness of light eternal."

Piccionastro: "And Jesus said: 'I am the living bread which came down from heaven. If anyone eats this bread he will live forever. And the bread that I shall give is My own Flesh for the life of the world. I solemnly assure you, he who feeds on My Flesh and drinks My Blood has life eternal. And I shall raise him up on the last day.' "

A server went forward and picked up the wafer which he put on Hoffmann's tongue, and tipped the goblet to his lips so he could drink.

Monks: "Lord Jesus Christ, King of Glory, deliver the soul of this faithful departed from the pains of hell and the deep pit; deliver his soul from the lion's mouth, may hell not swallow it up, nor may it fall into darkness, but may

Michael, the holy standard bearer, bring them into the holy light: which you once promised to Abraham and to his seed. We offer You, O Lord, sacrifices and prayers of praise; receive them for the soul of Benito Mussolini whom we remember this night."

Piccionastro: "Grant, O Lord, that it may pass from death to life. Which You once promised to Abraham and to his seed. Promise now to Benito Mussolini, seed of Abraham."

Slowly now Hoffmann rose to his thin height, as did the monks. His eyes closed, his head back now, he spread his arms, the white silk falling into winged folds, and in a voice of great depth and resonance, he called to the heavens: "My Christ, I have eaten Your flesh and drunk Your blood as I have every night since the death of our great leader, Benito Mussolini, who lays here before You without blood and without living flesh. I stand before You, humbly and with full love, as his proxy, the keeper of his soul which has entered my body and which our prayers and devotionals have kept here in this house, which is a house of God. Thank you, O Christ, for making me the host of the soul of Your devoted servant, Benito Mussolini. I now beseech You, as You have been beseeched every night since his passing, to grant our beloved Mussolini resurrection, so that his soul may reenter his body and give it life and restore him to the world. Take me in his stead, My Christ, take me in sweet surrender, and let Mussolini rise from this cradle of death once again to rule his people, lambs of Your flock who need him as Your lieutenant on this earth. O Christ, I have eaten Your flesh as proxy for Mussolini, and I have drunk Your blood with Mussolini's mouth, and I have sung Your praises with Mussolini's voice, and my hands in supplication are the hands of Mussolini. Hear my voice! I call loud to the heavens! Grant us some sign of hope that the corpus will be infused with life. A sign, O Christ, so that we may believe . . ."

He dropped to his knees and the monks and Black Shirts followed suit. Father Piccionastro and his two servers knelt behind the altar. There was absolute silence. So quiet I could hear the wax-hot sound of the candles. Hoffmann's face was toward the crucifix and his arms were in supplication. No one stirred. In this silence, the metallic sound on the glass was magnified. Hoffmann started—his head jerked around and he sprang to his feet. A gold coin had dropped from the ceiling onto the glass. I deduced from his behavior that after long years of having repeated this entreaty, night after night—this beseechment for a sign had for the first time been answered.

The server nearest the glass reached for the fallen coin.

"No!" Whispered fiercely. "You would dare touch the sign of God!" Hoffmann on his feet, arms stretched upward, exalted. "The sign of God! It will be! It will be!"

Tears on his face. Veins on his temples distended. His hands clenched.

Then his eyes rolled upward and he gasped for breath and he was seized with an epileptic attack. The two officers moved to him quickly with obviously long-practiced efficiency. They knelt over him—secured his tongue and ministered to him.

Father Piccionastro moved in front of Hoffmann and the two men. "I await the resurrection of the dead. And the life of the world to come. Amen."

Monks: "Amen."

The Black Shirts lifted Hoffmann's stiff and convulsive body and carried him to the rear of the altar; I lost sight of them as they descended the altar stairs. Father Piccionastro blessed the corpus and the soul with sprinkled holy water, and the servers held high their silver incense standards, the jasmine smoke swirling over the heads of the monks as they sang:

> "To Jesus Christ, our sov'reign King,
> Who is the world's salvation,
> All praise and homage do we bring,
> And thanks and adoration.
> Christ Je-sus, Victor!
> Christ Je-sus, Ruler!
> Christ Je-sus, Lord and Re-deem-er!"

One last look at the coffin-wall of jewels, moving my eyes reluctantly from jewel to jewel to jewel, memorizing each emerald, diamond, ruby, trying to match the jewels to remembered items in the inventory, trying to place which had been part of the cache buried in the organ pit: chain gold covered with diamonds—Order of the Annunciation; the diamond shield of the Persian Order; the German order of emeralds and rubies. I was too concentrated on the jewels. Look away, monk, look away. Turn your eyes toward the heavens—where the gold is.

The Black Shirts broke formation, a squad moving toward the door to escort the monks back to their quarters; the other squads squared sharply left and right and disappeared through side doors.

Ted took hold of the bottom of my sleeve and guided us into the forming file, so that we would not be parted in the pairings. As we came to the door leading out of the crypt, a Black Shirt looked right at me, eyes into mine, but I slipped off his gaze and lowered my head and resumed my shuffled silence.

chapter twenty-four

It was not yet light when I pulled into the courtyard but as I walked from the car to the villa door, the sky streaked suddenly, a curtain rising on a pink cyclorama.

I started up the stairs, but stopped, too fearful that she wouldn't be there. The throttled silence suggested she had gone. I felt a deep stab of loneliness. Of terrible despair. Of defeat. Paralyzing. After a while, listening, hoping to hear something, I forced myself to continue up the stairs, the feeling of loneliness and defeat intensifying.

The door to our room was closed. I turned the knob slowly, my chest compressed, and softly opened the door. The shutters were closed, the room too dark to see. I folded back the iron shutters and the deep pink light fell on the unslept-in bed.

I went to the bed and ran my hand over the coverlet, the flat lifeless silk convincing me she was not there. Not there sleeping as I saw her each morning before she woke, her hair patterned across the pillow, her face without makeup, tranquil and suffused with its true beauty.

Not there.

Oh, Christ! I pulled the coverlet from the bed and ripped

it, length and width, the sound of the ripping silk a soft shrill of protest, ripping it deliberately, just ripping it for the sake of it, not angry, not self-pitied, just ripping it for the sound.

I went to the balcony doors to shut out the morning sounds that came in from the garden, sounds she woke to and loved, but when I put my hand on the door handle the sounds pulled me out onto the balcony. The looming day was glorious. Already the sun had lit the water far below and I could see the early boats moving on the lake.

And there at the end of the garden, down the slope at the edge of the bluff which overlooked the water, where the garden path ended and the privet grew high, she sat on a stone bench looking up at the burgeoning sky.

My breath wouldn't catch for a moment, but I felt exalted. The fatigue and the tension suddenly gone, I was suffused by the enormous feeling of loving her. Standing there on that balcony, overwhelmed with her beauty, with loving her, I made no effort to stop my tears.

She saw me. She stood up but neither of us moved. Yes, I am alive and, yes, you are here.

She started to run up the path toward me, as fast as she could. I stepped from the balcony and ran from the room and down the stairs two at a time and across the white marble foyer, and I could hear her calling, "Paul! Paul!" as I ran across the front lawn knowing that as I turned the corner she would be there.

 **About the Author**

A. E. HOTCHNER was born in St. Louis, Missouri, in 1920,
where he studied as an undergraduate at Washington
University and received his LL.B. After practicing law for
two years, Mr. Hotchner entered the Air Force in 1942
and eventually became Chief European Correspondent for
Air Force magazine. After the war he was articles editor
of *Cosmopolitan* magazine, and from 1950 on, as a free-
lance writer, he wrote more than 300 articles and short
stories in such national magazines as *Esquire, The Saturday
Evening Post* and *Collier's.* His play *The White House,*
starring Helen Hayes, was performed on Broadway in
1964. He has written many original dramas for television,
most memorably a Playhouse 90 *Last Clear Chance,* with
Paul Muni; he also wrote the highly acclaimed television
dramatization of Ernest Hemingway's *For Whom the Bell
Tolls.* Mr. Hotchner's memoir, *Papa Hemingway,* became
a national best-seller when it was published by Random
House in 1966, and an international best-seller when
published later in England, France, Germany and fifteen
other countries.

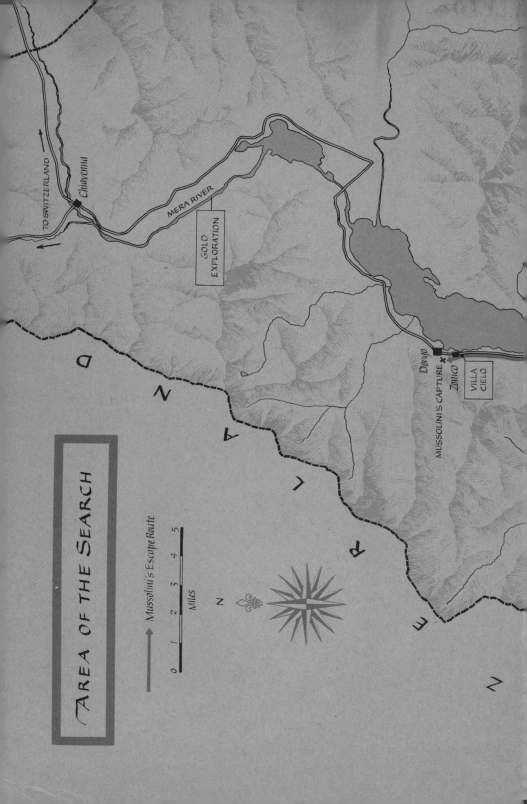

AREA OF THE SEARCH

Mussolini's Escape Route

Miles

0 1 2 3 4 5

TO SWITZERLAND

Chiavenna

MERA RIVER

GOLD EXPLORATION

Dongo

MUSSOLINI'S CAPTURE ✕

Zonico

VILLA CIELO